HAVE
YOU
SEEN
HER?

BOOKS BY DEA POIRIER

The Marriage Counselor

HAVE YOU SEEN HER?

DEA POIRIER

bookouture

Published by Bookouture in 2023

An imprint of Storyfire Ltd.
Carmelite House
50 Victoria Embankment
London EC4Y 0DZ

www.bookouture.com

ISBN: 978-1-83790-740-3
eBook ISBN: 978-1-83790-739-7

For everyone who's lived in a shadow

1

There's something about living in a shadow, being the second fiddle, the one who could never be enough—no matter what. Over the years, it's gotten easier. I've stepped out of the darkness. I've learned to make my own light. But there's always a draw, an invisible rope that tugs at me, that that makes me miss *her*, that makes me wonder if I could be the one to save her. In my quiet moments, I always find my fingers straying, googling her name, like a moth to flame. Though we've gone our separate ways, she's imprinted on me. She's a part of me. It's something I know I'll never shake, no matter how hard I might try.

The turbulence on the flight jolts me, everything in the cabin rattling at once in response. I grit my teeth against it, a lightning bolt of pain arching from my tooth to my jaw and up to my temple. Trying to calculate the odds of dying on a flight, I wrack my brain for the last time I heard of a commercial flight crashing, the flaming wreckage littering the Midwest. The fact that I come up blank makes me feel a little better. Though this isn't my first flight, the jarring movements put me on edge. Another violent shake makes me all too aware of the dull roar of the engines, the collective breath held by everyone in the cabin; we all wait together, a shared experience, wondering if we'll make the transition as one—if the cabin will become a coffin.

We lurch again, the fuselage jumping, and my stomach bottoms out, as if I'm on a roller coaster—I swear it feels like we've fallen fifty feet. Creaks and groans reverberate through the air around me, and I clench my jaw harder, my entire body rigid. The sounds around me act like a warning siren, the airplane screaming that it's past its limit. It feels like a monster has the plane in its grip and is threatening to rip it apart. My fingers curl around the armrest, my nails grinding against the metal or plastic—or whatever the cold surface is. For a moment, I swear I smell smoke mixed with the sharp scent of alcohol that keeps wafting toward me from the man to my left. But it must be my mind playing tricks on me, because I'm sure if there was *actually* a fire, by now alarms would be echoing through the cabin.

It'd be just my luck to die like this, after my sister dragged me across the country. At least it'd make good content for her social media pages. We've barely spoken in the last decade, that is, until five days ago when she called me eight times in a row. Out of a misplaced hope that she finally wanted to reconnect, I answered.

Cancer.

That's why she was calling, to deliver bad news—the worst. I'll never forget the way she said *terminal*, the vowels thick in her throat. I'd never heard her like that, vulnerable, fragile. As if she was just waiting to die. I always hear of people having years, a while to prepare, to get their affairs in order. But Eviana had weeks, maybe months if she was lucky. There are people who leave their mark on the world, and somehow nothing ever leaves a mark on them. My sister is one of those people. But somehow, I could hear the echoes of it in her words. I imagine it painted on her flesh. It was like Icarus finally crashing back down to earth. Life finally caught up with her—for once, my sister was mortal.

Terminal. My big sister. The person I clung to for years while she always shoved me away. She was dying. My gut reaction, well, I'm not proud of it. It's an ending I never expected for her. I always assumed Eviana would die in a glamorous way—her Jag falling off a cliff after she lost control, a poisoning by a crazed fan, her helicopter smashing into the side of a mountain. Because the very last thing I ever thought about my sister was that she was just like everyone else. It wasn't possible that she could die of something so—normal. Something that others die from.

The plane jolts again, but this time it's the wheels touching down. I want to breathe a sigh of relief, but I can't. No, instead, there's a tangle of anxiety, a bramble bush that expands every time I take a breath. I'll calm down once I get back to my apartment—at least that's what I keep telling myself. But the truth is, the anxiety never leaves me. There's always an invisible force living inside me, telling me that everything is about to go terribly, horribly wrong. That my time is almost up, that everything I've built is just seconds from crashing down around me.

I turn my phone back on as we taxi, carving toward the terminal at Seattle-Tacoma International Airport. My phone buzzes over and over as it comes back to life. My chest tightens, and I chew on my left thumbnail as I look over the notifications —nine missed calls and a few text messages wait on the screen from a number I don't recognize. The texts explain who's sending all the mystery communications. Simon, my brother-in-law. Despite my sister and Simon having been married for over five years, I've never spoken to him. I didn't even have his number saved in my phone.

My thoughts instantly sour with a force that is so palpable that I swear other people in the cabin turn to look at me. Can they feel it too? Do they know something has happened? Did she already die? Is this *the call*—the one that will change every-thing? I navigate to my voicemail, and though he's called so many times, he's only left one message. I suck in a shaky breath before I press the phone to my ear.

"Hi, um, Blair?" His voice is low and uneasy. He says my name like he's unsure of it, like he hasn't said it aloud in a very long time—maybe ever. Like maybe he isn't even sure if it's my name. "Have you heard from Eviana? She went for a walk this afternoon and she never came back. I don't want to worry you... But I'm worried." He lets out a nervous laugh. "So, yeah, if you could call me back, please." The line goes dead.

My heart seizes in my chest, an invisible fist clenching it tight. Five days ago, I thought my sister was going to die.

But now... she's missing?

My call to Simon is short, loaded with all the words I can't say, all the questions I don't want to ask. But when your brother-in-law practically begs you to come help find your sister, how can you say no? I know my weakness is fixing things, saving people. I know that I need to build better boundaries, but today—my sister needs me, and that's all that matters. This is the first time Eviana has ever *needed* me, so of course I'll do whatever I can to help.

Getting a last-minute flight to Florida nearly maxed my credit card when Eviana called five days ago—and getting another now is an entirely different story. Anxiety tightens around me as I look at the cost on the screen. It's more than a month of my rent. I barely make enough as a social worker to keep my lights on. Though I'm sure I could ask Simon to send me money for a ticket, I'm too proud for that. It's not as if he and Eviana are hard up. They have more money than I'd ever know what to do with. I'm not that person though, the one who asks for help, the one who admits that I'm drowning. So, instead of groveling, I raise my credit limit while I stress-eat a brownie in an empty wing of the airport. There's no way I'll ever be able to pay this off.

Goodbye again, Seattle. Goodbye to the kids who need me, who I could help. Right now, there's someone else who needs saving. My sister is beckoning me, again. That's the way it's always been, I suppose. She calls and I come running, and deep down I know it'll always be that way.

The flight is somehow fast and slow at the same time, as if I'm stuck in some kind of limbo. I keep going over what he said again and again, because it can't be real. I must have imagined all of this, and I'll eventually wake up. My mind is a jumble as I try to make sense of it. I keep waiting for someone to yell that this was all a stupid prank. Because how can she really be missing?

Simon is waiting for me in arrivals. I only recognize him from pictures that my sister has posted on social media, a fact that embarrasses me to my core. Simon wasn't here during my last trip. Eviana told me that he was out of town. He's tall, his broad form leans against his black Escalade as if he's a model waiting for a photographer to snap the perfect shot. If there were ever a person who looked nothing like their name, it would be Simon. With his wide jaw, muscles, and long hair that's currently swept up into a bun, I'd peg him as a Thor or maybe Fabio. But he's the perfect match for my sister, honestly, more of a statue and less of a spouse. That's what she needs. My sister wouldn't thrive with someone who was practical, someone who was a little more normal. They've been inseparable since they met at a workshop on how to get rich quick in the age of influencers. He tried to be a *hustle for life* influencer, but never gained the traction my sister did. And from some of the scathing comments I've read online about him, my sister isn't the first successful woman he's latched onto. His first wife was also well-known online. I tried to dig for more details on what happened to that relationship but came up empty.

I drag my luggage forward, the wheels grinding against the pavement too loudly, as if it too is protesting this second trip that neither of us agreed to. I tighten the muscles in my neck as I brace myself against the noise. Simon grabs me, pinning my arms to my sides as he hugs me. My mouth and nose are smothered into his shoulder, the sharp woody scent of his cologne adding a caustic layer to the ordeal. I hold my breath until he releases me. There is nothing worse than a hug you didn't ask for and certainly didn't want. This is beyond awkward; we definitely don't know each other well enough for hugs. But Simon is the kind of guy who I'm sure will refer to me as *sis* the entire time I'm here, and force affection on me because we're *family*. I see these types of guys in my office from time to time. Though, they usually like to describe themselves as *the cool dad*. Simon just isn't quite there yet.

"How was your trip, sis?" he asks, and I grind my teeth.

I groan. "Harder the second time," I say as he takes my bag from my hand.

"The second time?" he echoes as he throws my bag into the back of the Escalade, as if it weighs nothing—it weighs at least thirty pounds. There's no way I have the upper-body strength to fling it around like he does.

I cross my arms and raise my brow at his question. "I literally just landed when I called you back," I say.

"Landed where?" he asks as he turns, planting his hands on his hips as his eyebrows quirk with confusion. Why isn't he following the conversation at all? Did he think my flight landed earlier in the day?

"Back in Seattle. My flight from Orlando left less than twenty-four hours ago," I explain, trying desperately not to let my frustration reach my voice—but I'm not quite sure I succeed. Exhaustion and anxiety are making me moody, to say the least.

"I just got back too. I was in London," he explains, but I already know this. Eviana told me about his trip. That's why I didn't get to meet him during my last visit. Did she not tell him about mine? Did she not want him to know I was visiting? I wish she would have told me so I could have kept my mouth shut. "Why were you in Orlando?"

I quirk my brows at him now, I'm sure mirroring his own confusion. "I was here visiting Eviana. Didn't she tell you?" Why didn't she mention my visit to him? Or did it slip his mind with everything that's going on with my sister? I know a lot of people have memory lapses when dealing with trauma, so I try to cut him some slack. It can't be easy having your sick wife just disappear.

"She didn't tell me that you were flying in," he explains. There are more questions swimming behind his eyes, but he doesn't voice them. "That's weird. We could have had a little family bonding time," he says before shooting some finger guns in my general direction, then punching me lightly in the arm.

I sigh, trying to piece this all together, and brush off his weird behavior. It all seems like a farce. Maybe he's acting this way because he doesn't know how to deal with Eviana's diagnosis. I shouldn't be so hard on him. "I came to visit because Eviana told me about the cancer."

He motions for me to climb into the Escalade. I slide into the passenger side. The heat of the vehicle presses against me while I wait for him to turn on the AC.

"Cancer? Who has cancer?" He eyes me for a moment. "Are *you* sick? You don't look sick."

The frustration is getting the better of me. My jaw aches with the pressure I keep putting it under. Feeling like someone isn't *really* listening while I'm talking is one of my biggest pet peeves. Why is he not understanding anything I'm saying? "No, I'm not. Eviana's cancer..."

He laughs as he starts the car, then rolls out of the parking garage. "Eviana doesn't have cancer, sis. Don't be stupid," he says. His brows aren't even crinkled. Confusion pierces my mind as I process his words.

A bad feeling blooms inside me, a warning sharpening my thoughts. What does he mean that Eviana doesn't have cancer? There must be some kind of miscommunication happening. That's the entire reason that she dragged me back here in the first place. I can't make sense of it. She told me that she was dying, that she had less than a couple months to live. I relay all this to him, to which he just laughs and shrugs it off, as if I told him some kind of joke. What the hell is even happening right now? Did she not tell him? Eviana didn't seem like she was having that much trouble processing all of it—if anything, it seemed like maybe she'd come to terms with it all. Did she not want Simon to know?

I rub the base of my neck reflexively. "Is she really missing?" I blurt the words out, and they're much harsher than I mean for them to be. After all my emotional intelligence training, I'm usually able to rein my feelings in, to sit with them and navigate the path to good communication. But I'm seriously confused. Does Eviana really not have cancer? Has she not told Simon because she isn't sure how he'd react? Maybe she didn't think that he could handle the news. I don't know what to think or what to believe. My mind is churning with the possibilities, none of which are good. At work I've seen parents keep the news of serious or terminal diagnoses from their children—but keeping it from a spouse is new to me.

He turns left out of the airport, then merges onto the turnpike. "Of course she's missing. Why would I have made you come all the way out here if she wasn't?"

My guts churn with anxiety, as a pit opens up inside of me. I gnaw on my thumbnail as I stare out the window. None of this feels right. But I have to push through it. There's no other way I'll get answers. I tell him about my trip, visiting my sister, but I keep thinking about the cancer. Was there a reason my sister didn't tell him? Though I know she's been one to exaggerate from time to time, to be dramatic, I don't think she'd lie about something so serious. Something about it all feels one-sided—off. There's no air of concern for Eviana like I would expect. I know we all work through shock and grief differently, but this seems callous. Maybe she didn't want to admit it—because it makes her seem too normal. It's the first time I'm seeing my sister as mortal, so it must be hard for her to reconcile too.

"Sorry she made you come all the way out here just for you to make a second trip. But yesterday evening, she went for a walk, which isn't something she does often. Since her social media following really started to take off, she's spent most of her time indoors, any trip out is calculated and planned based on the type of reach it's likely to get. Honestly, I don't think she's ever told me she was going to take a walk. She's a gym rat, so it's not like she doesn't exercise, but... walking? That's not like her. Maybe I should have questioned it more." He's rambling, but I don't stop him. It seems like he needs to get it all out, to talk to someone.

My sister is a professional influencer. She was actually one of the first dozen to get over a million followers, which I hate to give her credit for. Her social media following is now in the multiple millions, her yearly income from all of it is also in the seven figures. It may even be eight by now. Some part of me is jealous that she doesn't have to work a *normal* job, but then again, her entire life is built around this job. She's made herself into a product, and I think that may be more exhausting than sitting at a desk.

"So, what do the police have to say? Are they tracking her cards and stuff?" I grab my phone and scroll through my sister's social media, looking for a post that mentions she's missing so I can share it. She's got photo after photo of her cooking, holding products, walking through an orange grove with a little dog—a dog that I don't remember seeing when I visited, though I wouldn't put it past her to rent a dog. But there's absolutely nothing here about my sister being missing. I raise a brow as I keep scrolling, wondering why there isn't any mention of it.

He's silent for a long time, so long that I finally look up at him from my phone.

"Simon?" I press when he still doesn't answer me.

He clears his throat, and I swear his hesitation is palpable. I want to slap the armrest between us. Instead, I clench my hands tighter around my phone. My training has taught me better than to have outbursts like that. I have to stay calm, to coax the information that I need out of him.

"I haven't called the police," he finally admits.

I balk, my words completely lost in the torrent of my thoughts. How could he not call the police? What is he waiting for? Did he have something to do with Eviana's disappearance? Why else wouldn't he have called them?

"What do you mean *you haven't called the police?*" My tone is filed to a point, so sharp it could stab him. So when he flinches, I'm not surprised.

"Well, it's just not a good time," he says, his voice weaker than a wet paper towel. There's a hint of a whine there too, like a toddler who doesn't want it to be naptime.

"This isn't the kind of thing you just sit on. You have to call someone," I say, exasperated with him. I shouldn't have to explain this to a grown man. "Everyone knows that the first forty-eight hours are the most critical. We're burning valuable time." As soon as the words leave my mouth, I mentally question them. Is it forty-eight or twenty-four hours? I can't remember.

"I will. But not yet. Eviana had a temper. Sometimes, she just leaves for a few days to blow off some steam."

That's the first I'm hearing of this. When we were kids, Eviana was the opposite. She didn't take off. Instead, she'd stew, slam doors, and make sure that everyone knew she was upset. If she really took off often to *let off some steam*, then I don't know why he called me. I don't buy any of what I've heard so far. It's not adding up. He may have been with her recently, but I spent over twenty years studying my sister. She's cool, calculating, sometimes vicious. She's not the type to storm off. No, instead, she bundles everything up in the back of her mind to draw on later. If there's one thing I know for certain about my sister, it's that Eviana never forgives, and she certainly never forgets. I've never even seen her back down from a fight. If she left, there's a reason for it. But I don't think she's the type to do that—that's why I'm so worried here. If Eviana is sick, she may not be thinking clearly. Someone may have taken her, someone may have *hurt* her, or worse.

I look at Simon, the sharp edges of his jaw, the darkness swimming behind his eyes. It doesn't sit right with me. It's wrong. His lack of concern, the fact that he didn't call the police. Who is this man and what did he do to my sister?

3

AGE TEN

I've been hearing about the party for two months. If I were anyone else, I'd have been excited. But instead, there's been a pit of anxiety in my stomach since I heard about it. What's the point in celebrating my birthday, exactly? It's never the one that matters. It never compares to *her* birthday. Feeling like an afterthought used to upset me; but now, it's created an armor, a thick skin that protects me every single time Eviana gets attention. At least, that's what I tell myself.

"I need you ready in five minutes!" my mother's shrill voice calls from downstairs.

"I've been ready for an hour!"

My teeth clench together automatically. Eviana's words echo from the room next to mine, mirroring my mother's. The door to my room flies open, slams against the wall, then rattles. Eviana stands in the doorway, her hand on her hip. She flips her long brown hair back from her shoulder. I'm always envious of her perfect straight hair. My wavy tresses end up poofing out around me like a lion's mane. She's got on way too much makeup and a crop top, which I know my mother will yell at her about.

"Why such a sourpuss?" she asks as she tilts her head to the side. I hate the way she analyzes me, as if I'm a painting on the wall in a gallery. She doesn't find me that interesting. I know that she's just messing with me.

"Because I don't see the point in all this," I say. My voice cracks as I force the words out. Disappointment is already hanging heavy on my heart. The premonition for how today will end has already wormed its way into me, and no matter how much I might like to shed it, I won't. There's nothing that I can do about it now. Sadness has wrapped around me like a fist, and all day I've felt like I'm seconds from crying.

Eviana rolls her eyes at me. "Don't be so stupid. You should be excited about your birthday."

I cross my arms. "What is there to be excited about it?"

She throws her arms up and huffs, as if she's just so exhausted with my existence. "If you can't see why a birthday is exciting, you're beyond help, loser." She disappears, back into her room I expect, like a snake slithering back to its lair.

I descend the stairs before my mother can yell for me again. I know if she screams for a second time, that's when it'll all change, the real anger will emerge, and once that can of worms is open, it can't be closed again. I use the cloud of smoke hanging in the air as a trail to find her. She's leaning against the counter in the kitchen, her red acrylic nails clutching a long cigarette; she puffs on it as if the cigarette is the only thing tethering her to this world. She's got stacks of papers in front of her, to grade I expect. My mother is a professor at the university, a fact that she never shuts up about. My father was a professor too, before he died—and that's why she thinks that my sister and I are destined to be academics; there's no other acceptable option, we are clones of them or we are wasting our time on this planet. When the floor creaks beneath my feet, my mother glares at me, as if she didn't just ask me to come down here. Sometimes I wonder why she bothered having a second child, since Eviana was clearly all they ever wanted.

"Where are we going?" I finally ask.

She coughs out a laugh, smoke billowing from her lips. She looks like a dragon when she lets the smoke seep out. "Wherever Eviana wants to go."

A thread of anger shoots through me like a bolt of lightning. I hate her. I knew this was coming, and yet it still hurts. My muscles tighten as I try to fight against the rage. I don't want it to show on my face. I don't want her to see that I'm upset.

"Why is Eviana deciding where we go?" I thought that if it were my birthday, I'd have some kind of say—but I was stupid to even have that thought.

"Eviana got honor roll again. We have to celebrate," she explains, with a cruel smile. She knows exactly what she's doing.

Disappointment winds its way around me, squeezing so tightly I feel like I could collapse beneath it. "But it's my birthday," I manage after a long pause.

"And? That's not an achievement. I kept you alive for another year. I should celebrate that. Eviana got straight A's and managed to stay on honor roll. You managed to keep existing." She twirls her finger around in the air. "Good job. But last I checked your grades were all C's."

"But you said we were going to celebrate my birthday today." I can't help the whine that bleeds into my words. It stretches like sour taffy. I hate that it's cutting into me this way, that it still affects me. It's not as if I didn't know this would happen.

She shrugs and takes another long drag from her cigarette, her hawkish eyes piercing into me the entire time. "Maybe next year you'll remember that if you want to celebrate your birthday, you need to try harder in school. I don't celebrate losers. And neither does the rest of the world."

Eviana's feet thud against the stairs behind me. She's so close I know that she overheard our mother. She said it loud enough that I think someone on the front porch would have heard her. Mom ashes her cigarette, grabs her purse and keys, then stalks toward the door. It slams behind her, and I turn around to face my sister.

"Where do you want to go?" she asks me.

"Why do you care?" I spit the words at her.

"Because I'll let you pick this time."

I squint at her, not believing the offer. She's never offered something like this before. Why would she bother doing it now?

"Come on, we have to hurry," she says, glancing toward the door. "If she knows that I'm picking something you want, then we won't be able to go."

"I want to go to the arcade and then to get cupcakes from the bakery afterward, otherwise I know I won't get a cake." The words pour out of me, but the second they're out, I regret them. Because if I didn't tell anyone and it didn't happen, then it wouldn't be so hurtful. But now she knows what I want to do. She could decide that I get nothing that I want.

She turns and jogs toward the front door, and I follow closely behind. Eviana gets into the car, and I climb in behind my mother's seat. She hates when I sit on the other side. She told me she never wants to turn around and see my face.

"So, what did you decide?" she asks, looking in the rearview mirror at Eviana as she lights another cigarette.

Eviana makes a show of considering. My fists tighten at my sides, my nails digging into my palms, as I wait for the verdict. The fate of my birthday is in my sister's hands.

"I want to go to the arcade, then to get cupcakes afterward," she says, but she doesn't look at me when she says it. If she does, our mother will know what she did—what she's doing.

I look at my lap, trying to act as disappointed as possible. Though I feel mother's eyes on me, I don't look up until she throws the car into reverse, then backs down the driveway. I look to Eviana, who offers me the slightest nod.

Times like this, I remember I'm not alone.

Times like this, I realize that sometimes my sister is really on my side.

4

How do you sleep when secrets fill a house so entirely they move through it like a cloud of smoke? My sister owns what I would call a mansion. It's a 3,000-square-foot Tuscan-style monstrosity that is somehow entirely my sister, and yet not. I've paced the halls all night instead of sleeping, seeing her everywhere and yet nowhere at all. Her fingerprints, her imprints, they're on everything—and yet, this too is all a façade. This is a monument built to the lies my sister tells the world, her perfect life, her *dream*. But even nightmares are dreams. Every one of these *things* I know she picked out for the reaction, for how it would make the people who saw them feel—these hollow things, they tell a story about Eviana that I'm sure she didn't mean to write. The strange backdrop of her life, I didn't analyze it too closely while I was here the last time—all I could see in my shock was my sister—I tried to digest the whole of her life, all the years that stretched between us, how much and how little she'd changed. But now that I stop to really look, I wonder if there was any part of her life that was just authentically hers.

In the corners of most of the rooms, there are security cameras perched, watching my every move. The tiny globes are in the hallways, the living room, the formal dining room, but not in her office, the kitchen, bathrooms, or the guest rooms. There are even more cameras outside. And I wonder why my sister put up so many. She lives in a good area, locked away inside a gated community that has a guard on duty twenty-four hours a day.

The moon is high outside, casting shards of midnight light across the hardwood floor. I ask myself for the hundredth time why Simon didn't tell anyone—why her manager, Tom, also hasn't called the police. A stalker could have kidnapped her. A serial killer could have her tied up somewhere. Every single possible dark scenario has swarmed in the back of my mind for hours. His reservations also linger there, his silence, his ambivalence that his wife has disappeared. Eviana could have taken off for a few days, sure. But I call this whole *walk* idea into question. My sister's car isn't here. She drove somewhere, clearly. She's got friends in the neighborhood though. Maybe she's crashing with one of them. Maybe they drank too much wine, and she slept over—and now her phone is dead. I'm sure it's possible. Maybe this is all just a big misunderstanding.

Though my eyes have been roving the rooms softened by the darkened night for evidence, for any sign that Simon might have done something to my sister—I've found nothing. No blood, no broken glass, nothing that would intrigue a true crime podcast. And all the cameras in here, I'm not sure he could have killed her without getting recorded. As I stand in the kitchen, imagining Eviana taking the pictures for her social media accounts, my eyes grow tired. But I can't sleep. I won't sleep. I drag myself to the coffee machine, and struggle with it for a few minutes before it finally begins to gurgle. I have a ten-dollar coffeepot that I bought from Walmart. This stainless-steel William Sonoma monstrosity probably cost my sister a grand. As the golden liquid trickles into an oversized *Girl Boss/She-E-O* mug, I let out a bottled breath; though I hope to release the anxiety bound inside me with it, there's no relief, my chest is still tight, body and mind on edge. The muscles in my neck scream—they've been taut for too long—sending a dull ache all the way to my shoulder blade.

"Why are you up so early, sis?" Simon's voice behind me nearly makes me jump out of my skin. I hadn't heard him approach over the sounds of the coffee machine.

I whirl around with my heart racing and search for the right words. Eviana always had the perfect words ready, while I'm never certain quite what to say; even after my years of training, sometimes I find myself lost, unsure of what the best path forward is. "I just couldn't sleep," I finally manage. The nerves in my neck tingle, and I rub at it with my left hand. Simon puts me on edge, makes me nervous in a way I can't quite place. I'm uncertain if it's because he's a stranger or if there's something more. How long has he been there, watching me?

"That sucks, sis," he says. And my mind ruminates on *sis*. I hate it. But I won't interject. I won't correct him. Instead, I'll just swallow my frustration to keep the peace. "Do you want some Ambien? Eviana has a ton in the cabinet. She never slept well either. I wonder if it runs in the family. She's also got some Xanax and Valium," he rambles on. And it really bothers me that there isn't a hint of concern for my sister. Not at all. How can he think about Ambien and Xanax when she's missing?

"Do you wonder how she's sleeping now?" I ask as I turn around to retrieve my cup of coffee. "Do you wonder where she is?" My core tightens after I ask the questions. I wait for him to lash out at me, for him to raise his voice.

He scoffs at the question and waves his hand in the air like I'm being ridiculous. "Of course I do."

My shoulders fall a bit when he remains calm, his voice not even inching up. "So what really happened then?" I ask. I'm not sure if he expected me to not notice or if he doesn't have his story straight.

"What do you mean, *what really happened*?" he echoes, his

eyes narrowing on me. The look on his face dares me to accuse him of it, for me to utter aloud what I think he's really capable of.

"I can't help but notice that Eviana's car isn't out there. If she went for a walk in the neighborhood, then where is her car?"

His eyes go wide for a moment, then tighten again, as if this is the first time he's putting this piece of his lie together. No wonder he didn't call the cops.

"I don't know. Maybe she drove to one of the trails where she likes to walk."

There's no way he seriously didn't notice her car was missing. This guy knows something and he's just not being honest about it. But why?

"Most new cars have trackers. Did you even try to locate her car? Her phone?" There are so many ways to track someone down these days. It's not as if Eviana just disappeared without any trace.

He shakes his head and crosses his arms. "Eviana's car is older. It doesn't have tracking on it. And she always keeps tracking off on her phone because she's worried about hackers. Eviana didn't like the idea of Big Brother spying on her."

I don't buy any of it. He's obviously lying. She has cameras all over this house. If she were that paranoid about hacking or being watched, none of those would be here.

"So, why don't you call the police?" I test a sip of the coffee. It's dark and rich, without the bitterness I usually get from my coffeepot at home. Maybe there is something to this fancy coffee machine she bought. Not that I'd ever be able to afford one. When I finally look back to Simon, there's a war being waged on his face.

"Look, it's not that we aren't concerned about Eviana. We are." This is not a good start. And my mind goes over his use of the word *we*. Who the hell is *we*? He gestures a little too wildly with his hands, as if the movements will convince me when his words do not. "I know Eviana's wishes, and she wouldn't want anything like this to damage her brand."

Her brand? Her disappearance might damage her brand? I want to throw the coffee at him. But I don't, instead I grip the handle so hard my hand aches. I'm not sure why I even care this much. Eviana spent our entire lives pushing me away, making me feel like I wasn't enough—and here I am, still clinging to her skirt, worried about her, like we're in elementary school again. But this time, Eviana can't save me from this. And I'm not sure I can save her either. Why did Simon even want me here if we aren't going to call the police?

"Is her brand really all you can think about right now? What if she's dead?"

He huffs a laugh, as if the idea is the most ridiculous thing in the world. And I hate that I felt that way about the cancer. It just didn't seem possible. This though, her disappearing and being found dead, that's exactly the kind of death that I imagined for my sister. She's too glamourous to grow old. She's too dramatic to get sickly. She would fight the grim reaper off just to get the kind of death she *deserves*, the kind of end that would drive more engagement.

"She's not dead. She can't be. Don't be dramatic. Are you listening to too many true crime podcasts or something?" He rolls his eyes, and it enrages me.

How is he acting like his wife going missing is the most natural thing in the world? Is he so insulated with his wealth and this huge house that he really cannot see how fucked up this is? God, I hope this is some kind of weird coping mechanism, because otherwise, this guy has to be a sociopath.

"I'm going to the police if you won't." My words dare him to do something, anything. At this point I just want him to act like a normal person with a missing spouse.

He looks down at the floor and shakes his head slowly. When his eyes meet mine again, they're sharper, almost predatory. He takes a step toward me, and the tension between us thickens.

"And how will that look?"

"How will that look?" I echo because I can't make sense of his statement.

He takes another step toward me, the distance between us still at least four feet—but it feels too close. "You were the last person to see Eviana after all. You flew out a couple hours before I realized that she was gone. You could have easily done something to her."

Though the threat isn't spoken aloud, it's threaded in his words, his gestures. This is the reason he wanted me here. I look guiltier than he does. My stomach is in knots, because I wonder if he knows my secrets, *our* secrets. I wonder if he knows that deep down I really don't want to go to the police, because there are things about me and my past that I can't let them find. At the end of the day, with the facts presented right now, there's no one on the planet who would look more guilty of my sister's disappearance.

5

There's blood everywhere. The copper scent is sharp in my nostrils, nearly gagging me as I take it all in. Red mars the walls, congeals in pools on the carpet. Handprints trail across the furniture. It looks like a scene out of *The Shining*, and I wait for Jack to pop his head through the wall in my sister's living room. Jack Nicholson screaming, "Here's Johnny."

It's too hard for me to process it all, the scene in front of me. My thoughts feel thick, as if they're stuck in Jell-O. My emotions feel far away, as if someone has bottled them and put them away on a shelf.

"Eviana?" I manage as I take a step on shaky legs.

My heart finally awakens, pounding as I step between the pools, trying my best not to disturb the evidence. Each breath I suck in is sharp, as if the air is filled with razor blades. The sound of my own heart in my ears is too loud. I don't think that I could hear my sister even if she did call back out to me.

The trail of blood leads me through the house to my sister's bedroom. It's too much. There's no way this blood came from only one person. There must be gallons splashed across nearly every surface. I turn the corner, the curl of bone-white fingers catching my eye. A scream grows in the back of my throat.

There's a moment between sleeping and waking when everything seems real—when nightmares and dreams are woven into the same fabric, when reality can twist and morph, when anything is possible. In this space is where I find Eviana again and again, beautiful, haunting, and stolen. In most of my dreams, each time I reach for her, she disappears, evaporating into smoke that's carried off on the wind. Even my imagination can't find the answers. Even in dreams I can't hold on to her. In the worst ones, I find her body, the remnants of what a killer left of her.

When I finally wake, my brief stint of sleep has left me more exhausted than when I crawled into bed at two in the morning. After my unsettling talk with Simon in the kitchen, I decided there was no point in staying awake, in torturing myself longer. The midmorning sun is a visceral presence in Florida, the tendrils of sunlight cutting across the floor warming the room—the heat almost suffocating. I swear the guest bedroom gets no AC, and maybe that's purposeful so no one overstays their welcome. I feel like I'm being punished for occupying this space, as if despite the invite, Simon really doesn't want me here.

I glance at my phone, swiping away notifications from work that I'll catch up on later. I need to be in the right frame of mind to catch up on my client work, and I'm not there right now. Though I took some leave from my job as a social worker for the city of Seattle, PTO doesn't mean much to my team and I know I'll still end up with text messages daily for as long as I'm here—but at least I'm still getting paid, and my cases haven't been abandoned. Even from here, I can still do some good for the kids who need me. There's no way I could take unpaid leave, but thankfully I never use my vacation time, so I have several weeks to draw from. At the end of the bed, I rifle through my clothes, pull on a pair of leggings and a T-shirt, before slipping down the hall. I swear, the moment I leave the room, I can feel the cameras watching me. I wonder how long Simon surveilled me on the feed before he decided to approach me in the kitchen. The idea of him keeping tabs on me seriously creeps me out.

Two deep voices from the living room give me pause. I stop, hovering in the hallway as I eavesdrop. I recognize Simon's voice, but the other man, I'm not sure who he is.

"Look, it's best for everyone if we just let this work itself out. The sponsors, the planned endorsements, it's not going to look good—you know?" the mystery man says to Simon.

"Yeah, yeah, I know. This is just literally the worst time. You know that spring is the best time to get some of these outdoor shoots in Florida. We've got so much lined up. Why couldn't she disappear in July or August?" Simon is clearly exasperated, and though I can't see him, I imagine him throwing his hands up in the air in his frustration.

The fact that they're talking about my sister so callously, it sets me on edge and sends a warning down my spine. Do they know more than they're letting on? Did they get rid of my sister because she was causing problems for them? I'm going to watch and listen, collecting as much information from them as I can while I'm here. If I get enough, maybe then the police will listen to me. Maybe with enough evidence they'll overlook my past and instead focus on what happened to Eviana.

"How much content do we have? How long can it buy us?" the mystery man asks.

"I don't know, a few months? Maybe a little longer if we're smart about it."

"That's plenty. I'm sure everything will have sorted itself out by then. That gives us time to plan and figure out what the next best steps are. For now, just keep posting like normal and act like nothing is off."

"Yeah, I'll do that," Simon says.

I edge forward, finally looking into the living room, and that's when I see that Simon is on a conference call with someone on his laptop. My guess is it's Tom, Eviana's manager or agent, or whatever the hell she called him. She spoke so highly of him when I was here, but now I wonder what she'd think if she heard him talking this way. They're planning to keep her posts and social media going like she didn't disappear. Instead of going to the police they're worried about revenue and appearances. What the hell is wrong with these guys? How did Eviana manage to surround herself with the biggest sociopaths on the planet?

When the call ends, I watch Simon navigate to something on his laptop, and delete a bunch of files. From where I stand, I can't tell what they are. But I'd put my money on him deleting evidence. I finally step into the living room and Simon whips around, surveying me, obviously trying to figure out what I heard and saw—and how much. But I stroll through the kitchen with my head held high like I heard nothing at all. I wish I knew the full depth of what they are up to. His eyes bore through me with each step, the burn of his gaze stinging against my skin. It's bad enough that I know he's watching me through the cameras, but now he's going to watch me in person too.

I make a cup of coffee and slip out the front door onto the porch and unearth a cigarette from my pack. I hate that this is a habit that I picked up from my mother, but no matter how many times I try vapes, patches, gums, I just can't shake it. The only way I can rid myself of some of the anxiety bound up inside me is to let it out with a breath of smoke. My palm shields my eyes from the sun as I walk toward a sliver of shade cast by a palm tree. I don't want to smoke next to the door, where I'm sure Simon will throw a fit, though I bet it'd be easier for him to keep tabs on me there.

From the front yard, all the houses in the neighborhood feel more grand, taller. While in the Escalade, it didn't quite feel this way. But now, as I look over the imposing structures, the McMansions made of mostly stucco or stone, I wonder how many eyes can see me from all the windows. I feel like a fish stuck in a fishbowl, eyes and noses pressed against the glass as they survey me. It makes me miss my apartment. It may be small and expensive, but at least it's all mine and I can be alone.

The scuff of feet against the street and the gentle jingle of a collar draws my attention. I hear the woman before I see her, her path obscured by the large bushes between Eviana's house and her neighbors. When she comes into view, my eyes sharpen. The woman is tall, lean, clad in designer athleisure gear. Though it looks like she's dressed to work out, her hair is perfectly curled, and she's got on a full face of makeup over her pale skin. A long-haired dachshund trots along in front of her, clearly oblivious to my existence. With her attention so rapt by her phone, I don't expect the woman to notice me. But she glances to her right, directly at me, and freezes.

Her hand snaps to her heart and she gasps. I guess that I startled her.

"Oh, dear God, you about scared the bejesus out of me, girl," she says with a bit of a Southern drawl. She throws her curls over her left shoulder before facing me fully.

"Sorry," I say, taking another drag from my cigarette.

"Those things will kill you, you know," she says, pointing a long acrylic nail in the direction of my hand.

"We're all going to die. I like the idea of picking what kills me." My usual sarcasm doesn't reach my words, but I think the message still gets across. I'm well aware of my choices, but I hate the public need to mother me about it. I don't tell everyone with a cocktail in their hands that it'll lead them down the same path as my cigarettes.

"Do you know Eviana?" she asks, gesturing toward the house.

"Yeah, that's my sister," I say.

She raises her hand, shielding her face from the sun, and appraises me. Then she closes the distance between us, much to her dog's dismay. As she walks in the grass toward me, the dog fights every step, yanking the leash as if it's terrified of grass.

"I didn't know she had a sister." She props a hand on her hip. The way she says this, I feel like she's about to ask me for proof.

I let out an uncomfortable laugh. Though I'm unsurprised that Eviana wouldn't bring me up often, somehow the disappointment is still sharp.

"Do you know her well?" I ask, unsure if this is someone Eviana runs into often.

She scoffs, as if I should know exactly who she is.

"I'm Annabell Keller," she offers. But when my reaction doesn't match what she's going for, she adds, "Eviana and I get together at least once a week. We're great friends."

I nod and take another drag.

"Where is she? I tried texting her but she's been so bad about responding recently."

My mind slams to a halt. I hadn't even considered what I'd say to people if they asked me where my sister was. I didn't expect Simon to put me into a position where I'd have to lie. I didn't think I'd be running into her friends and having to continue on with life like Eviana didn't disappear. My mind screams for me to come up with something, but it takes Annabell clearing her throat for me to speak again.

"She's really busy shooting some new content, so she's going to be out of town for a little while," I say, trying to keep it vague. The moment the lie leaves my lips, I feel disgusting, dirty. I can't believe I'm lying for him—but what other choice do I have? He'll implicate me in this if I don't play along. I'll have to keep playing this role for as long as it takes me to find my sister. This is, until I find her.

"Oh!" she says, as she makes a show of smacking herself in

the forehead. "That's right. She told me she was going to be out of town for a while."

I sip my coffee as I process her words. I'm unsure if they're the truth or if it's some kind of show she's putting on to seem closer to my sister than she really is. How often did she even talk to this woman?

"You know, I did wonder if she was looking to leave town for other reasons," she says before pursing her lips with displeasure. Her dog starts to yank at her again, urging Annabell toward the street.

I raise a brow at her statement. "What do you mean?"

"Oop, I've got to go," she says, motioning toward the dog.

She looks back at me three times as she shuffles away, a smirk quirking her lips each time before she disappears from view, blocked by another fence made of bushes.

I stomp out my cigarette and grab my phone from my pocket. It takes me a few seconds to find Annabell on social media, to confirm what she's said about their friendship. My sister has never posted a picture with the woman. But they do follow each other. That begs the question, how close were they really and what did she mean about Eviana looking for other reasons to leave town?

After my chat with Annabell, I open the front door and nearly slam right into Simon. He stumbles backward, his eyes wide. Clearly I caught him off guard. My stomach twists. It's obvious he was watching me, keeping tabs on me as I was talking to Annabell. The warning sirens sound in the back of my mind again.

"Oh, sorry, I was just going to check the mail," he says. The lie could not be any less believable.

"Yeah, sure," I say as I orbit as far away from him as possible.

I head back to my room, feeling Simon watching me as I go. I wrack my brain for anything that Eviana might have said the last time I saw her, if there was anything that pointed to her disappearance. But there was nothing. She didn't mention anything to me. She talked about how desperate she was to find a treatment for her cancer, how she hoped that the doctors were wrong. And now, I wonder, did she leave because she didn't want to face a fight for her life in the spotlight? Did something more sinister happen to my sister? Did she really just leave? Why didn't she tell me what she was planning?

A bad feeling inside me warns me that Eviana is dead, and that Simon had something to do with it. How else could you possibly explain his detachment—his complete lack of concern around my sister's disappearance? I pull up her social media accounts on my phone to find that he's posted a new picture from her account. Eviana is standing on the beach. She's got on a teal stripped bikini with a crocheted coverup over the top. She's wearing sunglasses, a full face of makeup, and a wide-brim straw hat.

Nothing like a good beach day to reset the soul, the caption reads. I grind my teeth together as I read it over and over, until I can see the words imprinted on the back of my eyelids every time I blink. Under the post, there are already hundreds of comments. There are nice ones, obvious spam, and creepy guys who comment on every single thing my sister posts. I don't know how she deals with this deluge day in and day out. It's overwhelming to me just looking at it.

I click to the next post, then the next, scrolling and scrolling through the likes, the loves, the comments, the arguments of her fans, until it all blurs together. It isn't until I get to the fourth most recent post that I find what I'm looking for, a threat.

Stop posting this shit or it's gunna get you killed.

I keep reading and find a few others.

I know where you live.

You want me to find you, don't you?

What do you think I'll do to you when I find you?

What do you want me to do to you?

Are you a bad girl who deserves to be punished?

Are you a bad girl who deserves to die?

The threatening messages are on most of her posts, buried among the other innocuous messages. I notice that Eviana never replied to them, but she very rarely interacted with most of her following. I look at all the hate that's spewed her way, all the threats, what looks like stalking, and I catalog it in my mind.

Which of them are real threats, and which of them are bored? I can't help but think that the threats on the internet are nothing compared to the threat that's in this house—the threat that still can't seem even remotely concerned about my sister.

6

It's all fun and games pretending your famous wife isn't missing, until you miss a livestream that you didn't know she had planned. Simon has erupted, simmered, and is now pacing the living room and kitchen so frequently that I think he may wear a path into the floor. Turns out, three hours ago Eviana was supposed to do a livestream for her fans, a quick Q&A session to reconnect because she felt like they deserved a little *time* with her. Apparently, Eviana hadn't mentioned this session to either Tom or Simon, and they're absolutely *freaking out* about it.

I've been sitting at the way too modern kitchen table, something that looks more like a statue than something you'd eat on, watching as it's unraveled. I'm probably getting too much joy out of it, feeling like karma has come home to roost. Though Simon has thrown up a *Sorry, I'm not feeling well today* post to appease her followers, it's clear that quite a few aren't buying any of it. Social media is ablaze with speculation, anger, and a smattering of well wishes. Buried among the comments, as I search, I find the usual stalkers and threatening accounts. There are so many skeptical comments though, the dam won't hold for long. Simon didn't plan this well enough.

"I can't believe she didn't tell me that she had this livestream planned." Simon grinds the words out through his frustration. He keeps throwing his hands up in the air, and letting out guttural growls as if that will do anything to fix the situation. "And the goddamn cameras aren't working again. What the hell is happening with the Wi-Fi in this house?"

The cameras aren't working? Well, that makes me feel a little better. "Did she tell you about everything that she planned for her accounts?" I ask. I thought that Simon managed her calendar and had a lot of insights into what Eviana had planned —but now I'm wondering just how hands-on he'd been. Just how many secrets was my sister keeping from him?

"She didn't tell me everything that she had planned, that would be ridiculous. It's not like she answered to me. I didn't tell her what to do." His words are cutting, and the anger simmering behind his eyes takes me aback. He clenches his fists at his sides. How did Eviana live with this man? Was he always this angry beneath the surface? Did he ever hit my sister? And his comments that he didn't tell her what to do stick out to me— why would he even mention that? No one accused him of being Eviana's boss.

I ignore his comments and turn my eyes back to my phone. The looming presence of his anger is like a third person in the room, and I don't want to set him off more than I already have. I have no idea what this guy is even capable of.

"It's fine. We're going to get ahead of this, and no one is going to suspect anything." He mumbles the words to himself like they're some kind of affirmation, as if he says them aloud, that will make it true. "They won't ever notice. It will all be fine. It has to be fine."

"Eviana posted a lot of videos; this can't go on forever. At some point she either has to reappear or..." I trail off, not really certain how I want my words to hit home with him. But they're true. Eviana can't just disappear. He and Tom can't pretend forever that she's home and fine. There's a limit to how long this façade will last. They can't never post another video of her. Though I'm sure they'll try to conjure up something with the help of AI, it won't look legitimate and that will make their case look even worse.

He whirls, his eyebrows inching up his forehead. "Don't you think I know that? Don't you think I've been sitting here calculating that exact fact? I'm well aware. You pointing it out a hundred times isn't going to fix anything." His rage fills the room like a toxic fog, and I take a couple steps back, wanting to put as much distance between us as possible.

I grind my teeth together until my jaw aches and a headache awakens behind my eyes. I'm not going to let him talk to me like this. Eviana might have put up with him running his mouth, but I'm not going to. "If you'd go to the police, that would bring her back faster. You're not even out there looking for her. So I don't know why you think she's just going to reappear on the doorstep. You should do something," I say.

He digs in his pocket and throws his car keys at me. "If you're so smart, you go do something then. Go find her yourself if it's that easy."

I catch the keys in midair, the cold metal digging into my palm. His words are so sharp, I flinch.

"What are you waiting for, Detective? Go on," he says, as his hand slashes the air, motioning toward the front door when I don't stand up right away. He can't be serious.

"You seriously think I'm going to go out there and find her? In this town?" I ask, baffled. Orlando is huge. It's sprawling with many surrounding cities that are also densely populated. She could be hiding anywhere, if she left of her own volition, that is. Maybe if she went missing in our hometown, back in Gainesville, I'd stand a chance. But here? There's no way.

"You're so certain I can do it, so you go. I'm sure you can find her within an hour. You seem so confident that it's easy."

His anger rises with every word. The muscles in my torso and arms tighten as he looms over me. A throbbing vein on the side of his neck pulses with a warning. I have to get out of here, away from him. I tuck the keys into my pocket, grab my purse, then walk out the front door, feeling his eyes on me with every step that I take. I half expect him to follow me, for him to stomp up the driveway right behind me. But he doesn't.

In the round driveway, I find the monstrous SUV casting a long shadow on the driveway. Though I've never driven something as large as Simon's Escalade, I climb in—what other choice do I have? The interior smells like leather and my sister's orange bergamot perfume. It makes my stomach clench, but I try not to think about it. I wonder, when was the last time she was in this car, whether or not she was alive, or if it's the last time I'll smell her perfume.

Stop being so morbid. Of course she's alive.

Not even I believe my own lies. If my sister were alive, she would have posted something on social media. She would have texted Tom or Simon. Eviana wouldn't just disappear, she wouldn't run away, and she certainly wouldn't abandon the accounts that she worked for years on. That, at least, I know about her. Eviana worked for this, she fought to build the life that she has. She wouldn't throw it all away because she was pissed at Simon.

I press the button to start the engine while I consider what to do and where to go. When I glance back at the house, I see Simon standing in the foyer, glowering through the glass door at me. The look on his face is filled with such hate that I immediately throw the car into drive and press the gas. I need to put distance between the two of us, give him time to cool down. My mind flashes back to the crime shows that I've watched before; how do they find missing people? First, they always try to retrace the person's last steps. But I don't know what my sister did before she disappeared. All I know is that allegedly she went for a walk. That should mean that the neighborhood is the best starting point—but Eviana's car is gone. So, she must have driven to wherever it is that she went for a walk.

I work my way through the curving roads, passing under towering oak trees, oversized houses, and past driveways stuffed with luxury cars. I side-eye Porsches, McClarens, and the odd Bentley. I can't imagine what these people do to afford these cars. On my salary, I'm able to keep myself in a one-bedroom apartment with public transportation and that's pretty much it. Though I'll indulge in coffee I don't need and takeout sometimes, otherwise I live a pretty frugal life.

At the gate I nod to the guard, then I turn left out of the neighborhood and drive toward the coffee shop my sister took me to during my visit. A few minutes' drive from her house, there's a shopping center with a coffee shop, a grocery store, a gym, and several small restaurants. I know she came here at least once a day, so it seems like a good first stop. Though I scan the parking lot for her electric blue Range Rover, there's nothing remotely close.

I park at the edge of the lot and climb out of the Escalade, then walk toward the coffee shop. Though it's barely ten in the morning, the air is already hot, thick with humidity. Despite the walk being only a minute or so, my skin is damp with sweat when I open the door to the shop. The smell of vanilla and coffee hits me the moment I step inside, and I relish the fragrance. Inside the shop, to my left, there are clusters of tables, a few filled with patrons who are typing away on laptops. To my right, there's a long counter with several baristas behind it, swarming around a hissing espresso machine, a whirring blender, and a long line of canisters filled with drip coffee.

A woman with light brown skin and curly black hair approaches the counter when I step forward. Her smile is warm when she greets me. "Hey, what can I get you?" she asks.

I order my usual, then ask, "I know it might be a weird question, but have you seen this woman in here recently?" I ask as I show the barista a picture of my sister.

She scrutinizes the picture, then looks to me with an eyebrow raised—though she doesn't say anything. A woman approaches, squeezing between me and the counter to see the picture I'm showing to the barista. The woman is a bit shorter than me, with pale skin that's covered in colorful tattoos. She's got on a tank top displaying full sleeves and artwork that carves across her collarbones.

"Sorry, just being nosy," she says as she wrinkles her nose at the picture then slinks away.

"It's my sister. I was in here with her a few days ago," I clarify, though I don't want to give her any indication that Eviana is missing. I glance over my shoulder to see where the woman went and find her sitting at a table not far from me.

"Oh, right. She's usually in here most mornings around nine, but I don't think I've seen her in here today," she explains. "Is everything okay?"

I nod. "Yeah, I thought she might have left something here. Her laptop is missing." The lie doesn't land, and I can see the confusion clearly on her face, so I let the conversation die.

"Okay, well, your coffee will be done in a few," she says as she points toward the pickup area.

While I wait for my coffee, I google any local walking trails nearby. And the tattooed woman approaches me again.

"Hi, I'm Claire. I couldn't help but overhear about your sister. Is everything okay?" She raises a brow, and I find her interest a bit odd.

I nod quickly. "Of course, she just lost her laptop, so I'm trying to help her track it down."

"Eviana always was very forgetful," she says with an unamused arch of her brow.

"You know Eviana?"

She lets out a tense laugh. It looks like she wants to smile, but I'm not sure her Botox will allow it. "Of course I know her." The tone of her voice hints that it's not a good thing that she knows my sister.

"Oh?" I finally say when Claire doesn't continue.

She props her hand on her hip, as if to says she's frustrated I haven't already heard the story. "Eviana and I were really close. I was an influencer before her, until she decided to destroy my career."

This is the first I'm hearing of something like this. Why would Eviana bother to destroy her career? "How did she do that?"

"She spread lies and rumors about me. I'm sure if you find that laptop of hers, you'll find the details of it. Good luck with finding it, but I'm sure karma took care of that for you." She looks me up and down with disdain before she throws her hair over her shoulder and stalks toward the door.

I watch her disappear then turn my attention back to my phone, to my search for trails Eviana might have driven to. There are a few, both none close enough to Eviana's house that I'd consider them a stop. Instead, I look at the parks that are all within a ten-minute drive of her house; I'll start at those instead. Though I'm still not sure I buy Simon's story about my sister going for a walk, I need to cover all of my bases.

With my coffee in hand, I head out of the shop and climb back into the SUV. I scan the parking lot, wondering if Claire is waiting out here for me, but I don't see her. I refresh my sister's social media page, and find much of the same—more speculation, more questions, more disbelief that she didn't show for her livestream. I look through her pictures to see if she's mentioned any trails or any parks that she frequents until I finally find two. I put those at the top of my list and pull out of the shopping center.

I turn toward the first park, a three-minute drive from my sister's house. The lot is empty when I turn in. It's eerily deserted in a way that I didn't expect. Usually in the mornings parks like this are packed with families and people walking their dogs. I pull in under a canopy of oak branches that are heavy with Spanish moss. Cold seeps from my iced coffee, chilling my fingers as I slip from the car and walk toward the boardwalk that slinks through the dense forest behind the park. Eviana has several pictures on her social media accounts of her at this park, posing on the boardwalk, the thick oak trees spreading behind her like the outstretched legs of giant spiders.

As I step carefully through the grass toward the path, it occurs to me just how out of character this would be for my sister. And I wonder again if I'm getting any truths from my brother-in-law. Eviana was never a *nature* person. She hated the outdoors, bugs, the heat. I'm honestly not certain why she stayed in Florida. Maybe she liked the beach enough to redeem it. But everything in my sister's life seems like something on a checklist, not something she actually enjoyed. She didn't *lounge* at the beach; she just took pictures there. This whole state was just a backdrop—one big photoshoot. She didn't eat the baked goods she posted on social media; she just needed the content. I wonder if there was anything she really loved or if her entire life had become a performative list of tasks—what a sad way to live, if that were the case.

When I reach the trees, under the dense blanket of branches, the temperature drops a few degrees. Though it's a nice reprieve, my neck is still slicked with sweat. My shirt sticks to my back as I walk, and I regret not changing into something more suited to the weather. A boardwalk emerges from the dirt path in front of me, and I continue, my steps sounding hollow on the weather-beaten lumber. Wooden handrails rise alongside the boardwalk, creating a separation between the path and the wild forest that stretches beyond. The handrails are thick with spiderwebs, and tiny lizards dart in and out of my path as I walk. Though I know I'm alone out here, the constant rustling far off in the trees is unsettling.

It's just squirrels, I tell myself over and over, but some of the movements sound so loud, I know I'm lying to myself. The path curves in front of me, and I follow it, walking slowly. Shards of light spill from the gaps in the branches above, freckling the wooden deck in front of me. Ahead of me, probably twenty feet away, metal gleams in a pool of light, capturing my attention. I slow my pace as I approach, then realize that there's something metal stuck between the wooden planks. I shoo a lizard out of the way as I kneel down, then use my fingernails to free the piece of metal. The gleam of gold sparkles as I retrieve it, and as I hold it up, I realize that it's a small bracelet—one that I recognize. It's my sister's bracelet, a golden linked chain with a small charm on the end. Her initials are carved into the small charm. As I lay it in my palm, examining it, my stomach drops. The charm doesn't just have her initials, next to the *E* there's a smudge—a brown circle that I swear can't be anything but dried blood.

7

INSTAGRAM

DizzyGirl23: *@EvianaPendelton I hope you feel better soon! I was looking forward to your livestream but it's so important to feel well.*

Ttturner2: *@EvianaPendelton Are you sure you're okay? It's so not like you to just bail on a planned event. I really hope you're okay, but something seems off*

BiggestFanGurlll: *@EvianaPendelton lol liar. U aren't sick.*

Mistery: *@EvianaPendelton The pic you posted today wasn't even a recent pic. You have the same nail polish on that you wore in a pic on March 3, 2021, and the shirt is a repost too. You never repeat outfits or nail colors, so I think this pic is old. Why are you not posting a new pic? Are you really that sick?*

ValHalGal: *@EvianaPendelton Feel better hun!*

Dudeudeude02: *@EvianaPendelton u dumb bitch u deserve to be sick, I hope it's fatal. Trash like you shouldn't even be on the internet. Serves u right.*

DizzyGirl23: *@Dudeudeude02 Grow up and get off her page if you don't like it.*

ValHalGal: *@Dudeudeude02 you only have one life to live and this is how you choose to live it? Maybe log off.*

EvianaPendelton: *Everyone, I am so appreciative of your concern, but I promise that I'm fine. There's nothing to worry about. I'll be back to my usual self in a few days!*

BiggestFanGurlll: *@EvianaPendelton ur responding to stuff now? Weird. You never bothered before. Guess u are sick. LOL*

8

Unease slithers through me as I wait for the gate to Eviana's neighborhood to rumble to life and allow me entry. Every time I sit here, my palms slick with sweat as if the guard will finally decide this time that I'm not allowed back in. I expect for him to figure out that I'm a fraud, that I don't belong in a neighborhood like this. When it finally opens, I hit the gas a little too hard, lurching forward. My heart is pounding as I close in on Eviana's house. I worry about what's waiting for me inside—if Simon is still angry with me. I don't trust him, he makes me uneasy, and there's always a warning prickling in the back of my mind. *You can't trust him.*

I'm not sure that I really want to be alone in there with him again. But as I approach the house, I notice a small white BMW convertible in the driveway. A chicly dressed Asian woman is leaning against the car. She's got on a flowy green top. Her glossy shoulder-length hair is swept back from her face with a thin gold headband. She's focused her attention on her cellphone.

The more I look at her, the more it nags at me. I know this woman. She's one of Eviana's closest friends, Tia. We ran into

her at a coffee shop while I was visiting. I pull in beside her in
the driveway, carefully maneuvering the huge SUV. When I
climb out she glances to me but it takes a few seconds for recog-
nition to ripple across her features.

"Blair!" she says as I approach. "I thought you went home."
Her brows furrow with confusion.

"I did, but I came back," I say, hoping that she doesn't
ask why.

"Did you get Eviana all settled back in Seattle? I assume
that's why she's not answering the door."

I'm struck silent by her comment, not entirely sure what to
say. What does she mean? Why would Eviana be back in
Seattle?

She takes a step closer and lowers her voice. "Eviana
mentioned with all the financial issues going on that she might
go stay with you for a while." She glances back toward the
house, as if she's checking to see if Simon is watching us. And
I'm sure he is. I swear I always feel his eyes on me. He's watching, looming, keeping tabs on my every move.

I almost laugh because I've never heard anything so ridiculous. The thought of my sister spending any amount of time
back in my tiny apartment is absurd. My place is smaller than
her closet. She wouldn't know what to do with herself back
home. Where would Tia even get that idea? There's no way that
Eviana really hatched a plan to go back west with me.

"You know what, let's go over to my place to chat," Tia says,
when I'm still silent.

I climb into the passenger seat of her car. It smells like
leather and floral perfume inside. She starts to drive as soon as I
buckle my seatbelt. The interior has soft blue leather and
orange stitching. A huge glowing screen slices across the dash,
accented by metal and ambient lighting. It reminds me of a
spaceship. It's a nicer car than I could ever imagine owning.
Hell, I don't even own a car back home.

"So, I'm guessing based on your face that Eviana didn't give you all of the details she should have." She glances at me expectantly, as if I'll divulge all my sister's secrets. I wish that I knew them, but Eviana wouldn't have even trusted me with a house key.

I decide to play along, hoping that Tia will catch me up. But I don't want to admit that my sister didn't let me in on these conversations, that over the years we've grown apart as if we're both standing on opposite sides of a canyon that widens each year. I hate being left in the dark.

"Eviana had mentioned visiting, but she didn't say anything hinting that it might be long-term, or that she was having any financial problems." The lie is bitter on my tongue, but it's the closest that I can stay to the truth. Tia seems like a good friend to my sister. I don't want to lie to her. But the less she knows about Eviana's disappearance, the better. I have to keep all of this a secret until I have solid evidence against Simon.

"Eviana had been having a lot of issues recently. It wasn't just the money, there was some influencer friend that she used to have who started threatening her. She was convinced that Eviana sank her career or something—but Eviana wasn't that kind of person. There's no way she would have done something like that."

I wish I agreed with her, but my sister is definitely capable of destroying someone else's career, so instead of speaking up, I press my lips together.

She makes a tisking sound as she turns into a driveway. The house is at the far edge of the neighborhood, the lot shadowed by towering oak trees. She slides out of the car and motions for me to follow her. The house is about the size of my sister's, but the exterior isn't similar. The stucco and tile roof that are so common throughout the rest of the neighborhood have been traded out for a contemporary exterior. This house looks much more homey if you ask me. I follow her into the foyer. The interior is filled with blues and golds, intricately decorated like a fancy hotel. We work our way from the living room to the back of the house.

The living room is open to the kitchen. A high ceiling towers above us, with ancient wooden beams stretching to a peak. Floor-to-ceiling windows line the full length of the walls. Usually they'd be obscured by curtains or draperies, but these look straight out into the backyard. From where I stand I can see a sparkling pool, a sitting area, and the woods that flank the property line.

Tia waves me into the kitchen connected to the living room. Royal blue cabinets line the walls, a light stone filled with veins in the same shade of blue forms the countertops, and golden handles sparkle on each cabinet. It amazes me how uncluttered her whole home is. The counters of my kitchen back at home are filled with *stuff*. This feels so open, so nice. My sister's house is the same way. I guess that's what space buys you.

"Sorry, but I didn't want to get into the details out there where we could be heard." She motions toward the front door.

I nod, waiting for her to continue. I figure she's more likely to give me information if I stay quiet—the bonus is I also won't put my foot in my mouth.

"About six months ago, Eviana told me that she and Simon were having money issues. She thought that foreclosure was likely." She moves over to the small table that sits beside the windows looking out to the backyard, and signals for me to take a seat. I follow her and slide onto the soft chair.

When she looks at me for a response, I can't stop the truth from tumbling out. I'm sure it's already written all over my face. "She didn't tell me about any of this," I say, feeling good that this at least isn't a lie.

She clicks her tongue, a sound that's somehow sympathetic. "Eviana was an intensely private person. I'm sure she didn't mean anything by it. I know that she wouldn't want to have sounded like she was begging for money or anything. Any honestly, she didn't like to admit that anything was wrong." She reaches over and squeezes my hand atop the table. I guess my face is telling a story. She's trying to make me feel better.

"Yeah, I know. Eviana has never been one to discuss things like that—especially not with me."

"Well, you're her little sister. She doesn't want to look like a failure. She knows that you look up to her, that you used to idolize her."

I ignore the comment, because even though it's true, it feels like a jab. I'm too sensitive when it comes to my sister.

"Where is all the money going?" I ask. I know that Eviana was a millionaire. She's making six or seven figures at a minimum from all of her ad deals and sponsorships. So if she's pulling in that kind of money, where did it all go? Her house is nice, but I know she didn't blow all of it on that.

She shakes her head and sucks her teeth. "Simon has a gambling addiction from what I understand. He spends a ridiculous amount on scratch-off tickets, online gambling, casinos, sports betting—if he can bet on it, he'll try."

"Can't say I'm surprised," I say, I knew there was something off about him. I could absolutely see him blowing all of my sister's money on something so stupid.

"Eviana also has a penchant for spending. She says it's necessary for her lifestyle and for her following. But I know that it's not—not to the extent that she takes it anyway. She's always buying new designer bags, outfits."

I'm getting a bit of a picture already. But there's something I haven't figured out yet.

"Is she planning to leave Simon?" That's the only way this would all make sense. There's no way she was planning to move Simon into my apartment too.

She offers me a one-shouldered shrug. "Who really knows.

Some days it sounded like it. But recently she sounded like she was planning to maybe do it for real this time."

Tia looks at her phone as it lights up in her hand.

"Shit, this is my kid's school. I've got to take this. Sorry we have to cut this short," she says as she follows me toward the front door.

9

The backyard of my sister's house was built as a retreat. It's the kind of thing I've never seen in person before, but I've seen so many times on all the Real Housewives shows. It's one of those oasis backyards, with a rock-lined pool, a hot tub, several gazebos and lounging spaces, surrounded by large shrubs and towering bamboo along the back. On either side of the yard though, only a low metal fence separates her from the neighbors. From the spot I'm sitting in one of the gazebos, I can see into both backyards, noting how similar they are to my sister's. I wonder if the insides of the houses are identical too.

I've been out here for hours, hiding from Simon, as I try to figure out what to do with the bracelet. Obviously, I can't go to the cops yet. This isn't enough evidence—and after I picked it up with my bare hands, I'm not sure that having my fingerprints on my sister's bloody jewelry is going to look so hot. Simon is still on high alert, trying to recover from Eviana's missed livestream. The longer it goes on, the more speculation is rising on social media. It's clear that he's in over his head—a fact that I know he'll never admit to. I guess he thinks someone with millions of followers can drop off of the face of the planet and no one will notice.

"Good afternoon," a soft voice says from the other side of the fence. I look over to find a woman with long hair and a wide smile. She's tall, curvy, wearing a brightly colored sundress. Her skin is startlingly pale, especially for a place like Florida. How does she avoid the sun? I slathered myself in sunscreen as soon as I got off the plane and I still ended up with a sunburn on my shoulders. When I study her, I realize she looks eerily similar to my sister, in a way that's almost unnerving.

"Hi," I chirp back. I haven't seen any of Eviana's next-door neighbors since I've been here. And I wonder if Eviana spent much time talking to them. "I'm Blair Casteel. I'm Eviana's sister." I shove up from my seat in the gazebo and walk over toward the fence. The moment I step out of the shade, the heat of the sun warms my neck. Sweat prickles on my back and I curse this weather. Sure, I might have grown up with it, but I've been in Seattle for so long that I swear I've lost my ability to deal with the heat.

"Oh! It's so good to meet you. I'm Danica Fullerton. I've lived next to Eviana for, God, what, like three or four years now?" she says, clearly trying to do the mental math. "Are you visiting?"

I nod.

"Where from?" she asks.

"Seattle," I say.

"Oof, what a change. Am I right? I'm from Portland. Some days I miss the weather, to be honest. It gets so damn hot here," she says, rambling a little bit. "There are times I swear I'd pay a million just to get an overcast day."

"I love Portland. I try to get down there every couple months. I love the ride down there on the train."

"Oh, I miss that train." She offers me a warm smile and steps closer, but lucky for her, she's still in the shade of her house. "How's your sister doing?" She crosses her arms and looks to the house.

"Oh, she's..." I trail off, not entirely sure what to say. I'm still not accustomed to lying about things like this. How am I supposed to go on pretending that Eviana isn't gone? Someone is going to notice. There's only so long I can get away with saying she's out doing a shoot.

"She's having a hard time, isn't she?" she asks, lowering her voice, like she's concerned we might be overheard.

I look back to the house to be sure that I can't see Simon in any of the windows. When I'm sure he's not watching, or likely listening, I turn my attention back to Danica. "What do you mean? Why would you say that?" I ask, really hoping that she might have had some kind of friendship with Eviana. I'm desperate to find someone who my sister opened up to. While Tia knew some things about my sister, I feel like Eviana wasn't giving her the entire picture.

"I'm not the kind to spread rumors or gossip. I really don't try to eavesdrop," she says.

"Of course, I totally understand. It's not gossip at all. To be honest, I've been a bit skeptical of Simon," I admit, hoping that it'll get her to open up.

She nods. "Okay, so, a lot of the time I hear them arguing... well, maybe not arguing. I don't think that's the right way to explain it. I hear him yelling. I hear things break sometimes. I don't ever hear Eviana. I just hear Simon. It seems like they have been having a lot of fights lately."

With his attitude he's flipped on and off over the last forty-eight hours, I can't say that I'm at all surprised. I've seen his rage burst out. I can't imagine what he was like when he was alone with Eviana. How often was he yelling at her? And for what?

"When was the last time you heard them fighting?" I ask.

"Three days ago, I think?" she says, her voice lifting with uncertainty.

Three days ago... Simon wasn't supposed to be back three days ago. That'd mean he got back right after I left. So, I wasn't the last person to see my sister. He was. The lie doesn't surprise me, but it still sends a bolt of anger through me. The last time I saw Eviana, she opened up about wanting to step back from being an influencer. She was getting exhausted with so much of her life being performative. But she didn't think that Simon or Tom would take kindly to her wanting to take a break. Could she have told him she was quitting? Could that be what the fight was about? Did they do something to prevent her from quitting?

"Could you hear any of what was being said?"

"I heard bits and pieces. It sounded like he was accusing her of lying about something. But I wasn't able to garner what he thought she was lying about." She shakes her head and looks back toward the house. "I wonder if he thought she was cheating. I don't know how she could. They were always together—it seemed like she barely left the house, while he ran all over creation. But he felt like the kind of guy who'd accuse his wife of cheating."

I swallow hard, wondering what kind of life my sister was really leading—what she was dealing with on a daily basis. When I used to scroll through her feed, it looked on the surface like she was living the perfect life, like she had it all, the perfect husband, a huge house, more money than anyone could ever ask for. I envied her. The life that she'd built for herself. But what if even with her millions of followers, she was suffering in silence? Maybe she felt like there was no one she could truly be honest with. Was she trapped in this life?

"What makes you say that?"

She offers a casual shrug. "He yells at kids who get too close to the house. I've seen him yelling at their landscapers, the cleaning people they've hired, delivery people. It seems like he's always taking his anger out on someone. There's just something really off about him."

It's interesting since he's really tried to play a different role around me.

"Actually, there was one time that he screamed at me too. He caused quite the commotion."

"Oh?" I ask when she doesn't continue. It's clear that she needs interaction to share stories. She's not the kind of person to monologue.

"I had a few people over for a holiday party. I guess one of my guests parked in front of their house. Simon came over, banged on the door. He started shouting about how disrespectful it was for there to be a car on the street in front of his house. He said if the car wasn't moved in five minutes, he'd slash the tires and have it towed. Eviana was trailing after him, begging him to calm down, but he wouldn't listen."

"God, that's terrible. I'm so sorry."

"It was very tense. He ended up peeing on the car before we got it moved. But it was sorted out and he finally calmed down."

She takes another step forward. As she gets closer to the light, I can see that she's got green eyes, a thin nose, cheekbones that are a little too sharp. I'd guess she's about ten or so years older than I am.

"Did my sister ever talk to you about Simon?" I know she's overheard things, but I want to know if she ever heard anything come from my sister's lips directly.

She shakes her head. "No, she never opened up to me about anything like that specifically. But I would see her out here crying from time to time. I invited her over, and we'd have wine occasionally. We weren't close enough for her to give me all the details about her dirty laundry," she explains. "But, a few days ago, I did hear a lot of doors slamming after the fight."

"Did you see anything?" I ask.

"You know, my security cameras did go off in the middle of the night because I think Simon was leaving," she explains. "It was around two a.m. or so, I think." That's right around the time that I got the first texts from him.

My heart seizes. This isn't good. Unless he was having an affair or was up to something there was no reason for him to be leaving at that hour. "Leaving in the middle of the night? Could you see what he was doing?"

"It looked like he brought something to his car, then went back in the house, then he left. My camera went back off when he came home a few hours later."

"Would you mind sending me a copy of those videos?"

She nods. "Sure, just give me your number and I'll text them to you," she says.

"Thank you." I give her my number and save her contact info in my phone. A few seconds later, I've got the video.

"Blair, seriously, is Eviana okay?" she presses as she looks at me. There's concern swimming behind her eyes. And I don't want to tell her the truth, I can't. It's too dangerous for me if the police get involved at this point—there's no way that this ends well for anyone. I know the best thing now is for me to build my case about Simon's involvement. It's clear that he did something to my sister, and I'm going to prove it. Once I have the evidence, then I'll go to the police.

"Yeah, Eviana is fine. She just needed to get away for a little bit. Everything was just getting to be a bit too much for her, so she needed some space." Though I feel uneasy about the lie, it comes out smooth, as if I've practiced the lines. "She's a big girl. I know she can take care of herself."

She nods, though I can tell that she doesn't quite believe me.

"If you remember anything else, or if you come across any other videos about the fighting, it'd really help me out if you could send them."

"You know, there was something else, now that I think about it," she says, her brow furrowed with concentration.

"Oh?" I ask, anticipation swirling in the pit of my belly.

"I did hear Eviana arguing with a woman on the porch a few days ago. The voice was familiar, though I don't know her name. She had a lot of tattoos. That's really all I could see."

Tattoos. I wonder if it was the woman from the coffee shop... What was her name? Claire. I think it was Claire. "Did you get a sense of what they were arguing about?"

"I came outside in the midst of it all. I heard some accusations of backstabbing, being two-faced, before the woman stormed off before the sliding glass doors were slammed closed. She wasn't happy with Eviana, that's for sure."

"That's helpful, thank you," I say, realizing that I've probably gotten all the information that there is to get out of Danica, for now anyway.

A sick smile twists her lips. "Are you trying to get her to ditch his ass for good?"

I nod. "That's what I'm hoping for. I know he doesn't treat her the way she should be treated. Especially if he's yelling at her all the time," I say.

"Let's nail his ass to the wall."

Danica signals that she's going to head back into the house, and I offer her a little wave as she goes. She was far more helpful than I ever expected a neighbor to be. There are a couple friends of Eviana's who I met while I was visiting. I should talk to them too, but I don't have their contact information. Somehow, I need to figure out how to get in touch with them. I need to learn about what my sister's life was really like, and what Simon was up to.

But how angry did she make her friends? Eviana has always had rather tenuous friendships. Did she take it too far this time?

10

AGE THIRTEEN

The lights are dim, the living room illuminated only by the glow of the television, the flickering spotlighting the sharp edges of the couch beside me, the boy sitting only a foot to my right. The air is tight, as if we're both holding our breath—though I know it's in my head alone. Eviana brought this boy, Josh, home to watch a movie tonight, and though I expected that she'd want time alone with him, she begged me to watch a movie with them. My body feels too tight, rigid, as I sit up too straight next to Josh. I hate this. Feeling so awkward, so out of place. He's in tenth grade. He looks too grown up to be this close to me. It's exciting and strange all at the same time.

Ten minutes ago, Eviana got up and said she had to go upstairs for a minute. And here I've sat, like an obedient puppy while I've waited for her. I should be watching the movie, but instead, all I can do is keep looking up the stairs wondering when she'll come back down, when I'll be able to finally breathe again. I feel like a rabbit trapped with a lion.

"She's been gone for a while," Josh says, and in my periphery, I can see that he's turned his head to look at me.

He's got dark hair that dusts his ears, ice-blue eyes, and

plump lips. His jaw is square, dusted by dark stubble. I'm not surprised that Eviana brought a guy like this home. He's super cute and clearly her type.

I nod and press my lips together, not wanting to say the wrong thing. Josh is a few years older than me, and completely out of my league. I barely talk to guys in my own grade. The fact that he's talking to me right now—I could literally die. *He's just talking to you to be polite*, I tell myself to try and calm my racing heart. I'm all too aware of the sweat prickling my palms and the back of my neck.

"Yeah, I guess," I finally manage when he continues to look at me expectantly.

He scoots a little closer, closing the gap of about a foot between us. Only six inches separates us now. Tension tightens across my skin, as if I've been shrink-wrapped. I'm too aware of his proximity, the sharp edges of his cheekbones, the heat blooming in my chest as he nears. Can he hear how hard my heart is beating? Does he know I'm absolutely freaking out right now?

"You're prettier than her," he says, and I swear I need to clean my ears out. Because there's no way that he actually said that. He has to be lying. There's no way anyone could honestly believe that. I swallow hard as I try to settle my churning guts. He reaches up and pushes a strand of my hair behind my ear, and goosebumps prickle on my skin at his touch. I want this to be real, but a nagging feeling in the back of my mind just won't shut up.

He leans in, the heat of his breath feathering my lips. I can't breathe or move. I feel like a deer frozen before a car slams into it on the highway. His lips press hard against mine, but it doesn't feel nice, or right. It's like kissing a statue that's soaking wet. So much of his spit coats my lips, and spreads down to my chin. I just wait, counting in my head until it's over. *Shouldn't I have enjoyed that?* I ask myself over and over as he pulls away.

Did he enjoy it? Did I do something wrong? Is there something wrong with me?

His lips curve into a smile, then his eyes flash up to the landing that skirts along the edges of the living room. Eviana stands, leaning against the railing. The way she's looking down at me, I know that she saw everything. Laughter erupts from both of them at the same time, as if I'm surrounded by a pack of hyenas.

"How was that, Josh?" she asks, venom lacing through her words.

"I've had better kisses from a dog," he says, then howls with laughter.

I shove up from the couch and yank my hand back. Before I can stop myself, I smack him hard across the cheek. It's not like I asked for this. I could sink into the floor right now. Humiliation threatens to crumple me to the floor. I didn't even want to kiss him. He kissed me.

"Don't ever touch me again." I spit the words at him.

"Ha, as if I'd even want to. You fell for that line about being prettier than your sister. There's not a chance, you'll never measure up to her. You're fugly."

"Believe me, I know," I say, tears stinging my eyes. Though I hit him, I feel like he's punched me. The damage he's done is far worse.

I run up the stairs, and Eviana gets in my way, trying to block me from getting into my room. She holds her arms out. I try to duck to the right, but she sidesteps, making me stumble back.

"Let me go to my room," I say, an edge to my words. I hate when she sees me cry. My eyes sing, and my nose already feels stuffy.

"Why, so you can cry? You poor baby," she says, her tone high and mocking.

I dodge to the left, then to the right when Eviana tries to

follow me. But her reflexes are a little slower than mine. I manage to squeeze past her and get into my room. She wheels around, trying to stop me, but I grab the edge of my door and slam it closed. Eviana screams as the door shuts hard on her fingers.

I grind my teeth together as she screams for our mother. I'll get in trouble, I know it—but in the end, it was worth it.

11

It's been four days. Four days since my sister went missing. Four days since I think Simon or someone else did something to her. But I still don't have enough evidence to prove it yet. There's also a voice nagging in the back of my mind about the argument with Claire. How is all of this connected? This morning when I got up, I started combing through Eviana's social media pages for more updates. It seems her stalkers are out in force. There are so many threatening comments. A few are a little too on the nose, mentioning they know where Eviana lives in Orlando. Though the messages aren't specific enough to list an address, it still makes me wonder if someone did find it. There are so many shady sites where someone could have bought her information. I'm not naive enough to believe in privacy. There are a few snide comments from a name I recognize as well, Claire. I click onto the account and navigate through a few minutes' worth of her content—but I don't find anything particularly helpful.

I tap away from social media and look through my contacts. In high school, Lucia Arenas and I were super close. We still keep in touch, talking at least a few times a month. After college, she moved to Orlando and became a cop. I don't know if she's the right person to go to about my sister, but I do wonder if she could give me any insight.

Instead of calling, I shoot her a text. It takes a few back-and-forth messages for us to agree to meet at a place in Kissimmee for lunch. I pace the guest room until it's time for me to climb back into Simon's car. I debate again, if I should grab my own rental car—but for now, I'm more than happy to burn his gas and avoid another hit to my credit card. It takes me almost an hour to battle traffic from Orlando to Kissimmee. When I finally pull into the parking lot of the small Colombian restaurant, it's packed, but I know from the reviews online that's usual for this place. You can't call it a lunch rush if it's this busy from open to close.

I climb out of the car, just as the dark clouds huddled above the restaurant begin to open. Rain pelts the pavement, and I curse not getting here a few minutes earlier. I slam the car door and dart toward the front of the restaurant. A woman with dark hair holds the door open for me and I thank her as I duck inside. I run my hands over my hair, trying to wipe away the rain that's collected there.

The restaurant smells delicious, like meat, roasted garlic, and spices I can't quite place. I glance around at the busy tables until I finally spot Lucia and offer her a little wave as I walk over to the table. She watches me as I move. She stands to give me a hug before we both sit down.

"Oh my God, you look exactly the same," she says with a smile.

I offer her a laugh. Though we talk all the time, this is the first time I'm seeing her in person in years. "I'm not so sure that's a compliment." I was an incredibly awkward teenager who was insecure and had no idea who I was. If I'm still giving off those vibes, I might need to make some adjustments. "You look amazing though," I say.

Lucia's skin is light brown, flawless. She's a bit taller than I am, which is saying something. Her dark hair is cut into a pixie style, showing off her sharp jaw and angled cheekbones. She's straightened her hair. When we were growing up, she had long curls. Though I expected to find her in a beat cop uniform, instead she's got on a button-up and slacks.

"Oh, come on! You know I meant it in a good way," she says with a little laugh.

"Oh, I'm sure." I half roll my eyes at her, but I make it clear in my tone that I'm joking. "How are things?" I ask as she pushes a menu toward me. The last time we spoke, she was dealing with drama at the precinct: a detective and a sergeant were rumored to be having an affair.

Before she can answer, a waitress arrives to take our order. We order our food, then Lucia jumps right back into our conversation.

"Oh, you know." She flashes her wedding ring at me, wiggling her fingers. Our usual chats have been fewer as Lucia was planning her wedding and it was getting close. They went to Cuba so her grandparents could attend the ceremony. I wish I could have gone, but it wasn't in my budget and I've never bothered to get a passport. "It was so nice having my *abuela* and *abuelo* there."

"I saw that online! How did it all go? The pictures looked so nice."

"It was great. My wife had a really good time. It was her first time going to Cuba."

I offer her a smile, because I'm genuinely excited for her. She's glowing from the inside, as if she's never been happier—and I'm really glad she was able to find her person. It's so important.

"Did you go on a honeymoon?" I ask. When my sister got married, she went on a forty-five-day cruise that went halfway around the world, but I know that's not typical. I'm really curious where Lucia would have decided to go. The last time we spoke, Lucia hadn't known what the honeymoon would be. Her wife, Prue, wanted to surprise her. Lucia was stressing for weeks. She's too type A to let someone else plan a trip for her.

"We did. We went to New York. We both have family up there. It was good to go see everyone," she explains.

"Oh, that's so nice."

"We did all the stupid touristy stuff we never did as kids. God, it was so fun but we felt so stupid. It was perfect, honestly. Prue did such a good job."

I laugh at that. I haven't gone to New York to do any of the tourist stuff, but I've seen the pictures posted online so many times in the past I feel like I've been there myself.

"So, are we going to talk about what you're doing here? And why you didn't tell me that you were visiting?" she asks.

I knew this was coming. If this trip had been planned, obviously I would have mentioned it to her. The idea of lying to Lucia, it makes my stomach turn sour. Guilt leadens my thoughts. Lucia is too good of a friend. She doesn't deserve to be lied to.

"And—how are things going with Eviana?" she asks, raising a brow.

That, at least, has an easy answer. "Complicated." Lucia knows my relationship with my sister well, so there's no reason for me to pretend anything otherwise.

She lets out a throaty laugh. "So, no different than usual then?"

"She's off doing a shoot for some new deal that she got." I roll my eyes, as if it's ridiculous.

She raises a brow. "So, what are you doing back here then?"

"I was here before she took off. I'm staying a few extra days." The lie comes out so smooth, I surprise myself.

"How are things at work?" she asks. "Are you still a social worker?"

"Yeah, I am. Nothing new. Most of the cases are pretty similar. Sometimes I feel like I'm working the same cases over and over again. How about you?" I ask.

"I actually have news. I just got promoted to detective for Osceola County." She looks down at the table. Our food arrives and we pause to allow for the server to slide our plates onto the table.

"That is so amazing, congratulations." I'm not surprised at all, and I also won't be surprised when she ends up being a sheriff in a few years. Lucia has always excelled at everything. She did great in school. She knew from the moment she graduated that she wanted to go into law enforcement. And that's exactly what she did.

We both take a few bites of our food, and I lean in, trying to lower my voice but still speak over the noise.

"I was hoping I could run a scenario by you. I'm working on writing a novel, my first, and I'm not sure how something would play out in law enforcement," I say. I've gone over the question in my mind several times, wanting to make sure that I asked it the right way. Though I've practiced it, it still sounds a little uneasy.

"Oh, you're going to write a book? Why didn't you tell me before? That's so exciting. Of course, hit me with it."

"Okay, so let's say that two of my characters knew that someone was missing. This missing person had been gone for several days, but neither party let the police know that the person was missing. What kind of trouble could they be in for that?" I ask.

She sits a little straighter in her chair. "Well, I think it depends. If they ended up having something to do with the disappearance, then they could be charged with obstructing an investigation, tampering with evidence, hindering an investigation, conspiracy, things like that—it really would depend on the circumstances and what they knew. The more they know, the more trouble they'd get into. It also depends on the age of the missing person. There are different laws if the missing person is a minor."

I nod. So, I really can't come forth with this now. I would get into trouble. "What if someone knew about the missing person, didn't report it, but now they suspect that a person is responsible for that disappearance?"

She tilts her head as if she's trying to decipher what I've said, and I wonder if I was clear enough. It's hard to ask questions about this without incriminating myself.

"Well, I would say that usually in a situation like that, if someone comes forward with evidence of a crime, we typically try to not charge them if we can help it. Sometimes, the witness who comes forward will be offered immunity against charges if the guilty party is connected—if enough evidence warrants it. But there are no guarantees, it really depends on the prosecutor, the type of crime—is it really a missing person or does it end up being a homicide investigation? Sorry, it's hard to break it down into distinct terms unless I really know all the details." She takes a bite of her plantains.

I feel like someone has tied a million-pound anchor around my waist, and I've lost a bit of my appetite. I know that anything I could offer up against Simon isn't real evidence at this point. My fingerprints will be all over my sister's bracelet. Then it's my word against his about her disappearance.

I finish up my lunch with Lucia, with regret brewing inside me. I wish that I had gone to the police as soon as I heard from Simon—maybe that would have gotten me out of this mess. But for now, it looks like I was complicit in my sister's kidnapping, disappearance, or whatever this is—and a bloody bracelet makes it look like I was complicit in her death.

On my way back to Orlando, my cellphone rings with a number that I don't recognize. Usually, I'd let it go to voicemail, but it's a Florida number, so I answer it.

"Hello," I say, uncertainty clinging to my words.

"Is this Blair?"

"Yeah," I confirm. "Who's this?" I navigate onto the highway as I talk.

"Eviana's sister?"

I want to sigh. I hate that my defining characteristic is just being a sibling. No accomplishments, no achievements, just who I share DNA with. I wonder who I would have been if I didn't spend my entire life as *Eviana's sister*.

"Tia told me that you were in town and she gave me your number. This is Camila Rivera. I'm worried about Eviana and I haven't been able to get ahold of her. I was hoping that maybe you could get her to call me."

A lump swells in my throat, and I try hard to swallow. But it does nothing to clear it. "I don't know if Tia told you, but Eviana is out of town doing a shoot. She's also on a digital detox, you know. I'm sure she mentioned it. She just feels like she's never really present anymore—she doesn't want to live through devices."

"That makes total sense," she says without skipping a beat. "So, I just want to make sure she's not mad at me or Fiona."

"Why would she be mad at you?" I don't know much about this Fiona person. I don't think I've met her.

"There was just a misunderstanding. Just have her call me when she can? Okay?" There's a thread of urgency to her words.

She rushes off the phone and I'm left wondering what it is that Camila really wanted to say to my sister.

There's a car I don't recognize in the driveway when I pull up. It's a tiny yellow sports car with lashes over the headlights. When I get closer, I can finally make out the silver letters on the back spelling out *Porsche*. I park Simon's car, then walk toward the house, confusion gripping my thoughts with each step. As I slip in through the front door, I remain as quiet as possible. The low volume of voices tells me that Simon is talking to someone in the kitchen.

I skirt along the wall separating the foyer from the living room and kitchen, knowing that there's no direct sight line to where I am. I'm hyperaware of my movements, trying to stay as silent as possible so I can overhear their conversation.

"Oh, come on, we could have a little fun," the woman purrs. "The cameras are off, right?"

"Yes, like I said, they've been off for like a week. They're not connecting to our network for some reason. But Fiona, believe me, now is not the time," Simon says, and I'm surprised to hear him rebuff another woman, honestly. I definitely pegged Simon as the cheating type.

I step a little closer, trying to peek into the kitchen. I want to see who this Fiona woman is. My bag thuds against the wall, and I trip, knowing my cover is blown. I catch myself on the wall, cursing how clumsy I am as I try to regain my composure. Simon clears his throat, then silence falls in the kitchen.

Casual. Act casual, I tell myself as I walk into the room and glance between Fiona and Simon, offering them each a tight smile. Fiona is a bit shorter than me with wide shoulders and muscular arms. She's wearing a tight tank top to show off her muscular figure. A tennis skirt reveals toned legs. I walk past them wordlessly to the fridge and grab a bottle of water. When I turn, Simon's eyes have sharpened.

"Fiona, this is Blair, Eviana's sister," Simon says, his words as sharp as his eyes.

"Nice to meet you," she says, a little too sweetly. She glances around the house, her head tilting to the side as her ponytail swishes behind her. "Where is your sister?" Her words are pointed in a way that makes me wonder what she's getting it.

"I'm sure she's around here somewhere," I say with a shrug. I crack open my water, nod to them both, then leave the room. I'm not sure what I interrupted, but I wish I had heard more.

12

There's always a crisis on the internet. In the world of social media, there is not a single dull moment—and if there is, it's inevitable that some internet celebrity will start some shit just to get a thousand likes. That's the way that it goes, day in and day out like the tides. As I open social media and navigate to my sister's accounts, I feel a bit like a drug addict searching for a fix. I don't know why I'm still doing this to myself, what I expect to find. All I'm going to see are the contrived posts that are set up by Simon, but I guess some part of me is curious what he's going to do to keep her following interested and convinced that Eviana hasn't disappeared. The other part of me is probably hoping for some evidence that I know won't come.

As my eyes finally focus on the first post, I realize that something is off. The snapshot doesn't look like a typical post on my sister's page, which almost always is a picture of her. A grainy black-and-white picture sits in the first square. It takes too long for me to realize what the picture is—a sonogram. I click on the picture, then read the caption.

I'm so excited to announce #BabyPendelton will be joining our brood on 10/17/2023.

My throat goes bone dry. I zoom in on the details on the sonogram, and find my sister's name in the top corner. She's pregnant? Why didn't she tell me? Why didn't *he* tell me? Finding out your sister is pregnant at the same time as millions on social media is heart-wrenching. And on top of this, she's sick. Is she going to delay treatment for the baby? Is that why she called me here—in case something goes wrong? I shove off the bed and throw open the door before storming down the hall. When I reach the living room, I find Simon leaning back on the couch drinking what looks like whiskey from a very full highball glass. His hair is a mess, stubble creeps up his cheeks, and the dark circles beneath his eyes are intense. I'm not sure if this is a symptom of stress or if this is a normal morning ritual for him.

"It's ten a.m. and you're drinking?" I ask, though that's not at all what I came out here for. But I didn't realize he was a drinking-whiskey-at-ten kind of guy.

"Life is a little stressful right now, Blair, thank you for asking." He rolls his eyes at me before taking another swig. When his eyes settle back into their sockets, he glowers at me. All his swagger, his charm from the night I landed, has drained away. I guess this is the real Simon. The one I met at the airport was the façade he throws on for everyone else.

I step closer and plant my hand on my hip. "Why didn't you tell me that Eviana is pregnant? How could you post this without talking to me first?" I'm absolutely baffled that he's so self-centered that he wouldn't think to tell me—the aunt of this child—that my sister is pregnant. I never knew she even wanted kids. She never mentioned it. It definitely didn't come up during my visit.

He sputters a laugh. "Pregnant? What are you talking about?"

"The post that you just threw up a few minutes ago. The one of Eviana's sonogram. It announces that she's having a baby," I say. Sometimes I wonder if he lives on the same planet as me, he's so spacy.

He grabs his phone and taps on the screen several times. Then his eyes bulge.

"I didn't post this," he finally manages.

My heart seizes in my chest. If he didn't post it, that means that Eviana did. So she's still out there somewhere then? Well enough that she can post. If she can post, why hasn't she texted me back? Why hasn't she answered my calls? Maybe she really did leave just to get a break from him. But if that's the case, where is she and why isn't she answering anyone?

"So then she did? You think that she's okay then?"

He shrugs. "I don't know. Let me look at the details of the post," he says.

I refresh the post, but as soon as I do, it's gone. I squint, wondering if I really saw what I think I saw—or if I was imagining it. It's ridiculous when I gaslight myself. But I try again and again, as if it might make the post reappear.

"What do you see?" I ask when he doesn't tell me what he sees about the post.

"Nothing, I just deleted it," he says, frustration edging on his words.

My stomach drops. "What if Eviana posted it? Don't we need to know that?" I swear, it's like he wants Eviana gone and doesn't bother to put in even the most minimal effort to find her. "If we can figure out where she posted it, then we can find out where she—"

"It doesn't matter!" He throws his arms up in the air, cutting me off. "I deleted it. I bet no one even saw it. Move on! She's gone and there's nothing we can do about it. If she wanted to be found, we'd already know where she is." He slams his palm on the table, jumps up from the couch, then storms out of the room.

I grind my teeth together until my jaw protests. How did she stay married to this guy? I'll have to put together the pieces here by myself. It's not uncommon for influencers to use tools to schedule posts and manage their calendar, so that could be how the image ended up posted today. We haven't found Eviana's phone though, so I suppose it's also possible that she has her phone and is still posting like normal. But why would she choose this and why now? Why post a sonogram but bail on a livestream? Is it because if she did a livestream, we might be able to track her down? None of it adds up.

The feed refreshes, and I check to see if Eviana's sonogram reappears—my jaw clenched with hope—but it doesn't. A small part of me had prayed it would get reposted, that I'd get the signal I'm after that Eviana is still alive, that she's still out there, that I should keep searching for her. I know I can't stop, not until I know she's alive or dead—at least. But the tiniest hint that she's still out there would help so much.

In the other room, I can hear Simon mumbling. I pad quietly toward the hall so I can eavesdrop on what he's saying.

"I just deleted it!"

He's got the call on speaker. I think talking to Eviana's manager.

"You should have let me take a look before you deleted it."

"We can't afford to let something like that stay up," Simon says, as if the possibility of my sister being pregnant is just an inconvenience, a speed bump along his path to pretend that she's not missing.

"We could hire someone. If we could photoshop some pictures... instead of months of content, we could have years." When he says this, I know that it's Tom for sure.

My throat goes bone dry as I process his words. Years. He's planning to keep this all going while my sister could possibly be gone for years? There's no way they think that she's missing.

They clearly know something that they're not being honest about. They must be thinking what I did all along—she's dead.

"Yeah, I think that's a good idea. We need to start thinking longer term."

Long term. They want to plan for a future where my sister doesn't come back. I should have gone to the police. I should have let them know my suspicions when I had the chance. It might destroy my life, if they find out about my past—but I'd risk that if it meant finding my sister. Some part of me knew that Eviana was likely dead, and they were covering it up. But now I know for sure, I'll have to prove that they killed her myself—otherwise, it'll look like I was involved. I can't just go into a police station with no evidence. I've got to play this the right way. I grab Eviana's laptop and squirrel it away in my bag with my own. Tomorrow I need to try and go through it. My phone vibrates with text messages from several of Eviana's friends. They've added me to a group chat apparently. On my phone sits a screenshot of Eviana's sonogram. If they managed to grab this, chances are it was snagged by hundreds of her fans too. I mute the thread and try to process my racing thoughts.

My sister's secrets are waiting, and I'm the only one willing to delve into them. I'm the only one who cares about saving her.

13

Caught between waking and dreaming, I'm not sure what's real. I've been chasing Eviana in my dreams, trying to bring her back, as she runs ahead of me through a maze. Though I know I'll never catch her, I'll never bring her back, I can't stop trying. I can't give up on her, not like everyone else always has. Tension blooms in my chest, and I know that I need to prove to Eviana that I'm the sister who she needs, the one who can protect her, save her.

The rustling of something rouses me again, and my eyes flutter. Midnight moonlight streams in through the curtains, and a shifting shape startles me. For a moment, I think it's the shadow of the oak tree in the backyard swaying in the wind. But my heart jumps when I realize that it's a person. Simon. He's near the door to the guestroom digging through my suitcase. I bolt upright in bed as I try to make sense of what I'm seeing.

"What the fuck are you doing?" I ask as I throw the light on.

"I'm looking for evidence," he says, the words almost a growl through his gritted teeth.

"Evidence of what?" I throw the blankets aside and surge out of the bed. Going through my suitcase is a huge invasion of privacy. Anger flares inside me, white hot. My fists ball at my sides. I knew he was an asshole, but this is just a whole new level I wasn't expecting.

"Of what you did to Eviana! I know that you did something to her," he says. "She told me what you did, the kind of person you really are."

I don't ask him to elaborate because I know what he's likely getting at. But I can't believe that Eviana would have told him our secrets—if she did, I doubt that he ever would have invited me here. He wouldn't have dared. She must have told him something else.

"I would have never done anything to my sister," I say as I shove him away from my suitcase. I can't say that about anyone else—it seems my sister has collected a long list of enemies—but I never would have hurt her.

"Bullshit. She told me that you hated her, how jealous you were of her." He spits the words at me.

Jealous, yes—I can't deny that. But hate? I didn't hate my sister. I just wished that Eviana loved me the same way that I loved her. We'll never have that kind of relationship though. It's just not in the cards for us. Not after everything that's happened. Every day I wish that things were different, that it was safe for us to be close again. But after what we did, it's safer that we're *estranged*.

"You have no idea what you're talking about."

Simon is an only child. He can't possibly understand the dynamics of having a sibling—more, he definitely can't understand what it's like to be the younger sibling of a golden child. And he sure as hell didn't have the kind of upbringing that we did.

"The hell I don't." He reaches out, trying to push me out of the way so he can get back to my suitcase. I elbow him and snap it shut. He grabs the back of my hair and yanks me away from the luggage. I yelp in pain as shock seizes me. Did he seriously just do that? I throw myself in front of my bag before he can dig back into it again.

"Do you think I have a bloody knife in here or something? Do you have any idea how ridiculous you're being?" I ask as I zipper my luggage closed. "You know what, I'm leaving. You can't do this. I've been out here trying to find out where Eviana is while you play house on Instagram and pretend everything is fine. You don't even want her back. You don't care that she's gone," I say, the words like glass in my throat as I force them out. I thought that Eviana had the perfect marriage, someone who loved her. But now I wish I knew the truth before. I wish she'd told me how controlling Simon was, how he treated her—about the constant anger, the paranoia, the drinking. How did she deal with this?

"Get out of my house! You're crazy. I don't want to see you again. You're lucky I haven't gone to the cops to tell them what you did to her," he snaps at me. He's too close to me, so close I can see the yellow of his teeth, smell the sour stench of his breath, see the rage simmering behind his eyes, the veins bulging in his neck. My whole body tenses. I expect him to grab me again the moment I turn my back.

I scoop up my things while he watches. I'd already felt like I'd overstayed my welcome. Now I know for sure that I never need to step foot in this house again. I'll go find Eviana by myself. Good riddance. I hope I can get this guy locked up.

"Don't worry, I'll get out, and I'll let the police know what I've seen here—I'll let them know exactly what you did to my sister," I threaten as I throw the last of my clothes into my bag.

"You won't dare," he says as he stalks my steps around the room. Every place I turn, he's there, like a goddamn shadow. I know he's not going to give me an inch of freedom until I'm out of the house. His aura is imposing, it presses against me—a looming threat that I can't escape.

I grab my phone and order an Uber, then snatch the last of

my things. I sling my laptop bag with both my and Eviana's computers inside over my shoulder and wheel my suitcase from the room. The weight of the laptops bites into my flesh, but it's nothing compared to the ache that still throbs in my skull where he grabbed me.

"Oh, yes, I will. I'm going to tell them everything I've witnessed. I'm going to tell them exactly the type of person you are. I spoke to Danica next door. I know how you treated Eviana. I know about the screaming, the fights. How you were here the night she disappeared," I say, my words as threatening as I can manage. I hate that my nerves make my voice tremble. But who knows what this guy is capable of. The idea that I'm alone in a house with the man who may have killed my sister is not lost on me. He could very easily do the same to me. Eventually my work will realize that I'm missing—but until then, no one would have any idea what he's done. I'd have to hope Eviana's friends or Danica mention that I was here. He might be able to get away with this for years, pretending my sister is still alive, profiting off her image.

"Bullshit," he rages, as I powerwalk toward the front of the house with my stuff in tow. His anger is rising behind me, a wave that's threatening to take me with it. His hand fists the back of my shirt, and he throws me against a wall, my suitcase thudding to the floor. His teeth are bared. He's panting as his feral eyes meet mine. Primal fear rises inside me, and I calculate the damage I can do to him with my nails, my fists. Maybe I could kick him in the balls and run for it if I have to. I try to remember every way I've heard of a woman escaping an attacker, but my mind comes up with absolutely nothing.

He raises his fist, then hits me hard in the cheek. Though I try to dodge out of the way, it does me little good. I'm pinned against the wall. There's nowhere for me to go. Stars explode behind my eyes as pain radiates through my face. I can't believe he hit me. I've never been hit in the face before—well, not as an adult—and it takes my breath away.

Tears pool in my eyes, not from sadness or anger, but from pain. I want to wipe them away, knowing that they make me look like a scared little girl, but I don't. My lips pull back, exposing my teeth, and I jerk my leg up, hitting him hard in the balls with my knee. He groans and both his hand instinctually move to his crotch, as if they'll do anything about the agony I just caused him. I run toward the door, my suitcase bouncing behind me, the wheels protesting, the plastic body careening into the wall several times. The impacts don't slow me. If anything, they propel me faster—because I know if I slow, the collisions won't be my suitcase anymore. It's my body that will be pummeled instead.

If Simon raised his fists to me, I know that he was fully capable of doing the same to my sister. I wonder if there's evidence of it on her pages, bruises that she covered with makeup, or if he deleted security footage with evidence of his abuse. Maybe I should just kill Simon and save her the trouble. I should release her from this marriage that has become her prison. There's no other way for her to get out, for her to save herself—I'm sure he'll fight for her money if she has any left, the house. He'll drag her name through the mud just to try and destroy her.

When I throw open the front door, I can hear Simon behind me. I know that he's coming, I swear I can hear the plan formulating in his mind—he'll destroy me if I give him the chance. The burst of air against my face, somehow it's calming. It centers me. He can't beat me to death in the front yard, on the driveway. Danica's cameras at least would see it. There's no way he'd get away with it out here. When I make it to the paved driveway, the door slams behind me, then locks. A closed door, the end of a chapter, our relationship terminated. Good riddance, douchebag.

At the edge of the road, I wait with my heart hammering. I glance back at the house over and over again, waiting, anticipating that Simon will emerge from the front door to try and drag me back inside. But each time, I only see him glowering from the door. My cheek throbs, I bet it'll bruise. I thread my fingers into my hair, massaging my scalp where Simon pulled it. It takes a few agonizing minutes for the Uber to pull up, and by the time I climb into the back, my heartbeat has slowed a bit, but the pain in my cheek has only gotten more intense. Each beat of my heart sends a fresh wave of pain, and I swear I can feel it swelling, the bruise building beneath the surface of my skin. Though it's dark, I look at my reflection in my phone screen, noticing the telltale red mark beneath my eye. I doubt that the driver could see it if he glanced at me in the rearview mirror.

The trip to the hotel takes twenty minutes, not because of traffic, but because the driver keeps ignoring the GPS, swearing that he's a local and knows a better route. When I finally climb out of the car, it's almost two in the morning. My eyes burn with exhaustion, and it feels like even my soul is tired. The wheels of my suitcase protest, squealing behind me as the doors to the hotel hiss open in front of me. This was the closest place to my sister's house without resorting to the tourist district—though I have nothing against that section of Orlando, I know that it'll be so much more expensive to stay over there, and I'm overextended as it is. I'm not sure my credit card will let me push it much further.

At the front desk, I find a woman with her dark hair in two French braids. Her light brown skin is radiant, flawless, with a sparkle of highlighter atop each of her sharp cheekbones. My eyes widen. I was not expecting to see Valentina here. She's one of Eviana's closest friends. I met her a few days ago.

"Just getting into town?" she asks as I approach, then she laughs when she finally looks up at me.

"Blair, what are you doing here? I thought you went back to Seattle."

"It's a long story. But I'll catch you up after I get a room," I say, not wanting to be rude, but also desperately needing to catch my breath. Can she see the red welt growing on my cheek? I hadn't planned to see any of Eviana's friends, and I don't know how I can get away with lying to her. Eviana kept most people at arm's length, but not Valentina.

"Shit, I'm so sorry, but we're all booked up solid for the night," she says with a grimace. "We've got a convention going on right now, so we've been filled up for a few days. I will have a room that'll open up at four p.m., though I know that's not a whole lot of help right now."

I didn't think that a hotel like this would be full.

"Can I hang out in the lobby until a room is ready? I don't have anywhere else to go," I say, too exhausted to hop from hotel to hotel until I can find an open room tonight.

"Okay, you aren't waiting for a room. I get off in thirty minutes. You're going to come stay at my place," she says.

I tense up automatically. She wants me to stay with her? I wasn't expecting that. I don't want to impose.

"Oh, come on," she says, urging me to take the offer, probably registering the shock on my face. She leans closer to me, leaning against the counter between us. "What happened? Why aren't you staying with Eviana?"

"It's a really long story. I'll tell you about it after I get some sleep, if that's all right." I feel bad, but at the same time, I'm not sure I can give her a coherent account of what's happened right now. My brain feels like it's been dipped in molasses, all my thoughts are slowed down, as if I can't access them all. I also really hate the idea of lying to her.

She leans against the counter, closing the distance between us a bit. Her eyes scan the lobby before snapping back to me. "It was Simon, wasn't it?" she presses.

I give her the little nod that I know she's looking for. But the entire story, well, she'll have to settle for that later.

Valentina's house is in the same neighborhood as my sister's. She lives two streets over, in one of the few houses that isn't a Tuscan-style McMansion. Instead, her house is contemporary, a sleek modern house with sharp lines and huge windows that glow against the inky night.

"Man, this house is nice," I say as I slip from her Range Rover. The air outside is cool and damp, so moist that I can feel it on my skin. A gentle breeze sweeps through the palm trees in her front yard and it's strange how at ease I feel here. I know just two streets over danger looms—I'm sure if Simon knew I was here, he'd come over and harass me.

She offers me a smile. "The hotel has been doing great since I bought it. I actually got to buy two other locations. It helped me buy this," she says as she motions toward the house.

"You own three hotels?" I ask, shocked. She doesn't look like she's even in her forties yet. I can't even imagine owning my own home, let alone being responsible for three businesses.

"Yep, I'm thinking about buying a bed-and-breakfast out in St. Augustine next. They do so well out there, though the hotels struggle. Here, B&Bs don't do so well. It's funny how different markets support different things." She talks as she leads me up her front path toward the front door. When she opens the door, the scent of oranges and vanilla is heavy in the air.

"You manage all of that yourself?" I ask, baffled.

She nods. "I have employees, of course, but I rotate through the properties to make sure everything is running to my standards. And to make sure every employee feels valued and that they're all treated well."

I follow her through the sparse but well-decorated living room. On the floor there's a fluffy rug under sleek couches.

Ornate metal and glass tables punctuate the ends of the furniture. Stained-glass lamps illuminate the room, casting shards of color on the high ceilings. Large paintings adorn every stretch of wall, their colors adding vibrance and life to the room. In the kitchen, every surface is white, the counters, the cabinets, the walls, even the floor. Though I'd expect for something so austere to look clinical, somehow it doesn't. She's got pops of color in vases, knickknacks, and the hardware. It gives it a very contemporary feel. She opens the fridge, grabs a couple sparkling waters and hands me one.

When we left the hotel, I was still bone tired, but now as the late night creeps toward morning, I've gotten a second wind. The house is dim, lit only by LED accent lighting that runs along the cabinets and the tops of the crown molding. I take a seat at the small table that's in the kitchen, and Valentina joins me.

"When's the last time that you heard from my sister?" I ask her. I don't know yet how much Valentina could know—or how much I should trust her. But if my sister was close to her, then I assume Valentina is someone who might be able to help me. I know they spoke while I was visiting, but I wonder if Eviana reached out after that.

She unlocks her phone, and glances at her messages. "Um, six days ago," she says, then curses under her breath. "How has it been that long? I could have sworn that I spoke to her more recently than that. Damn, now I feel like a bad friend."

"You're not a bad friend." I look down at the sparkling water, finding it much easier to look at the bottle than it is to look at her right now. If I make eye contact, I think she might see more behind my eyes than I mean to reveal. "I need to tell you something, but for now, I need you to promise to keep it between the two of us," I say. I don't know why I lied to everyone else and I'm going to tell her the truth. But I swear that last interaction with Simon knocked some sense into me. I need some outside perspective, help from someone who really knew my sister—and isn't Simon. There has to be a way out of this, a way that I can take him down.

"Sure, of course, I'll keep anything between us that you need," she explains. "Is everything okay? Is Eviana in some kind of trouble? She mentioned that she was getting some threats from a woman named Claire, who was convinced that Eviana cost her her influencing career. I guess she was Simon's first wife, so now she has a huge grudge against Eviana and thinks every terrible thing in her life is caused by your sister."

It takes me a long time to digest what she's saying. Claire? The woman who I ran into in the coffee shop? The same woman who Danica saw? It seems like there might be more going on here than I realized.

"When did those threats start?" I ask. Eviana didn't mention anything to me about it.

"Months ago. But I guess it all kind of came to a head a few weeks ago. Claire approached Eviana outside of her favorite coffee shop. She slapped Eviana and told her that she was going to take her down." She shakes her head, like it's all just too much.

"That's a lot to process," I say. Is it possible that I've got this all wrong and that Simon didn't do something to my sister? Did Claire have something to do with this—or were they working together? "I need to ask you about something else."

She nods. "Of course, anything."

"Did Eviana mention anything about any health problems to you?"

I look back at Valentina. She shakes her head as her eyes bulge with surprise. "About a month ago we went to Puerto Rico together, she needed to get away for a little bit. It was just the two of us for a week and she didn't mention anything about her health," she says. "She talked a lot of shit about Claire, Fiona, and Simon though."

That's odd. I didn't see anything about a trip to Puerto Rico on Eviana's social media. That seems like the kind of trip that she would have plastered all over her feed. Did she really keep some parts of her life private? I've never seen her post any of her close friends on her pages. She gives me a brief overview of some of the beef she had with Claire and Fiona, but it doesn't amount to anything I think would lead to my sister's disappearance.

"Did she talk about anything else while you two were on the trip?" I ask. I'm really not sure anymore what to believe about Eviana's cancer scare. Was it real? Was it just a ploy to lure me back to see if the two of us could reconcile? What was the real reason? What about the pregnancy?

She laces her fingers together atop the table. "She was having some major issues with Simon and Tom. The two of them were really pushing for her to post more on social media, to spend more of her time trying to pump as much money out her page as possible. They were never satisfied and kept telling her that the shelf life of an influencer was so limited that she really needed to maximize income while she could, because she wouldn't be able to choose when the money would stop flowing." She sighs and shakes her head. "Honestly, she was kind of over the entire thing. She really wanted to take a break or to step back from it altogether. But anytime she told Simon that she was thinking along those lines, he'd get mad at her and start fights. He always kept pushing her. Nothing she did was ever good enough. He was telling her that her good looks would only last for so long... and then why would anyone bother following her."

Anger flares in my core, and I grind my teeth together. I hate that my sister wanted to take a break from a life that was stressing her out, and her husband and manager forced her to keep going. Both of them were profiting off of every move she made, so why would they let her take a break? They had no incentive to actually take care of Eviana. She mentioned to me that she wanted to take a step back, but I wish she said she was running into their resistance.

"Was Eviana pregnant?" I ask.

She shrugs. "Not that she told me. It could be possible though. She talked about wanting to have kids eventually, but it didn't seem like it was the right time... not with everything that was going on with Simon. I always asked if it wasn't the right time or if it wasn't the right guy and she always got annoyed with me." She takes a swig of her water. "What's going on, Blair?" There's concern in her voice, and I know that I can't drag this on forever.

"When I came to visit she told me that she had cancer. We'd had a strained relationship for many years. It felt like she was trying to make amends before the end—or that's how it felt anyway. I got on my flight to go back home, everything seemed normal, but when I landed I had a call from Simon saying that Eviana went for a walk and never came home." I take several sips of my water, but no matter how many I take my throat still feels too dry. All this has been begging for me to spill it to someone for days. But now that it's out, I'm not sure I should have said anything. "And I don't know yet if Eviana took off to clear her head for a bit or..."

"Eviana went for a walk? Bullshit," she says before shaking her head. "Eviana's missing?" she asks pointedly, as if that part of my comment just finally sunk in.

I nod. "No one has seen her in almost a week now. I've tried looking for her. With what you've told me, I think that maybe she took off to teach Simon and Tom a lesson. I think that she was trying to get some space from everything. Simon told me point blank that he will tell the police that I did something to Eviana. He's saying I was the last person to see her before she disappeared. So I've kept my mouth shut while I've been looking for evidence of where she might be."

"What if something happened to her?" There's an edge to her voice when she asks it. Frustration is threaded into her words—and I don't blame her. That's how I feel too.

"I know, I've thought the same thing. But Simon and Tom don't want to go to the police. They don't want Eviana to get into any trouble if she left on her own. They don't want it to reflect badly on her brand," I explain. I don't mention the bracelet, because I know that Valentina will go to the police. If I were in her position, I'd do the same thing. "Look, like I said, I really need this to stay between us. When I told Simon I was going to go to the police, he told me that if something happened to Eviana, that he was going to make sure that this all came back on me—he's going to make it look like I did something to my sister." I don't tell her about the rest, about what else the police might find if they look hard enough at Eviana's life and mine.

She throws her hands up in the air. "This is ridiculous. We can't just not go to the police."

"Valentina, please," I plead. I can't have her go to the cops. I need a little more time, and I'm sure my desperation is written all over my face. "I think I can find her. I just need a few more days to keep piecing everything together. Eviana posted something on her Instagram account, a sonogram. I know that she's still alive, she still has access to her accounts, and she posted. If anything really serious had happened, she wouldn't have been able to post." At least that's what I keep telling myself. "I think she just needs a little more time, more space, and she'll come back on her own." I don't believe the words, though I say them aloud without faltering. While I'm hopeful about the recent post, I know it could have been scheduled with software, Eviana could have planned it months or weeks ago. But if something happened to her—I need time to prove that I'm not the one who hurt her.

"I guess you're right," she says, though I'm not sure that she believes me. "Did you and Eviana fight while you were here visiting?"

I shake my head, but she looks at me like she doesn't believe me.

"We didn't have anything to fight about, not anymore anyway." The words aren't entirely true, but not entirely a lie either. We got our arguments out of the way years ago, when our relationship burned to the ground. Neither one of us is the type to revisit trauma, to let it rise to the surface and consume us again and again. And I don't think we even know each other well enough to fight anymore.

"Do you know Fiona, Annabell, and Tia?" I ask.

She makes a face like she just smelled a rotten lemon. "Unfortunately."

"What do you mean by that?"

"Don't get me wrong. Tia is a good person. But I wouldn't trust Fiona or Annabell at all. Fiona is a fitness influencer. That's how she got in with Eviana. She's got twice as many followers as your sister. Annabell is just a hanger-on of Fiona's. She brings nothing of value to anything."

I nod, trying to digest everything she's said. I'll have to find Fiona's social media accounts.

"Fiona is always causing problems and starting drama with everyone else. So, I stay as far away from her as possible."

I take in all the information, making mental notes of who to approach and who to avoid. Valentina and I talk for another half an hour about my sister and my suspicions about Simon before I head to the guest room and fall asleep.

14

YOUTUBE

A woman sits at a desk, her face a little too bright under the glow of a ring light. Glowing circles illuminate her pupils, and her teeth shine as she offers the camera a smile. Her bright blue hair falls stick-straight to her shoulders. She tilts her head to the right, then takes a sip from an ornate teacup.

"Thanks for joining me for another episode of *Tea with Tiffany*." She holds the teacup up and tips it toward the camera, the amber liquid inside almost sloshing over the rim.

"So, who wants to talk about Eviana Pendelton?" She raises a brow, then her smile turns feral. "I just find it interesting how she missed a livestream that she said was going to be so important to her platform, one that we absolutely could not miss—then, suddenly, she's too sick to appear on the stream."

The woman rolls her eyes.

"We all know that there's something strange going on. Eviana has never shied away from the camera before. She's one of the most annoyingly *online* internet celebrities that there is. She documents every moment of her life, including when she's sick. Does anyone remember her two-week minute-by-minute log of having a breakthrough case of the measles? Normally she would have hammed up not feeling well for the camera to make us all feel so grateful that she still managed to turn on a video feed to listen to her cough."

She takes another sip of her tea, then props her elbow on her desk to lean against it.

"Then, I don't know if anyone else saw the post that was up for about fifteen minutes yesterday..."

A screen capture of the post with Eviana's sonogram appears in the video frame next to Tiffany's face. The image zooms in, showing Eviana's name on the top right of the sonogram.

"So, right here, we found out—for about fifteen minutes— that Eviana is expecting. We've got her sonogram here, when the baby is due, all that jazz. But the funny thing is, the thing that I just cannot stop kicking around in my mind... the post was deleted. Why on earth would she delete that post after making that kind of announcement?" Tiffany takes an exaggerated slurp of her tea.

"It's just so strange. I mean, her canceling the livestream because she was feeling sick, that adds up with the pregnancy. But why delete it? Why have none of her other posts referenced the pregnancy? You can't make an announcement like that and then just take it back. That's not how it works. She's posted three times since then without a single reference to the pregnancy."

The image of the sonogram disappears and Tiffany's face is recentered in the screen. Her eyebrows are cocked with confusion, as if she can't put all the pieces together herself.

"I've seen some speculation that Eviana isn't okay—that maybe someone else is messing with her accounts. I don't like to make accusations like that. But it really seems like something is off. Some of the posts are clearly recycled."

She offers a sly smile to the camera. "Need proof?" she asks with a wink.

Next to Tiffany, another post makes its appearance on screen. The image is of Eviana at the beach in a bright red bikini. She's got on a straw hat and oversized sunglasses.

"This picture looked familiar to me. As you see, Eviana's account posted this picture twelve hours ago. The bikini has been retouched or recolored," Tiffany explains as another image that's almost identical appears, but in this one Eviana is wearing a teal bikini.

"I'm not going to say it's impossible for Eviana to have taken two incredibly similar photos, but you guys, it's clear these were taken on the same day—they're the exact same bathing suit. She's got on the same nail polish, makeup is the same, her hair is highlighted the exact same—same length too. These pictures were taken during her anklet phase, which she hasn't been in for at least seven months. I think that this picture has been doctored to look new, but it's the same one."

Another picture appears on screen, this one of Eviana sitting in a coffee shop posing with a latte. The latte is topped with a high mound of whipped cream that's also slathered in chocolate sauce. Next to that picture, one from another angle is posted.

"So, this picture, posted twenty-four hours ago... We've got Eviana in her favorite coffee shop. This is the kind of content she posted a lot a year ago, but now is pretty rare. Most of her photos now are of her in her house, or at a location where she's got some kind of sponsorship going. We can see she's wearing the same outfit. The shirt is recolored again. But everything else is the same. Whoever did this did not have an eye for detail, because as we see, the exact same person is in the background waiting for their coffee in a mustard-color dress. Mustard is so not in season now, and it's just too coincidental that she'd be at the coffee shop a year apart and the same person would be in the background. And we can see some of the recolor bleeding onto her coffee mug right here."

She draws a phantom circle on the video, highlighting the error.

Tiffany pauses to take a long drink from her tea.

"I don't ever want to be the kind of person who screams fire. That's not at all what I try to do on my channel. But there are some very obvious signs here that are starting to surface. I'm really concerned for Eviana, because what I'm seeing—well, it makes me think that Eviana isn't in control of her account anymore. It makes me think that maybe she's not the one posting. And if that's the case, I have to ask—what happened to Eviana?"

15

Valentina woke me up at eleven to tell me that she had to get going. She was dropping in at a couple of her properties, but to make myself at home. It's catching me off guard that she's being so nice, so helpful. When we were kids, none of Eviana's friends were nice to me. They terrorized me, played pranks on me, and it led to a deep-seated distrust of anyone who aligned themselves too closely with my sister. But Valentina seems genuine, and I like to think that my sister grew out of terrorizing me. Most of Eviana's friends in Florida have been fine, but not super welcoming like this.

I find a pot of coffee brewed in the immaculate kitchen, then search the cupboards for a cup so I can pour some. I test a sip, finding a dark roast that lights up my tastebuds. I scroll through emails from work as I drink and answer all the urgent ones. Back in my room, I unearth Eviana's laptop from my bag. I wonder if that's what Simon was searching for, if he realized that I had taken it—but then again, he's so self-involved, I seriously doubt that he would have noticed that it was missing at all.

My phone dings with a notification, and I glance at it to find an email with alerts that I set up. I wanted to be sure that I got any new information on my sister the moment it was posted, and now, thanks to these handy alerts, I get updates almost hourly, so I don't have to sit and refresh feeds on my phone every five minutes. The list isn't long, so I scan through it. There are new YouTube videos speculating about my sister, her pregnancy, and what's been happening on her social media. I'm happy to see that her fans have picked up on my sister's departure from her usual posting habits, and quite a few picked up on the fact that Simon is recycling photos. I hope it's making his life a living hell. If he did something to my sister, he never deserves a moment of peace again. There might have been moments in my life when I wanted to kill my sister—but that's my right as a sibling. Daydreaming about smothering your sister with a pillow when you're a teenager is not the same as what Simon has done. Valentina's words whisper in the back of my mind—Claire. Claire also threatened my sister. Could she have something do with this? I need to check to see if there's anything on Eviana's laptop.

I remember Valentina also brought up Fiona. I finally navigate to Fiona's social media accounts. The posts vary, displaying short videos of workouts, Fiona making a lot of smoothies, but no real food—then lots of pictures of her flexing and posing in front of various backdrops. Every post has a ton of engagement, likes, comments. But Eviana wasn't a person who cared at all about fitness—what did she and Fiona even talk about?

I wonder if at any point the police will be involved, if they might show up at Simon's doorstep and demand to see Eviana. That idea makes a smile slither across my lips. I'd love to witness that, to see my brother-in-law dragged from his front stoop and thrown into the back of a police car while his neighbors watch.

With one last sip of my coffee, I finally crack open my sister's laptop. It's a clunky and yet sleek thing, a new MacBook that's better than anything I would ever be able to afford. The screen glows, and splashes of color appear across the screen as it comes to life. My sister's name and photo stare back at me from the screen, making my stomach clench. Pictures of her have always had a bad effect on me.

There's something about seeing the better version of yourself, the person you almost were, the person you could have been if you were born a year earlier. Eviana took all of the good genes when she tore her way out of our mother. I was left with hair that's too thick, legs that are too long, shoulders that are too broad, and dark arm hair that I got teased relentlessly for. My smile has too many gums and my nose is just—well, awful. I always wonder if I'd looked like her, if I would have turned out the same, vapid, vain. Some days I envy her because she's so pretty, because she was always better at everything than I was. Eviana got told she could grow up to do anything—while I got told that they were sure I had potential... for *something*, that one day I'd *find my way*. That's the nice way of telling you that you're stupid, and they're not sure you'll ever add any value to society. But at least you can do the jobs all the *special* people don't want.

I try a few passwords, trying to figure out how to get into my sister's laptop. Each incorrect attempt makes the screen shake, then settle back down with a sound marking the failure. I grab my phone, and put in a call to Melvin, our IT help desk genius who's always able to help me when I'm at work. He's saved machines for me, recovered files, worked tech miracles. If there's anyone who can fix this for me, it's Melvin.

"Hey, Blair, how are you doing?" he asks as soon as he answers the phone.

I spend a couple minutes catching up with him, before

delving into my question. "Hey, how could I get into a Mac if I don't have the password?" I ask.

"There are a few options," he says, with a little laugh.

Melvin talks me through finding an account that Eviana had on her laptop that wasn't protected with a password, and within fifteen minutes I'm in the machine. He also talks me through how to find any missing files, thinking that I'm trying to recover something from my own laptop—I'd guess. But I don't bother to correct him. It's for the best he doesn't know what I'm actually up to.

"I owe you coffee when I'm back!" I say, then thank Melvin and end the call. I follow his instructions to use this secondary account to unlock Eviana's, turn off the password, then I log in to her account.

I hold my breath as I wait for the machine to boot up and log in to her account. My shoulders are tense, my whole body rigid as I wait to see if I was successful. Finally, when her desktop icons load, the stress in my body unravels. I'm thankful that Eviana wasn't more diligent with her security. When I start to sift through her folders, I find hundreds of pictures—her shoots for her social media accounts it looks like. Many of the pictures I've seen before. These are the same images that Simon is relying on at this very moment.

In one of the recent folders, I find something that I'm not expecting. I click on a photo, and it opens to reveal my sister holding a growing belly. She looks like she's got to be at least eight months pregnant. Confusion spears my mind as I look for any evidence that the image is photoshopped—but it can't be, it's too convincing. I keep clicking on picture after picture, watching a timeline of Eviana go from barely pregnant to well into her ninth month. She's got it all cataloged, clearly ready to post. There are sonograms, images of her posing in a nursery, holding signs showing how far she's along, and that baby

Pendelton is the size of an apple, a grapefruit, a pineapple, a watermelon.

I feel sick to my stomach, lost for words. Simon denied it. He said he didn't know anything about a pregnancy, but someone had to help her set this up, someone had to take all these pictures. It's clear that she never was pregnant. There's no baby. Even her best friend didn't know about a pregnancy. There isn't even a nursery in that huge house of hers. This is all clearly contrived for social media. The idea that my sister is the kind of person to fake an entire pregnancy for social media, that makes me sick. But on the other hand, I have never been less surprised in my life. I swear I think she has some kind of Munchausen's.

What kind of person is my sister really if she's willing to lie about cancer, a pregnancy, if she's willing to deceive the entire world—for what, likes? For some sponsorship deals? Throughout the images I can see products decorating a nursery, obvious tie-ins that would help her generate revenue. But Jesus Christ, inventing a child to make money—I don't know if it'd be worse to have a child to exploit it or to just pretend that you did.

Why was she trying to deceive me though? Why did she reel me back into her life with a lie? She must have known that if she really needed me, I would have come.

I open her browser and look through the tabs. She's got every one of her social media feeds open. They're all logged in. If I wanted to, I could end this all now. I could post as my sister. I could ruin Simon. Some part of me wants to find a picture of my sister in tears, then tell every one of her followers that she's scared of her husband—but I already know that she'd never take a picture of herself crying. I don't think I can remember a single time when Eviana genuinely cried, I only recall tears that were meant to get me into trouble, ones to get her exactly what it was that she wanted, crocodile tears.

When I get to her software that she uses to schedule posts, I see that she scheduled all of the pregnancy photos—from announcement to... the last post I read takes my breath away. Eviana was planning to fake an entire pregnancy just to tell her followers that the baby was stillborn. There never was a baby, and yet, she wanted to use her platform to manipulate millions of people into being sympathetic and donating toward the funeral for her baby.

Bile claws at my throat, and I want to be sick. I want to throw up until I rid myself of these feelings, until I can be numb to what a horrible person my sister is. This is a sickness. When I find her, I'm going to get her help, because this is not normal—this is an addiction.

The rational part of me wants to give up on her, to walk away, to go back to my life and pretend that none of this ever happened. But I can't do that. If she's dead, to the police that would look like I killed my sister and then fled the state when it started to look bad for me. And even though my sister is twisted, even though I don't trust her, even though most of the time I envy her—there is that primal part of me that just wants her to love me, to fix everything between us. I never got that from our parents. I've never gotten that from anyone. But I need it from her. I need Eviana to tell me she's proud of me, that she loves me, and that even though I'll never be her—that's fine.

I keep scrolling through post after post, watching my sister spiral in real time with the things she was planning to put on her feeds. She spent so much time orchestrating this, plotting for the world to grieve with her. In the last few shots saved on her hard drive, I can see Simon reflected in the mirror behind my sister. His eyes are wild, feral. Anger rages on his face, and I swear it looks like he took a picture right as he was about to scream at my sister. Was this not her plan? Was it his? Did he put Eviana up to this?

Looking at it all strikes a chord with me. I can't hear my sister's fear, but in a few of the photos I can see it. She cataloged it here, as if she was trying to make sure that someone saw it. She wanted there to be some record of what she was going through. I know that Eviana didn't run off. She's the one who scheduled all these posts and then threw them back into the draft folder—as if at the last moment she defied him.

If I don't figure out what happened soon, the world won't be grieving with Eviana, they'll be grieving for her.

My phone rings and the name on the screen makes me feel like my snooping summoned Fiona. I swipe the call, accepting it. The moment I press the phone to my ear, Fiona is already talking. Simon must have given her my number.

"Where can we meet? I need to talk to you. Now," she says.

I clear my throat, only to find it's gone bone dry.

"Why?" I manage. I can't flat-out refuse because I am curious about what it is that she wants.

"Need to talk to you about Eviana." There's an authority to her words, making it clear that this is a demand that I will not be arguing with. If I wasn't so intent on finding out everything I can about my sister, I'd decline. But as it stands, I need all the help that I can get.

"And we can't discuss this over the phone?"

She scoffs. "Absolutely not. There's no way to be sure of who might be listening."

That's quite an alarming bout of paranoia. I coordinate with Fiona to meet with her at a coffee shop named Phoenix Tail. Within a half hour of her call, I climb out of an Uber to find a concrete building with large windows. Flowerbeds in front are overflowing with hydrangeas. As I walk toward the door, I feel like someone is watching me. Down the street, I notice a woman with familiar tattoos twisting up her arms watching me from beside her car. Claire. What is she doing here? I want to ask her about what Valentina said, but as I hurry my steps toward her, she climbs into her shiny SUV and pulls away before I've even made it twenty feet.

The jingle of the coffee shop door opening draws my attention. Though I'm disappointed that I couldn't talk to Claire, I need to get to Fiona. I open the front door and get hit with the rich aroma of coffee. There's a dull roar inside from several espresso machines. To my left, there's a large coffee bar, stocked with coffee machines and paraphernalia.

I order a coffee and take a seat at one of the many empty tables spread around the space. The interior is very industrial, with pipes sticking out of the walls to hold up shelves. Rustic wooden tables are scattered around the room, mismatched chairs shoved against them. On each table, there's a small vase with a single yellow rose.

After I've got my coffee, I sip it slowly and wait for Fiona. She's late, of course. I recognize her when she strolls in. She's wearing a tight tank top, leggings, and running shoes. Her long blonde hair falls in ringlets that make it clear she's probably lying to me about why she's late. Her perfect makeup leaves me feeling a bit unsure about my own appearance.

"Thank God you're here," she says as she plops down in front of me. "You didn't get me a coffee?" she asks with a wrinkle of her nose.

I don't respond because I'm so taken aback. Why would I have ordered her a coffee? I barely know this woman.

"Anyway. Where the fuck is Eviana?" She straightens in her chair, her eyes wild in a way that edges on being unhinged. This close, I can see that her nose is a little too straight, which makes me wonder if it's genetics or a good plastic surgeon. Her lips are over-plumped, and overlined—she looks a bit like a goldfish.

"Why are you asking me and not Simon? The two of you seem close," I say, a little disdain slipping into my words. I wonder just how far the relationship with my brother-in-law has gone.

"I don't know what you mean by that, but Simon said that I should talk to you about it."

That bastard.

"Like I've told everyone—" I start.

"Cut the shit," she says, smacking her hand on the table, interrupting me. "*Your* sister is screwing me over right now. And you're going to help set this right. Actually, I don't care if it's you or Simon or Tom. One of you is going to fix this."

I feel all eyes on us from her outburst, and I try not to glance around. My eyes hold steady on Fiona, accessing her.

"I'm not following," I finally say, not at all wanting to indulge this attitude of hers.

"Eviana was supposed to announce our partnership during her livestream. I held up my end of the bargain. It got her over five hundred thousand new followers. But she didn't post anything in return. She was supposed to be part of my product launch."

I'm way out of my depth here. "I'm sure you saw that she was sick." Why am I suddenly my sister's manager here? She should be working this out with Simon, not with me. "I'm sure if you speak to Tom—"

"Tom isn't getting me anywhere and neither is Simon. So, you're going to. Simon said that you're the only person who Eviana will listen to."

I take a sip of my coffee as I try to process what she's said and how to proceed. I need to be careful with this one. I can tell that already.

I channel my sister's spirit, her confidence. "Eviana isn't taking calls right now. She's on a digital detox, so there really isn't much that I can do. But I'm sure once she decides to get back online this will all get sorted out." My offering isn't what she wants, and I know it—but there isn't anything else I can give her.

She lets out a cold laugh. "Why? Because she's pregnant?

Give me a break." She shoves up from the table. "I better hear from her tomorrow or I'm going to make all of your lives hell."

Something tells me that she definitely means it. And as I watch Fiona disappear out of the coffee shop, I wonder what exactly she's capable of.

16

I don't know how I'm going to get Fiona to calm down. But then again, maybe I shouldn't. Maybe I should let her make Simon's life a living hell. Personally, the rise or downfall of my sister's social media empire doesn't affect me at all. But I don't quite understand Fiona's anger. I tried to process what happened with her on my way to pick up a rental car and on my entire drive back to Valentina's house, but I'm still coming up short. None of it makes sense. Is Eviana missing a livestream really the end of the world? Surely this woman has better things to do with her time than threaten me. But until I find my sister, there's not much I can do about it anyway.

The background noise of the TV has entertained me as I've dug through my sister's laptop and tried to figure out what to do about Fiona. But it's the sound of breaking news that draws my attention. I look up to the TV, the two female anchors coming into focus as they sit behind a desk. A white woman with dark hair sits next to a Black woman who has her braids woven into an intricate bun atop her head. Both women are clad in different shades of pink and offer the camera tight smiles.

"I'm Jasmine Jenson," the white woman says. "And this is Lena Lorenzo."

"Thanks for joining us for the five o'clock news. We've got a breaking story for you at the top of the hour," Lena says.

The camera focuses in on Lena, and a square appears next to her on the screen along with the words *Violence Strikes Lakeview Shores*.

Panic crackles through me as I read the caption. That's my sister's neighborhood, the one I'm in right now. I haven't heard sirens, anything to indicate that anything has happened here. Did someone realize that Eviana is missing? Is this what I've been waiting for? My heart pounds and time slows down as I wait for the news.

"Reports are coming in that last night, Danica Fullerton, a resident of Lakeview Shores, was attacked in her backyard in what police are now calling an attempted kidnapping. This incident has deeply disturbed the gated community that has never seen so much as a break-in in the past. We've reached out to the security company that employs an armed guard at the entrance for comment, but we haven't received a response. For now, police are asking if anyone has any information on what transpired in Lakeview Shores to please call Crimeline with information."

I click the TV off as the segment ends and my thoughts linger on what was said. Danica looked so similar to my sister, almost eerily so. And now someone has attacked her in her backyard? I wonder if my sister was the intended target. I need to get over to Danica's house and make sure that she's okay.

It takes me a few minutes to get from Valentina's house to Danica's. On the way, I pass three Orlando PD patrol cars parked down the street, and I know at least for now, they'll likely swarm the neighborhood until the storm has passed. I park my rental car out front of Danica's house and walk up her cobblestone path toward the front door. A wrought-iron gate stands in front of the wooden door, a security measure that didn't seem necessary in a neighborhood like this days ago.

I listen intently for signs of life in the house after I've rang the doorbell. The lock grinds as Danica opens the door and peers out at me through the ornate metal. She looks tense, tired, with dark bags hanging beneath her eyes. But when she recognizes me, her brows lift, and she throws open the gate to wave me inside.

"Oh, Blair, thank God it's you and not another cop or someone from the news," she grumbles as she locks the door behind me. "They've been hounding me all day, as if what happened isn't bad enough."

"Are you doing okay? I just saw what happened on TV," I say, looking her over for any obvious injuries. Her neck is angry, raw. In the bright light of the foyer, once inside, I can see purple marks on Danica's throat and arms, exposed by the white tank top that she wears. Her long hair is pulled back into a low ponytail.

"Ugh, it's a long story," she says, exasperated.

She's got on baggy beige lounge pants, but her feet are bare, and they make a sticking noise against the tile as she walks through her house toward the kitchen. When I stand frozen at the front door, she pauses to look back at me.

"Well, come on then." Her voice makes it clear she's surprised I didn't follow her automatically.

I walk past ornate pieces of antique furniture that look like they're not only at least a hundred years old, but also so substantial that if they tipped over, I'd die under the weight. Everything oozes wealth, from the plush carpets to the sleek couches that look as though no one has ever sat on them. Everything is embossed, embroidered, edged, or gilded. The kitchen looks very similar to my sister's, which leads me to believe they're the original kitchens the builders plopped into these houses. Danica finally stops on her porch, and signals for me to take a seat on one of the couches. She's got enough seating out here for thirty people. I wonder if she has people over that often.

The couch is softer than I expect when I sit. Danica offers me a glass of tea, which I take to be polite, though I don't particularly want it—most tea in Florida is overly sweet, and I prefer mine unsweetened. But I'm pleasantly surprised when I find it to be free of sugar.

"Are you sure that you want to be out here after what happened?" I ask as Danica sits across from me. She sets her tea down on the table between us and crosses her legs before she speaks.

"I am not going to let anyone make me feel unsafe or unwelcome in a part of my own home. What happened was terrible, but I'm not going to swear off my favorite part of this house because of something"—she wrinkles her nose—"unfortunate. I will not give that man any more power over me."

I nod, wishing that I had that same kind of fearlessness, but I know that I don't. I've always envied that in other people. Tenacity. Spunk. Those aren't words that I think I'd ever use to describe myself. If someone attacked me in my backyard, I'd sell my house and move to a high-rise condo. I'd probably never set foot in a backyard ever again. Then again, I'd never categorize myself as brave.

"I'm so sorry that this happened to you," I offer, not sure of what else to say. "Are you sure you're okay?"

She shakes her head and waves her hand, as if it's nothing. "We cannot let the horrible things that happened to us, define us. This will not change me. I will not let trauma carve me into a husk of my former self. I will move on. I will be stronger." She has so much conviction when she speaks, I swear she could do it for a living.

I nod. "I'm glad that it wasn't worse." She could have been killed, and I wonder if that was the intention or if she was really the intended target. Were they actually after my sister?

She smiles. "Exactly. It wasn't worse. I'm alive. I wasn't maimed, things could have ended horribly, but here I am." She holds her hands up. "Everything happens for a reason."

"Did you see who attacked you?" I ask, wondering if it's crass to ask something like this.

She takes a sip of her tea then shakes her head. "No. It was pretty dark, and our cameras were down because we've been having trouble with our Wi-Fi for the past couple weeks. I swear it goes out anytime the wind blows. I've tried to have them come out over and over but they say the problem is on our end. There aren't any issues with the service or hardware. Who knows."

"Would you mind telling me what happened?" I ask, hoping that maybe it'll give me some clues as to what may have happened to Eviana. I can't help but think that this is all related somehow. It's too much of a coincidence otherwise.

She nods. "Might as well. If they ever catch the guy, I'll have to go over it a thousand times in court." She sighs. "I was out here doing my evening wind-down routine. I like to sit out here, in the dark, with a glass of wine as I go over my day, what went the way I liked, what didn't, and what I hope for tomorrow." A sad smile crosses her lips. "It may be stupid, but it's something that my mother did every night, though she came out to have her evening cigarette, not wine, but still. It reminds me to be present, to appreciate things. Gratitude and introspection are so important."

"That sounds like a nice tradition," I say. I do something similar in the morning. I try to sit with my coffee on the small balcony of my apartment and take in the city before I go to work. "Yesterday, I'd gotten into a fight with Simon over the fence after I pointed out to him that I saw a tattooed woman sneaking around in his backyard." She rolls her eyes. But the tone of her voice tells me that this is nothing new.

A fight with Simon? A tattooed woman? Right before she

was attacked in her backyard? I was thinking that maybe someone had tried to kidnap Danica thinking that she was Eviana. But now I wonder if Simon was behind all of this or maybe Claire. I did tell him about Danica's video of him leaving. And the frequent arguments that he and Eviana had. I kick myself for saying anything to him. I could have put Danica in danger. But why would Claire have come over here, and more importantly—how could she have gotten into the neighborhood? The guard never would have let her in.

"About what?" I ask, trying not to sound as hungry for the answer as I actually am.

"He was upset that I was spending so much time in the backyard, and since I pointed out seeing that woman, he thinks that I'm watching the house. He thinks that I'm sitting back here to spy on him, since technically I could see into the kitchen and living room from where I usually sit over there." She motions toward the pagoda she's got set up toward the back of the property under an old oak tree. The pagoda is lined with market lights, and I know from experience that it looks very pretty in the evenings when she's got all the lights on.

"That's ridiculous," I say. Though I do hope that Danica was spying, I hope that she has more dirt on Simon that she can share with me. She's lived next door for long enough to give me good insight.

"I know! As if I give a shit about what's going on over there. But he got so mad when I mentioned I hadn't seen Eviana in a few days. I was asking if she'd gone on vacation with another one of her friends, since she just got back from her trip to Puerto Rico recently," she explains. When Danica speaks, she's a bit too animated with her hands. But she's so lively that I find it endearing.

"That seems like a very safe question. I'm not sure why he'd get angry about that," I say, though I know exactly why. I've seen the speculation online. Simon has a very dangerous house of cards that he's building. If he isn't careful, it's all going to come crashing down very soon. And I know these little jabs, the speculation, people noticing that Eviana isn't around—it's all starting to stack up in his mind. There's only so long that he can keep this charade going.

"I know. Asking about your neighbors and showing a bit of concern isn't a crime. But Simon acts like it is. He accused me of being one of Eviana's stalkers, of posting nasty messages all over her social media accounts. He tried to accuse me of wanting to hurt her." She throws her hands up with frustration then takes a sip of her tea. "That's the most ridiculous thing that I've ever heard. Why would I do that? As if I don't have enough stuff going on that I would resort to stalking my own neighbor?" A dry laugh erupts from her.

"I can tell that you're not that type of person." The words are necessary to keep her going. There's a hungry look in Danica's eyes that tells me she wants some type of validation from me, and I'm more than happy to give it to her to keep her talking.

"Exactly. No one in this neighborhood is that type of person. Except for maybe Simon. I've seen him in his car, sitting outside of houses, peering in the windows. He's the one stalking around the neighborhood, sniffing around. He always looks like he's up to something, watching."

It doesn't surprise me much. There have been several times that I've felt like Simon was watching, looming, just waiting for something. It wouldn't surprise me if he was doing that to other people who live here.

She looks down. "Look, there's something that I need to tell you. Something I feel like I should have told Eviana when I started to suspect... but I just couldn't bring myself to break her heart."

My stomach climbs my throat as she talks. I can feel the bad news brewing behind her words, I'm waiting for the last shoe to drop, for her to break something awful. My mind swarms with all the things that she could say, all the horrible things that I'm absolutely certain that Simon is capable of.

"What is it?" I finally ask when she's quiet for too long.

"I think that Simon is cheating on Eviana, or at least, that he's about to. He's always leering, looking at other women in the neighborhood. He sneaks out at late hours—like the night I showed you on the camera. He does that so often. I didn't want to say anything before, because I'm not the type to bad-mouth my neighbors, but after he screamed at me... well, the gloves are off. And with that tattooed woman lurking around... I really wonder if the two of them are meeting up. It seems like she's looking for opportunities to sneak in."

He was slipping out in the middle of the night often? Is that why he has all those sleeping pills that he offered me? I wish that Eviana had mentioned something to me while I was here. I wish she would have let me help her. Maybe making up the story about the cancer was her way of crying for help because she didn't want me to know about the real circumstances. I think that my sister was way too proud to tell me about what was really going on in her life. It's so painful to find out that you're being cheated on. It's humiliating, I'm not surprised she wasn't more open about it. Though I can't be certain that the cancer wasn't real, maybe she didn't tell me the entire truth because it was too embarrassing. Cancer isn't something you can control, but finding out your husband is a cheating dirtbag—that can feel like you did something wrong. I know so many women who are so hard on themselves when their husbands cheat. They ask themselves what they did wrong. Were they so awful that their husbands couldn't remain faithful? Was there something they could have done differently? If Eviana found out about the infidelity, I'm sure she went through the same thought process.

"How often was he going out?" I ask, realizing that the

conversation has really shifted away from her injuries—but maybe that's for the best. Danica didn't want to talk about her attack anymore anyway. Maybe giving me this information gives her some sort of comfort when she can't find it anywhere else.

"Three or four nights a week, it seemed like on average. There were some weeks when he went out almost every night," she explains then offers a little shrug. She finally meets my eyes again.

How was he going out so often and my sister didn't realize it? Or maybe they had some kind of arrangement? I'm not sure that it makes sense. I didn't know my sister well enough to know if she was a heavy sleeper. Could he really slip out nearly every night unnoticed?

"And Eviana never brought it up to you?" I ask.

She shakes her head. "No, but I do wonder if that's what all the fighting was about. Maybe he got caught. And maybe that's why it seems your sister hasn't been around in over a week now."

Danica's eyes sharpen, and a question lingers behind her eyes, a question that I cannot and will not answer. For now, I'm going to keep the secrets that I have, because for now, they're my secrets too.

17

YOUTUBE

The video opens to Tiffany sitting at her desk. She's got on a pink polka-dot dress that matches the teapot that's at her side. She pours herself a cup, and smirks at the camera before taking a sip. Tiffany gives a knowing smile to her viewers before tossing her hair over her shoulder dramatically.

"So," she says, stopping to sip her tea again. An image with the front of a neighborhood fills the screen next to Tiffany's face. Block letters atop an ornate brick sign spell out *Lakeview Shores*. Beneath the letters, water trickles into a fountain with turquoise water.

"Some of you may be aware that this is the neighborhood that Eviana lives in, in the Orlando area. She hasn't made it a secret. In fact, she covered the selection of the neighborhood and house-hunting there extensively five years ago, as I'm sure many of you remember." As Tiffany talks, the square with the image of the neighborhood fades and a short video plays of Eviana showing off the neighborhood and then her house.

She pauses to sip her tea again, then folds her hands atop her desk. The image on the screen shifts to a still from a news broadcast. An anchor stands in front of a house, and a banner printed beneath her face reads *Terror Strikes Lakeview Shores*.

"I'm not sure how many of you saw this. I live in Florida, so this has been running every five minutes all day long." She rolls her eyes. "Anyway, the woman who was attacked wasn't Eviana. No, it was her next-door neighbor—a woman who looks eerily similar to our queen. So, I have to ask—is this related to what's been happening on Eviana's channel?" She stops for effect. "Or I guess you could say—what hasn't been happening on Eviana's pages?"

She sighs and takes one last sip of her tea. "So, I have to ask... is Eviana okay?"

18

How many secrets can one woman keep? That's a question that I keep asking myself as I dig through my sister's digital history. I keep waiting to uncover something, for the evidence to be so clear that it will spell out exactly what happened to her—but I know that's a fever dream. There's no way something like that will happen in real life. I'm also not proud of the amount of time I've spent on Simon's social media. And while I can't prove he's cheating, the number of women he follows is highly suspect.

After my conversation with Danica yesterday, I know that the clock is ticking and that I'm running out of time. I have to find out what happened to Eviana before the police get involved, and I know that could be any second. My lies about vacations and offsite shoots will only go so far. With the attack on Danica, and the police already swarming her neighborhood, it's not a far leap for them to try and ask the neighbors if they saw anything happen at Danica's house. I wonder if Simon feels it too, the walls closing in, time slowly ticking to a halt. I hope he does. I hope what he did to my sister is eating him alive.

As I click through my sister's computer for what I swear is

the twelfth time, I feel like there's something here that I'm just not seeing. My sister was good at hiding things, so I wonder if she had files hidden away on this computer. She has always been so secretive. I open the Finder, then look at how much memory my sister used in the preferences. It takes me a few Google searches to figure out how to uncover hidden folders on Macs. Finally, I find a treasure trove of folders that I wasn't expecting.

My sister has folders upon folders of saved screenshots, threats that people sent her, videos of her upset about being stalked that I don't remember her ever posting. It looks like she was being terrorized by people on her social media accounts but decided not to let the world know about her struggles—not that I ever saw anyway.

In several of the folders, I find DMs that she's saved, images from other accounts, posts from competitors. She's got contracts and confidential records. Then, in a folder with no name, I find a Word document with nothing in it except for an address. I google the address and find what looks like an abandoned house. I save it and decide that I'll investigate more later.

After hours of searching, my stomach growls and my eyes have grown tired of staring at the computer; though there's so much more to go through, I need a break. I finally pull on some clothes and sling my bag over my shoulder. In the living room I'm surprised to find Valentina.

"Good afternoon," she says with a smile. "There's a fresh pot of coffee if you want some."

"I need to go get some food before I have any more coffee. Thank you, though. How's everything going? Thank you again for letting me crash here. If you want me to move on to the hotel, please let me know. I'm happy to go," I say, realizing halfway through my comments that I'm starting to ramble.

She dismisses my concerns with a wave of her hand. "Oh, don't even. It's no problem at all letting you stay here. I'm barely here most days. I practically live at my hotels, so don't worry about it."

"Why do you spend so much time there?" I ask.

She gives me a sad smile. "Because they mean a lot to me. Growing up in Florida, there are not a lot of opportunities outside of hospitality. I saw everyone working for these companies, busting their asses, getting paid nothing in return, getting laid off every time the economy dipped. And I told myself, I wasn't going to waste my whole life working for somebody else. I was going to help lift others up, not hold them down. I was going to bust my ass until my business was my own. I worked in marketing for years for hospitality companies until some small investments that I made on my own paid off big. I'm proud to own my own business, to be running a hotel—well, several now. It's my pride. It's my calling. And I try to treat my people right. I treat them better than other companies treat them. When there are struggles, we're all in it together."

I nod at that. "You do a great job. It's clear that your properties are loved. The hotel was immaculate when I went in. Some hotels here look really beat up, worn down by all the traffic that you see in Florida. I'm glad you were able to carve out your own space that you can be proud of. The way you talk about it, it's clear that you love it."

She nods and offers me a smile. "Thank you for that. I always tell my employees that people can see the difference, that it's the little details that matter. They always call me crazy and say I'm being too particular. But you get it!"

I nod. "It does matter."

She waves toward the door. "Where are you off to?" she asks.

"I was going to do another few loops through town, look for Eviana," I explain. Though I like Valentina and I trust her, I think telling her that I'm now resorting to chasing down addresses that my sister saved on her computer sounds a little extra crazy. So, I'm not going to drop that tidbit.

She nods. "I wish you luck. I really hope that everything turns out okay with Eviana. I'm getting really worried, especially after seeing that woman in the neighborhood was nearly kidnapped. Be careful out there, okay?"

I wish that news hadn't gotten out. Hell, I wish that it hadn't happened at all. But there's no fixing it. I hate that Danica was attacked. But now it calls into question everything I'd been thinking, everything that I'd been adding up in my mind. Was I wrong? Was I looking in the wrong place all along? Or are these two things connected?

I say my goodbyes to Valentina and head out the front door and climb into my rental car. As I weave through the streets, my nerves gnaw at me. My palms slick with sweat as I drive, and I wonder what I'll find once I reach the address on the GPS. I follow the directions, cutting through backroads on my way toward the northern edges of Orlando, where the city slowly fades to forest. This part of the city, it always throws me off, because while you'd expect for most of Florida to look like a swamp, instead up here it reminds me of the Northeast. There are hills, dense forest, there are even bears—it's like a whole different world.

The road curves into the trees, the pavement giving way to a dirt road that's wide enough for two cars. My hands clench the steering wheel until my knuckles flash white, my jaw tightens. A creeping feeling coils inside me, telling me that this is a bad plan. Maybe I should have been more specific, told Valentina exactly where I'd be. I glance at my cellphone, and notice that of course, I barely have any signal. The road curves, gobbled up by the trees. I follow it as closely as I can, my speed slowing to a crawl. I could probably walk faster than my car is moving right now. The body of the vehicle sways as the tires bounce into ruts and dips in the dirt road. Stray roots slash across the path, jolting me and the car. Ahead of me, a shape forms in the road, heavily shaded by large trees that curve over the trail—it's a blocky thing that I recognize almost immediately as my sister's Range Rover. My heart leaps, and I cannot believe that I actually found her car. I pull up close and climb out of my rental.

Thirty feet or so ahead of her car, a decaying house stands. Though it used to have white wooden siding, it's now covered mostly in green moss, lichen, and dirt, as though the forest is slowly reclaiming the house. Spanish moss clings to the sagging roofline, tickling the windows as a stray wind shifts. The front porch sags and looks as if any weight was placed on it, it may collapse. My heart thuds in my throat as I approach the vehicle. The windows are all fogged with condensation, and the door is yawning open. I take a peek inside. How long as it been out here? Since my sister disappeared? The keys are on the seat, my sister's phone next to them. But on the floor of the passenger side, I notice a phone that I've never seen before. I grab it and shove it into my pocket after checking if it still has battery—it doesn't.

I've seen enough crime shows to know that I shouldn't take my sister's phone. That will be way too much evidence pointing in my direction if something happened to her. And even though Simon said the tracking was turned off, I don't believe him—he has no reason to tell the truth. This other phone though... well, my curiosity is too piqued to leave it here. If my sister had a second phone, I need to know what's on it, and what she was hiding. Or maybe someone was in the car with her. Either way, this device may give me exactly what I'm looking for.

I scour the rest of the car, finding nothing of note. My attention turns toward the house, and I wonder if Eviana could have been desperate enough to stay in here. The dirt is soft as I approach the house, and I worry about how muddy my shoes will get. I'm not usually precious about what I'm wearing, but the more dirt and mud I track around, the more evidence there will be that I was here. I can't remember the last time it rained, and yet, it feels as if I'm sinking into the wet ground, the mud sucking me down with each step. I don't dare tread on the sagging porch, and instead shift along the side of the house toward the window. The smell of moss and damp invades my nostrils but puts me at ease. It smells like the forest back in Washington, where I like to hike—getting away from the city, being out in nature, it really helps settle my mind and my soul. And somehow, even though I'm looking for Eviana out here, I find a slice of peace I didn't expect.

Farther in the forest, the popping of branches alerts me to squirrels chittering in the canopy. Though I look up trying to find them, the house is blocking my view, so I try to tune it out. When I reach the first window, I stand on my tiptoes to peer inside. The glass is grimy, and I try to use my palm to clear away the muck. My heart pounds as tension compounds in the air around me. My aura of anxiety is so palpable I swear that it's a physical thing, pressing against me, tightening around my skin like cling wrap. I peer inside the smeared window, and movement catches my eye. Adrenaline floods into my veins as my stomach leaps in response.

I stagger back from the house, my foot catching on a protruding root. The world whizzes past as I tumble to the ground, pain shooting through my spine as I land hard on the ground. My teeth clack together and a jolt resonates through my skull. I force myself up, my mind whirring as I worry that whoever was in the house will rush out—that they'll come running for me. Maybe I shouldn't have come here by myself.

Once I've righted myself, I press my back against the house, just out of view of the windows. I force my breathing to steady, for my heart to slow, as I tell myself over and over that it'll be okay. My blood pressure is so high, my veins actually hurt. A sound echoes through the house, the noise vibrating against my back. I tense up, wanting so badly to look in the window, to see what's inside. Is it my sister? Has she been hiding out here?

The noises grow closer, and I glance to my left, seeing something move on the windowsill. But the shape is too small, it can't be a person. I stumble away, then turn to look into the house properly, and that's when I realize that it's a cat. It must have gotten into the house somehow—whether it's a stray, feral, or someone's pet, I cannot tell. The cat looks into the house, clearly not noticing my presence at all. I shake my head, cursing myself for being so startled by a damn cat. I walk back toward my rental, but as I approach, I realize something isn't right, there's a shape on the road behind my car. I stop dead in my tracks when I realize there's another vehicle pulled up behind mine—an Escalade.

Simon.

He's found me.

My mind whirls as I calculate the odds that my brother-in-law murdered Eviana and left her body in these woods. Then, I try to calculate the odds that he'll now do the same thing to me. And I've got to be honest, I think I'm more likely to win the lottery than I am to make it out of this alive. There's no other reason that he'd be out here, that he could have found me. If he knew that Eviana's car was out here all this time, then he must have done something to her. There are no other options. I wonder if he killed her by himself, if it was his plan all along, or if Tom was in on it too. Did Fiona help? Or one of Eviana's other friends? Did Simon's old ex Claire help?

He stalks forward, his footsteps heavy against the ground as he approaches. His hands are tucked away deep in his pockets, his eyes cast down on the ground as if he needs to watch where he walks to avoid tripping. But the confidence of his steps makes it look like this isn't his first venture out here. When he finally looks up at me, something dangerous swims behind his eyes, something I've seen before. It's the same way he looked at me before he attacked me.

"Fancy finding you out here," Simon says with a smile. He

pulls out his cellphone and takes a picture of me next to Eviana's car, before I have a chance to stop him. I grind my teeth together with frustration; yet another piece of evidence for him to add to the pile so he can frame me for her murder.

"What are you doing here?" I ask. "How did you even find me?"

"I followed you. I put a GPS tracker on your rental car after I noticed that you were staying with Valentina. I've been keeping an eye on you. I was hoping that you'd lead me to Eviana, or I'd at least be able to figure out what you did with her —and here you are, with her car," he says before adding a tisking sound, as if I'm a naughty child who's just been caught in the midst of something, as if he is just so disappointed in me. It reminds me of my mother.

I want to kick him in the balls again, to climb in my rental car and run him over—once or maybe five times. He's been tracking me? I shouldn't be surprised—and yet, the realization stings. We're so deep in the woods I don't think anyone would find him. But as that thought slithers through my mind, I realize the same goes for me—if Simon kills me out here, no one is going to find my body. That stray cat in the abandoned house will probably eat my corpse, and no one will ever know what happened. I can't let him do that. I can't let him get away with what he's done.

"You're following me now?" I ask as I cross my arms.

"My wife disappeared after she met up with you, and now you're sneaking around the town. Yeah, I don't think it takes a rocket scientist to figure out why I'm keeping tabs on you." Sarcasm drips from his words, and I want to punch him. "Did Eviana get all the brains too? I figured maybe she got the looks so you'd be smarter." He lets out a sad little laugh. "But clearly you're an idiot."

I internalize what he's said. I won't lash out. I know that's exactly what he wants. He wants proof that I'm the unhinged monster that he thinks—that'd make it so much easier to pin this all on me if I were that person. "You were the last person to see her, Simon. I've got videos of it, proof that you were there after me. Danica told me all about how you've been screaming at Eviana, how you've been sneaking out in the middle of the night. She knows you were there the night Eviana disappeared. Were you screwing someone else? Did you want Eviana out of the way so you could move on with your life? Or did you just decide it was time to get rid of her so you could take all her money since you were too much of a loser to make your own?" I throw the words at him, my accusations as sharp as daggers.

He barks a laugh, but the look in his eyes tells me that I've struck a little too close to home. His mouth is a thin line of disgust. Something I said was right on the mark, and it's made him uneasy. "That's ridiculous, you're bluffing. You don't have anything on me."

"I have proof," I say. I want him to know that I have info on him, but I don't want to completely show my hand. "I've got footage of you leaving the house. I know that you were there the night that Eviana disappeared."

His eye twitches. "No, you don't." He tries to call my bluff.

"Yes, I do," I say, my words punctuated. "And I've got footage with you screaming in the background. I believe you said something along the lines of *I'm going to make you regret this*." I parrot his words back to him.

He takes a step toward me, his movements stiff. "Don't go down this path, Blair. I will make you regret it." And my whole body tightens. I know what he's capable of. Is he going to attack me again?

"Just like you made Eviana regret it? What did you do to her?" I ask. Though my eye is still bruised from where he hit me the last time, I don't back down—I don't cower from his intrusion into my space. I will not let him think that I'm afraid of him, no matter what.

He grinds his teeth together so hard I can hear it. His anger makes me flinch internally, but I wrestle with my features, hoping that he can't see it.

"Get the fuck out of here, Blair. This is the last chance I'm giving you. It's time for you to go home. You're not going to find Eviana, and you're not going to help this situation."

"Do you have amnesia or something? You're the reason I'm here. You called me." I can't believe he has the audacity to try and send me home.

"I didn't call you. You showed up here, acting like you weren't the last person to see Eviana alive," he says before scoffing, as if the idea that he called me is ridiculous.

I grab my phone and go to my call log to prove to him that he called me, but all the phone calls and the voicemail he left me—they're gone. My mind spins, and I cannot process what I'm seeing. I know he called me, otherwise there's no reason I would have come back here. I would have never known that my sister was missing.

"You did something to my phone," I seethe.

He shrugs. "Prove it. It looks to me like you came back here to see if anyone would notice that you did something to your sister. They say criminals always return to the scene of the crime. Did you kill her? Did you decide that you were so jealous of Eviana that you couldn't stand for her to be alive anymore? I know that you and Eviana had your problems, but I would expect better of you, Blair."

I have to walk past him to get to my rental car, but I don't let that stop me. I storm past him, but he reaches out, grabbing my arm to stop me.

"This is all going to come crashing down on you," he says, his words clearly a promise. "And I can't wait to see you go down for this. You're going to get exactly what you deserve."

I look at him, my eyes sharpening so much that he drops my arm and takes a step back.

"This isn't going to turn out the way you think it will, Simon. I have a lot more information about you than you think. Just wait, we'll see who this really comes crashing down on."

Simon reaches out to grab me again, and I act automatically. I raise my fist and hit him hard in the nose. He stumbles back as blood trickles from his nose. My heart races and I run toward my car. Pain radiates from my knuckles, up my wrist, warning me that I may have done some serious damage to my hand. My heart pounds and my legs burn as I run toward my car. The sound of his footfalls behind me, the sharp crunch of twigs snapping beneath his feet spurs me on. I have to get away from him. I have to. Otherwise I know no one will ever figure out what happened to my sister.

His fingertips graze my shirt. But I'm so close, just seconds from my car. I just have to run a little faster. My heart pounds so hard it feels like it's struggling in my chest. The car beeps twice, recognizing that I've approached with the key tucked away in my pocket. My hands touch the metal of the door, my fingers curling around the handle. But Simon slams hard into me, pinning me against the door, my already injured hand screaming in pain.

A scream rips from my throat, but I know it's useless. There's no one close enough to hear me. If he kills me out here, they'll never find my body. I kick backward, trying to land my heel into Simon's shin but somehow he manages to dodge every attempt. His hand fists my hair and he slams my head into the car. Bone crunches in my nose with the impact, and warmth flooding onto my face tells me that my nose is bleeding.

Panic seizes me, and a primal energy takes over my body. It's as if someone else is controlling me, demanding that I fight back. I duck down and twist out of Simon's grip, then dodge around him. The car is a lost cause. I'm going to have to run through the woods. That's the only way I'll be able to get away from him. I force myself forward, sucking in a deep breath as I prepare myself to sprint.

Simon slams into me just as I start to run and knocks me to the ground. My body screams in pain, my hip, my thigh, my left shoulder blade all warning me that they're injured. His weight bears down on me, his too white teeth gnashing in my face. I swear it feels like I'm being attacked by a rabid animal, not a person. His fists fly at my face, and though I try to dodge them, several land, making black spots explode in my vision. I know I can't keep this up.

I force my uninjured arm straight up, my palm slamming into the bridge of his nose. Simon gasps and straightens enough to give me access to his throat. I aim my next punch for his Adam's apple. Simon lets out a sound that's half guttural, half gargle as he rolls off of me. This is my chance, the only moment that I have. Though my body protests, I flip over and force myself up from all fours.

"You bitch," he manages to growl after me as I stumble away.

It takes more steps than I'd like to gain momentum, to start to jog away from him. My body screams, but my mind is louder —the warnings telling me I have to get away, I have to keep going. *I can do this. I can do this. I can get away from him*, I tell myself over and over. Something hits me hard in the back, my body flies forward, and though I throw my hands out to catch myself, it does me no good. My head slams into the trunk of a tree. The world goes bright, the sounds of the forest too loud. Darkness ebbs in at the edge of my vision, as if night has suddenly started to fall—then suddenly, it's all gobbled up, the light snuffed out as my world goes black.

The smell of smoke finds me in the darkness. Fire and gas and pain—these are the only things with me in the ether. Agony throbs in my forehead as orange and gold dance on the back of my eyelids. It feels like I'm wading through syrup when I finally open my eyes. My whole body aches, pain shooting through my extremities like lightning.

Sirens pierce the air, drowning out the sounds of the crackling flames. Heat licks my face, and I realize I'm only a few feet from the flames licking at the vehicle in front of me. It takes too long for my mind to make sense of it all. Two burning cars in a forest, columns of smoke rising toward the sky. My mind swarms with a million questions and finally I remember what happened, that Simon came after me again. He did this. I know he set the cars on fire.

Smoke clouds the scene around me, darkening the sky. The shrill cry of sirens getting closer warns me that they're coming toward me. I can't get caught out here with my sister's burning car. My eyes flick between both vehicles, realizing that even if there was anything left in the car that I wanted to grab, it's too late now.

My eyes flick toward the house, then the woods. I have no idea how far it'll be to break through the other side. My phone stabs me in my hip as I take a step forward. I unsheathe it from my pocket and glance at my map app before slipping between the trees.

My phone vibrates, the screen lighting up with a call from my boss. I've barely got a bar of signal and somehow she can get through? I grind my teeth together as I debate whether or not I should ignore the call—but there's no chance my anxiety would let it go to voicemail.

"Hey, Amanda, what's up?" I ask, hoping that whatever she needs will be fast.

"Hey, Blair, I know you're dealing with stuff right now with your sister being sick, but do you have a minute?" There's a tension in her words that makes me uneasy.

My nerves tighten around me like a vice. I know that whatever she's got to say isn't good. I swallow hard, my whole body preparing for the worst.

"Sure, what can I help you with?" I ask, trying to sound helpful and not as stressed as I feel. If she tells me that I'm fired, I'm going to vomit.

"I got a strange email, followed by an even stranger phone call from a woman who claimed that you've been harassing her... she sent me quite a few screenshots."

My heart climbs into my throat as panic grips me. Someone is claiming that I harassed her? That's the most ridiculous thing I've ever heard. Something like this could be a nail in the coffin for my career. I work with children, if someone is spreading rumors and lies about me—I could lose everything I've worked so hard for. These kids need me. They need someone who understands what they're going through, how hard it can be.

"I would never do anything like that," I say, my voice faltering.

"I know," she says quickly. "The screenshots were clearly generated from an app or something. I mostly just wanted to warn you in case this person starts trying to call other people or to send these screenshots anywhere else."

"Thank you for letting me know. Who was it that sent them?"

"Her name was..." She pauses for a moment to think. "Fiona, I think?"

I wrap up the call with my boss just as I break through the trees. I get Fiona is keeping her promise to try to ruin my life—but she's going to regret it.

20

Valentina is out for the night, so I've snuggled up in the guest room with a thick blanket to combat the blasting AC, thankful that she's not here to ask me questions about my face. Maybe at least the cold will keep the swelling down. I've been back for at least an hour, trying to shake off the adrenaline still lingering in my blood from this afternoon. A dull ache still persists in my forehead, and my legs burn from my long walk through the forest. I've been flipping through the channels while I try to settle my mind. Though the sun set hours ago, the adrenaline from earlier today is still thick in my blood, threatening to keep me up all night. I stop clicking through when I see a reporter on the screen. A very familiar scene is behind her. Over her left shoulder, I can see the decaying white house I saw earlier today. To her right, there's the charred remains of two vehicles.

"We're here in the forest near Wekiva Springs, where a fire was reported by some concerned citizens who were driving by on the main road. While first responders have extinguished the fire and confirmed that no one was harmed, police are now trying to track down the owner of the vehicle. The VIN numbers have been scratched off, all the paperwork removed, even the license plate is gone. Law enforcement wants to call out what an odd situation this is, and their concerns regarding this vehicle. At this time, they're unsure if the car was stolen, and a thief decided to burn the vehicle before they were caught with it. Once law enforcement has investigated and given us an update, we'll let you all know what exactly happened here," the woman says before signing off.

I sit up straighter in bed and rewind the segment and play it again. Simon really went through a lot of trouble to ensure that no one would be able to track the car back to Eviana. And why would he bother burning my rental too? If he was trying to pin all of this on me, if that was the case, then why is he going through the trouble to destroy her car? That sends a very different message to me. Simon is trying to cover something up. He's trying to make sure that no one can track Eviana's last steps. I bet he took her phone too. I glance to the phone charging on my nightstand, the one I haven't been able to unlock yet—the one that I know may hold the answers to what happened to my sister.

My phone vibrates next to me several times, lighting up with text messages. I scoop it up and stare down at several messages from Fiona.

> Oh, honey, I hope everything is going okay at work.

> I heard that you might be getting fired??

> God that must be so rough.

> But also, I got some weird texts from Eviana. I'm just giving you and Simon both a heads-up. In 24 hours, I'm posting them.

Several screenshots appear in the text thread just as I finish reading her messages. The screenshots are text messages allegedly from my sister, admitting that she frequently creates fake accounts to attack herself and other creators for content. I've seen videos in the past of my sister addressing *hateful comments* and threats that were posted on her pages. Were they all fake? Were they all made up for attention? I don't respond to Fiona's message. At the end of the day, I don't care what she posts about my sister, as long as she doesn't figure out that Eviana is missing.

21

As morning light streams in through the large windows in Valentina's living room, I sit at her small table, drinking my first cup of coffee, waiting for her to wake up. All night, I had questions brewing in my mind. Though I told Valentina what I thought about my sister, I have yet to really get into the meat of what Eviana told her about Simon; I'll have to tell her what happened in the woods. I know she's going to have questions about my face; there's a cut across my forehead and bruises blooming on my cheeks, jaw, and arms. She needs to know what happened because there's no doubt in my mind that he'll kill me if given another chance. I need to talk to Eviana's friends more. I need to get some other viewpoints about what Eviana's life was really like. I know that Simon was involved, but I need more actual evidence to provide to the police—everything I've found so far is too circumstantial. And despite the growing bruises on my face, no one is going to believe me over him. That and if they ever connect my burned-up rental car back to me, I'm screwed. Thankfully the rental car company has no idea, and won't for a while—at least I had the foresight to get a long-term option.

Valentina emerges from her bedroom and yawns; she walks into the kitchen wearing leggings and an oversized T-shirt. Her eyes go wide when she appraises my face, which makes me think it got worse overnight. She offers me a smile before pouring a cup of coffee, then joins me at the small table. We exchange a few pleasantries, and she tells me about how she slept. Once I'm sure she's shed the remains of sleep, I finally tell her about what happened in the woods, then move on to my questions.

"Could I ask you a few questions about Simon?" I ask.

She stares at my black eye and the bruise on my forehead, and I swear I can feel it growing bigger under her stare. Finally she nods and waves her hand for me to continue.

"Will you answer a few of mine? I appreciate you telling me about what happened in the woods, but there's more I need to know."

I nod, albeit somewhat reluctantly. "What did Eviana tell you about her relationship with Simon? I need specifics," I say. "I spoke to her neighbor and she let me know that she heard lots of fighting." I point to my eye. "He clearly has no problem with violence toward women, so I need to know what he did to my sister in the past."

She presses her lips together before continuing. "She and Simon had a toxic relationship. For a while, I hate to say it, but I didn't really believe what she was saying, because if it were true, I didn't understand why she would stay."

"What was she saying?" I ask, desperate for the information. I hate that it's going to be a slow trickle, getting all of this information from her point of view. I'm too impatient for this.

"She told me that she never wanted to be an influencer. She started doing it because Simon pressed her to. He thought that she'd be really good at it and presented it as something that she really needed to do to make him happy. Eventually, she started an account just so he'd shut up about it. Simon made fake accounts to help build her account up fast, and it started growing at a rate that she didn't expect for it to. But he helped some of his exes get into the influencer game, so he knew what to do." She pauses to take a sip from her coffee. "It was getting to the point where posting and figuring out content was becoming a job, so Simon urged her to cut her hours at work. She was starting to make money off of her accounts, so eventually she agreed and did that since the company she was working for wasn't doing so well financially."

She takes a sip of her drink then continues. "He helped her make a lot of money. And he insinuated he might get bored if Eviana didn't start living a more exciting life. He'd apparently left his exes when their accounts stopped bringing in the kind of money that he wanted. He told her that being hot would only get her so far." She rolls her eyes. I'm not at all surprised he was a manipulative dirtbag. "She never really liked the influencer stuff, but she really liked Simon and felt like it was the only way to keep him interested in her. It seemed more like a drug addiction than a relationship to me, if I'm being honest. She was really burned out by the whole marketing thing too." She waves her hand as if to say *the rest is history*.

"What was she doing for work back then?" I ask. Eviana went to med school but dropped out. Other than being an influencer, I have no idea what she was doing for a job. I knew vaguely that she worked in marketing. We weren't in touch during those days.

"She was working for a small startup that made AI voice software, helping with their marketing and managing social media accounts, actually. She was very good at it professionally, but I don't think she ever imagined that she would be making her living off of influencing. She always spoke about it like it was temporary, fleeting, not something she wanted to do long term. I know deep down she really wanted to go back to medicine, but she didn't think that she had it in her to go back to school."

I swallow hard, knowing exactly why that was. But I'm not going to touch on any of that. Especially if Valentina doesn't bring it up. I seriously doubt that Eviana told her about what happened, how she got kicked out of medical school, and how our whole world fell apart after that.

I don't want her to dwell on this topic, so I continue on.

"So, after she started influencing full-time, what happened?"

"Simon quit his job pretty quickly after that. She didn't agree to it. He didn't mention that he was going to do it—he just didn't go to work one day and never went back again. For a while he told her that he got laid off. But then it was clear he wasn't looking for a new job. This was after they'd been married for two years. She ended up finding out that he lied about getting laid off. He quit because he thought her influencing could support them both. When Eviana asked him about it, he said that he needed to be home to help her with her content, and that they would both do it full-time." She shakes her head and presses her lips together again. "She was livid. She did not want him to stay home full-time with her. She knew that he was doing all this just to keep an eye on her. While he forced her to start doing the influencing shit, he became insanely jealous. There were times that when a man would comment on her posts, he'd scream at her and accuse her of cheating."

"That's awful," I say. But I can't say that I'm at all surprised.

She nods. "Yep. He's a piece of work if you ask me. He did that all the time. Someone would comment on her post, and whatever the person said was her fault. Eventually she had to give him access to all the accounts so that he could go through her direct messages to confirm that she wasn't talking to anyone on the side. He always had to have access to her phone, her computer. She couldn't keep anything secret," she explains.

That sounds so exhausting, and I hate that he treated her like that. "Why didn't she just leave?"

She offers me a one-shouldered shrug. "That's a good question. But I think it's because she didn't think he'd let her leave. He had his claws so deep into everything that she did, there wasn't really any way that she could get away. He could control her accounts, her money, her job, her image. There was nothing that was just hers. I knew I had to be careful about what I texted her, or what was said on the phone—because chances were he was always watching or listening. I do think that she likely considered it. But since he was a nonworking spouse, and she was so wealthy on paper, it wouldn't have gone well for her. She would have had to pay him alimony."

I pick at my fingernails as I listen. The things that she was dealing with, it makes me sick to my stomach. I wonder if that's why she lied to me. She was too proud to tell me the truth about what was going on in her life. Did she tell me she had cancer because she was considering killing herself just for a way to escape him?

"Things were really starting to come to a head with the social media stuff. I know you asked about the pregnancy... and I should have been more upfront with you about it, but I wasn't sure what your intentions were. I know you two weren't exactly close. But now that I know you didn't hurt her, that you're really looking for Eviana, I'll tell you the truth." She takes another sip of her coffee. "Simon wanted her to get into the baby market because there's so much money to be made there. But Eviana didn't want to have kids—not with him anyway. She wasn't willing to get pregnant, despite his constant nagging about it, and a few attempts on his part to get her pregnant. So their compromise was a fake pregnancy. He got her the fake bellies to wear, they hired someone to fake sonogram photos for her, then they lined up sponsors that would pay for the baby-gear posts."

She sighs and stops talking as she looks at the table.

"But the stillbirth stuff... don't you think that's taking it too far?"

She nods and looks back up at me. "Of course I do. Eviana did too, but Simon was forcing her. He told her that was the only way they could do this. It wasn't feasible for them to hire a child to pretend was theirs. They couldn't photoshop a fake kid into every photo shoot. So, the only way forward was for the baby to..." She trails off and doesn't continue.

"I can't believe that he talked her into doing this stuff," I say. I mean, I can believe that he came up with the ideas, but I just can't believe that Eviana would agree with it, no matter what. I thought that she had more conviction than that. There had to be some way for her to get out. To get away from him.

"Eviana tried to leave him because she hated the idea of this all so much. But Tom talked her into staying. He told her that divorce would damage her brand. She'd lose so much of her money, her house. She'd have to pay alimony to Simon—especially since he hadn't worked in over three years. She was going to get absolutely destroyed in the divorce."

I grimace, the idea of it all making me sick. He must have known exactly what he was doing when he quit his job. He must have known that Eviana would have to keep supporting him if they did end up getting a divorce.

"I think that she probably should have put her foot down more, but he just wore on her. He kept trying over and over and over again because he knew that if he didn't let something die, eventually if he nagged Eviana about it enough, he would get his way. He controlled the money, he controlled her friendships, he controlled what she ate. She didn't take a step in this world without him knowing about it."

"That's a horrible way to live." That makes me wonder if Eviana did take off. If this was what her life was really like, then no wonder she would have wanted to escape. I wouldn't suffer through letting a man control every single step that I took throughout the day. I wish she would have just told me what was really happening, I would have helped her.

"Eviana was looking for ways out recently, for ways to keep her brand and her income without being able to have Simon be along for the ride. I'm hoping... Well, I really hope that her disappearance is her first step to getting rid of him."

I nod. I hope that too. I don't want her to be hurt—or worse.

"There are a few of Eviana's other friends who you should speak to," she says, sliding her phone over to me with several contacts on the screen.

"These are all close friends of hers?" I ask, as I jot down the contacts on my own phone—the ones that I don't have already.

She nods. "I wasn't close with any of them. If they ask, you didn't get their contact info from me. Say that you got it from Eviana's phone."

I nod. "Of course, I won't tell anyone that it came from you," I say.

I finish drinking coffee with Valentina and tell her more details about what happened to my face, what Simon did when he found me in the woods. Though Valentina urges me to tell the police what's happened, I know they won't believe me—not when it's my word against his. Within the hour, she rushes off to get to the B&B she's considering buying, and I head back to the guest room. My phone vibrates next to me, and the name *Annabell* flashes across the screen. I remember the warnings about Fiona and Annabell as I swipe to answer the call.

"Blair, is that you? I swear I can never remember who I save in this phone."

"Yes, this is Blair," I say, wondering how she had my number saved if there wasn't a name. Then again, maybe she just picked me out of the group chat.

"Ugh, good, finally," she says, as if she's tried to call me forty times.

"What is it that you need?" I ask, trying not to be rude.

"Okay seriously, it's been forever. Where the hell is Eviana?" she asks with a bit of humor to her words.

When I don't answer right away because I'm not sure how else to lie, she asks, "Oh come on, isn't she done with her hiatus or whatever?"

I clear my throat, not sure that I should really get into the thick of the lies again. But I'm not sure how long I can keep up this act, especially when I start asking probing questions about my famous sister while she hasn't been seen for over a week. My guts churn as I realize there's only so long that I can keep doing this. I feel like I'm in so far over my head. If the tables were turned, and Eviana was in my place, I know that she'd handle it with no problem—but then again, I guess lying was second nature to her.

A spark of inspiration hits me, a thread of how I know my sister would handle the situation coming into my mind. "Why is it so imperative that you speak to Eviana? This obsession you have is a little disconcerting. Eviana mentioned—"

"Eviana mentioned what, exactly? Obsession? That is not even close," she cuts me off, temper sharpening her words as she speaks to me.

"I think you know exactly what she told me," I say, hoping that I can lead Annabell into revealing more information.

"That was all just a misunderstanding. She couldn't prove that I did anything. Someone was just spreading rumors about me leaving those comments."

It takes me a second to connect the dots. "So, you weren't leaving threats on Eviana's page then?" I press her. "Show me your accounts then." Someone has been leaving lots of threats on my sister's page and I know she received threatening messages as well. She mentioned as much to me while I was visiting. I wonder if this was a coordinated effort between these *friends* of hers.

She's silent for so long, I don't need her to admit her guilt, her silence is enough of a clue. "Look, it's just—" She trails off and goes silent, then the line goes dead.

Annabell may not have said anything of substance, but what she didn't say—that could fill volumes.

I've finally got a moment to catch up on work, to log in and slog through my inbox. Thankfully, my boss isn't taking the screenshots that Fiona sent her seriously—so as long as I keep up with my workload, it should all blow over. My phone rings, and I look down to see a call coming in from Tia. I swipe my phone to accept the call.

"Hey, Tia," I say.

"Thank God you answered. What's going on?" she asks, her words frantic.

I raise a brow, confusion gripping my thoughts. "What do you mean?"

"Eviana just called me. I've tried to call her back like twelve times, but she won't pick up the phone. I got this super weird text from her saying that I need to be honest with her about what's going on." Tia sounds like she's panicking, and I can tell by the cracks in her voice that she's telling the truth.

A bad feeling nags at me as I try to process what she's said. Eviana called her? The last I saw Eviana's phone, it was in the Range Rover before Simon set it on fire. While I was knocked out, he could have taken her phone. Or is it possible... No. It can't be. Why would she have abandoned her phone only to go grab it in the few minutes I was knocked out?

"Look, I know that she was having a hard time. That things were kinda messed up with Simon, but I need to talk to her. I need to know if she's okay."

"She's fine," I say, the lie practically burning my mouth on the way out. I try to keep my voice steady, but I'm not sure that I manage.

"Fine? I seriously doubt that she's fine. Before she disappeared, she told me that she had evidence that Simon was cheating on her. She was going to finally do something about it —that was about two weeks ago," she says.

The timeline concerns me. I wonder if she confronted Simon after he got back to Florida after his trip. I try to wrap up with Tia, assuring her the best that I can that Eviana is fine. But after I hang up with her, as the silence builds around me—I wonder what proof my sister found and what Simon did to her to keep her quiet.

22

I feel like a teenager sneaking out of Valentina's house in the middle of the night, even though Valentina is out. My heart feels like it's hiccupping in my chest as I creep across the dark lawn. The night is quiet, the sky slashed with a crescent of moonlight. I wish I had my rental so I could properly trail Simon, but I'll just have to watch him on foot.

I carve my way through the neighborhood, sticking to the shadows despite knowing it's doubtful that anyone is watching; I still feel the burn of eyes on my skin. I swear someone is out there, keeping tabs on my every movement. Light spills from the windows on the lower levels, pockmarking my path. My gut clenches as I finally round the corner to Eviana's street. The thunder of my heartbeat in my ears is so loud I half expect that everyone else in the neighborhood can hear it—but I know I'm just being stupid.

Eviana's house finally comes into view, the structure still imposing as I crouch behind the bushes across the street. But when I finally take a closer look at the house, I realize something's not right—Simon's car is gone.

Dammit.

But as I look up toward the house, I swear I see someone in the windows, the shape of a person. Who the hell is in the house if Simon is gone? Just moments after I saw it, it's gone. The movement stopped as if it never happened at all. Did I just imagine it? What if my sister is being held captive in the house? No. I shake that thought off. That'd make no sense.

I should have come out here earlier to watch. Though, then I probably would have been seen. I kick myself mentally. I have to figure out where Simon is going at night. I know he's been keeping tabs on me, and I've heard from Danica that he's slinking through the neighborhood spying on others. Is that what he's doing right now? Is he out here somewhere watching, waiting? Goosebumps needle my spine, fear prickling at me. What if he sneaks up behind me again? What if he attacks me? I'm not sure my body can take much more.

As I amble through the darkness back toward Valentina's house, I notice a familiar vehicle parked in front of Fiona's house. I swear that's Simon's Escalade. Though I want to creep closer to the house to see what they're doing in there, I can see the security cameras perched atop the roofline. I have to bide my time. Today is not the day, but I will figure out what the two of them are up to and what they did to my sister.

23

AGE SIXTEEN

My neck is slick with sweat. For the past hour, I've felt like I was going to vomit all over the seat in front of me. The bus lurches from side to side, swaying as the driver steers through a neighborhood. Though everyone around me is talking, I can't make out any of the words. I'm too lost in my own mind. In my backpack, I swear I can feel my horrible report card reaching out for me—I feel it looming there, like a storm that's brewing. I've never been great at school, but this semester, well, it's the worst so far.

Four D's, two F's, and an A—in art. My mother is going to murder me and bury my body in the backyard. That's the best I can hope for, honestly. I look up as the bus stops, glancing around to see if it's my stop—it's not. I lock eyes with Eviana for just a moment. She's toward the front of the bus, surrounded by friends, while I'm at the back of the bus, by myself, as always. There are questions in her eyes, but I don't know why. It's not as if Eviana has started giving two shits about me. She's about to leave for college, though I know she'll go to UF where our mom works—it's still likely that she'll move out. And then what... I'll be left here, alone, with our mother.

When we finally grind to a halt in front of our house, my face goes clammy. I can feel the dread pooling inside me for real. Eviana rises, and I force myself up too. I walk stiff-legged to the front of the bus. What if I just stayed on the bus, got off at the next stop, and ran away? How long would it take for my mother to realize that I'm missing? How long would it take for someone to find me?

Eviana finally looks back at me when I stand frozen at the front for too long, as if I can somehow change my fate if I wait long enough. Eventually, I realize I can't delay any longer, and I step off the bus onto the sidewalk. I walk toward our house, and Eviana stays beside me—usually she walks a few feet ahead.

"What happened?" she asks, looking down at her feet. She's got her thumbs looped into the straps of her backpack as she drags her feet against the concrete. I can't remember the last time she actually tried to talk to me while we walked home.

"I'll give you two guesses," I say sarcastically.

"Is it that bad?"

I nod, reluctantly. I know that she'll just end up rubbing her grades in my face, so I don't want to tell her.

"You know if you don't do better, you're not going to go to college."

A laugh erupts out of me. "You think that I'll even be able to hack it in college? I can barely make it through any of my classes now."

"Because you're not trying," she says as we turn onto our street.

I want to lash out at her because I am trying. I'm doing everything that I can to stay ahead in class—but it just doesn't take. It's too hard for me to focus, I can't remember anything that I read, it all just leaves my head as soon as I'm done reading. When we walk in the front door, the smell of cigarette smoke hits me, like I've walked into a wall of it. That's how I know she's home, that she's waiting.

"Girls," she says, her voice croaking from the kitchen table as soon as the front door opens. I swear, she's like a phantom, looming, waiting.

Eviana flashes me a look, then walks toward the kitchen. I follow behind her, as if she'll shield me somehow. I know she won't. It's only a matter of time before this all comes crashing down. I'm calculating the probabilities of punishments, how long I might end up grounded, if she'll slap me. She stops in front of the table, and I lag behind her. Our mother is sitting at the table, an ashtray vomiting old butts onto the tabletop, ashes scattered all around as if pepper has been spilled.

"Report cards?" she demands.

I drop my backpack to the ground and make a show of rummaging through it as Eviana grabs hers and hands it to our mother.

"All A's? Look at you go, girl," she says, standing up to give my sister a hug.

I finally grab the envelope from my bag, dread coiling inside me. No matter what, I can't delay this anymore. Eviana takes a step back and stands behind me after my mother releases her. I clench my jaw as I hand over the report card, bracing for something—impact maybe. God, it'd be easier if she just hit me. At least then it'd be over with faster.

She snatches the paper from my hand and tears the envelope open. Anxiety builds inside me as I watch her read it. Her eyes sharpen when she looks back up at me.

"This is a joke, right?" She spits the words at me as she slashes the air with the paper.

I flinch and take a step back automatically.

"This better be a joke, Blair." Her voice rises up octave after octave as she screeches at me.

Though I want to step back again, I can't, Eviana is behind me. There's nowhere I can go. I'm trapped between my sister and my mother's rage.

"You're better than this. You aren't an idiot. What the hell are you doing in school that you bring home grades like this?" She shakes the paper in my face as she screeches at me.

"I'm trying, I promise," I finally manage. I think this is the worst part. I am doing my best, and that's all I can do, especially when she won't help.

"Bullshit. If you were trying, you wouldn't be flunking out. Why are you even bothering to go? Just drop out and go work at the Waffle House. That'd be better for your future at this rate."

Tears sting my eyes as she screams at me. I want the ground to open and swallow me up. What I wouldn't give for a sinkhole to appear right beneath me.

"What do I have to do to get you to wake the fuck up? You're better than this. This is unacceptable. People are going to think that you're stupid, that there's something wrong with you. You can't build a future on grades like this. And what will the people at my school think? A professor raising a daughter who can't even make it through high school?"

"Mom, please," Eviana says behind me.

"No, don't you get involved in this. Blair, you are too smart for this. Until you get grades like your sister, you're grounded from everything. You're going to spend every moment of every single day reading textbooks and learning the material. You're going to write me papers about what you're reading. I will not have a daughter as stupid as you. I will not allow it."

"What kind of grades did you get in school?" I ask, then press my lips closed. I didn't mean to ask the question out loud, it just slipped out.

Eviana kicks the back of my shoe softly, as if to tell me subtly to shut up. But I can't. I'm sick of being a punching bag. I'm sick of never feeling good enough in this family no matter what I do.

"Don't be a smart-ass, Blair. I did well enough for myself. You know that you can't flunk out and get to where I am. I take

care of the two of you. I'm not under investigation here because
I'm not holding up my end of the bargain. That's you, child.
You're the one who fucks up time and time again."

"I fucked up because I'm not doing well in school? It's not
like I'm out doing drugs or getting pregnant. Jesus Christ, Mom.
I ask for help. I'm doing the best that I can. And you screaming
at me is not helping," I say, the words tumbling out of me. I'm so
sick of being second fiddle and only getting some kind of attention because my mother decides I'm not good enough.

"You don't need any help. You just need to apply yourself.
Why can't you just be more like your sister? Eviana is the
perfect child and you are just a nightmare. I shouldn't have had
a second daughter. It would have saved me so much trouble.
You ruined my body, you ruined my life. You are an ungrateful,
stupid brat." She spits the words at me so hard that I feel the
spittle hit my cheeks.

I want to lash out at her, to hit her. I clench my fists at my
sides and my nostrils flare. But before I can even take a step
toward her, Eviana grabs my arm and yanks me back a step. She
moves in front of me, stepping between my mother and me.

"That's enough, Mom. Blair doesn't need to be *me*. She is
her own person, and that's just fine. Don't tell her that she has
to be *me* to be better," Eviana says, glancing at me over her
shoulder. I'm taken completely aback by it. She's never stuck up
for me before like this. My mother and I have had this same
fight thousands of times by now, and Eviana has never inter-
jected. Why now? Why does she give a shit now?

"Oh, don't even try to rescue your sister, she needs to face
the problems that she created," my mother says, taking a step to
the side so that she can glare at me over Eviana's shoulder.

"This isn't a problem that she created. I see her studying
every night. She turns in her homework. I know that she's legiti-
mately trying her best. She's been asking you for help for years,
and you never help her with her homework, her projects, noth-

ing. Instead, you just leave her to her own devices and then get upset when she isn't perfect."

What she's saying isn't a lie. I've tried time and time again to get help. I just don't understand a lot of the stuff at school. Reading is hard for me, math doesn't make any sense, I just can't piece everything together—it all gets so overwhelming. And to know that no matter what I do I'll never be enough—it makes me wonder why I should even try.

"So now you two are going to team up against me? I'm the bad guy now?" She rolls her eyes as she unsheathes another cigarette from her pack and lights it. "I should have known better than to have children. Both of you ruined my lives. Eviana, you have promise, but if you start trying to intervene for your sister..." She shakes her head. "Well, then it'll be clear to me that you are both lost causes. I don't need either of you. You can both just leave this house, doomed to fail."

"Mom, don't do this, please," Eviana says, her voice cracking a bit. This is the first time Mom has ever talked to her this way. And I know she won't be able to handle it. She's done enough to try to intervene.

"I'm sorry, Mom. I'll study harder. I'll try to get my grades up. Maybe someone at school can help me," I say, deflating. I know I won't get the help that I need here. But it's just two more years. Two more years, and I'll be free. But for one of those, my mother and I will be alone together... and I'm not sure that both of us will survive that time alone.

24

As I sit in the guest room on my laptop, trying to get in a few minutes of work, my cellphone erupts, vibrating and dinging with notifications in a way that I am not at all used to. My pulse quickens as I swipe the phone from the bed and unlock it. I have a couple notifications from friends at work saying they're so sorry to hear the news about my sister. My heart climbs into my throat and lodges there, cutting off my breath. Did they find her? Is she dead?

I see I've got several alerts, ones that I set up for my sister's name. When I click on them, I find that it's not what I expected. The articles aren't about my sister's disappearance at all. I skim over headlines—*Beloved Influencer Spirals into the Depths of Addiction.* In the articles, I find screencaps of social media posts from Fiona. Apparently last night, Fiona made good on her threat to destroy Eviana. I'm not sure what of this is real and what's fabricated. But now Fiona has tainted Eviana's image in a way she will never recover from. Maybe I didn't respond well enough to the fake threats she made, so instead she decided to turn my sister into an addict.

The texts keep dinging on my phone, and I try to answer

them as soon as I see them. I'm not used to this amount of concern from anyone. My mind runs wild as my phone finally quiets down. It's clear to me that Fiona isn't going to back down, that she's going to continue to cause problems for me and my sister. But it really makes me wonder, if she's this angry at my sister for not keeping up her end of the bargain, could she really have something to do with Eviana's disappearance? Or is this all part of some kind of game that Fiona is playing? I don't know who to trust.

Warnings echo in the back of my mind. I know that this woman is trouble, I have no questions about that... but is she just trouble or is she dangerous? Is she more or less dangerous than Simon? What about the other threats my sister gets on a daily basis—or are those really faked?

I navigate to Fiona's social media pages, trying to see what else she's posted since she decided to wake up this morning and take Eviana down. She's posted at least twelve times since her post outing my sister. Three are tearful posts talking about how much she misses who my sister used to be—these posts make me roll my eyes so hard they nearly fall out of my head. If there's anything worse than crocodile tears, that's what Fiona has going on in these videos. Though there aren't any actual tears, it looks like she streaked her mascara down her cheeks for dramatic effect before she began filming.

The rest of the videos completely ignore her posts from the morning, instead digging into her workout routine, her weekly mindfulness challenge, and two new sponsorships she's just so excited about. As I scroll through the post, I begin looking at the comments, mostly focusing on the comments about my sister.

I hate that this happened to her.

There's something going on with Eviana, but this ain't it.

Everyone in show businesses gets there eventually.

Praying for her.

Bullshit, there's no way this is real.

This is fake, Fiona. Take this down.

It feels good that not everyone believes her. At least there's still some hope out there on the internet. I can't stand to look at it all anymore, so I order an Uber and tug on a wrinkled pair of jeans. In ten minutes, I'm in the back of a Civic that smells like French fries, and when the driver pulls up in front of the coffee shop, the stress inside me unwinds a bit. Thankfully the driver didn't even glance at my face, so I didn't have to come up with any lies—in the event my makeup isn't covering everything.

Heat presses against me from all sides as I stride toward the building. The afternoon sun bears down on me, warming my neck, stinging my flesh. It's a wonder to me at times like this that anyone still wants to live in this state; the sun and the heat are a constant unrelenting presence. A cloud of coffee-scented air puffs into my face as I throw open the door and step inside.

I order my coffee, grab it from the counter, and take a seat at a table near the window. Moments after I sit down on the hard wooden chair, the door jingles as it opens again and a woman with familiar tattoos strolls inside. She crosses the coffee shop, her eyes locked on me, and takes a seat across from me.

"I think it's time we have a chat," Claire says as she tilts her head and raises an eyebrow at me.

I nod, as anxiety tightens in my core. Thankfully, we're in public. But that still doesn't settle me much. This woman allegedly threatened my sister and was lurking around her house. What is she after? Why is she here?

"Where the hell is Eviana?" she asks.

I shrug my shoulder slightly. "Back at home, I think? I'm not sure. I'm not her keeper," I say. This woman wasn't close to my sister, so I'm not going to bother using any of my usual lies on her.

"Yeah right." She rolls her eyes. "She's been dodging me for weeks. She promised that she'd have my money by now."

Confusion clouds my thoughts, the questions that I had planned for this woman. "Money? What money?"

"Eviana promised that if I gave her the details of my past *experiences*, if that's what you want to call them, with Simon, she'd pay me fifty grand. I gave her everything she was after. Hell, I gave her some pretty damning videos I still had from when Simon and I were together."

I'm skeptical about what she has to say. "So, you were helping her?"

She lets out a little laugh. "Of course I was helping her. Hell, I'd help anyone get away from Simon. He's an absolute dirtbag."

I'm about stunned silent. "So, you weren't upset that Eviana helped destroy your career?"

She laughs a little louder. "My career? You mean the influencing garbage that Simon kept nagging me to do?" She rolls her eyes. "Look, I might have exaggerated a bit about the *career-destroying* when we first chatted. But Eviana had explained to me that *no one* was to know that she asked me for help, so sorry I had to lie to you like that. In reality, I quit that shortly after I broke up with him. No one destroyed my career. In fact, I own my own tattoo shop downtown. That's my career, not the crap he used to make me do on Instagram."

I want to apologize for what I'd thought about Claire, but she doesn't know, so instead, I press my lips together.

"So, when do you think your sister will be back with my money?" she presses, a little more insistent this time.

"She went out of town, but I'll shoot her a text and let her know that you need it."

Her eyes tighten, and I can tell that she's skeptical.

I raise my hands as if in surrender. "I promise. I don't care what she does or doesn't do with her money. But all I can do is pass along the message for you."

"I saw that she's on drugs or something on the news... Does she even have the money? She didn't seem like anything was off the last time we spoke..."

I shake my head. "It's all just rumors. I doubt any of it is true."

I finish up with Claire, surprised at the way the conversation has gone. Part of me wonders if it's all true, if it's real. But honestly, if Claire had something to do with my sister's disappearance, why would she be asking me for money now? None of that adds up. So for now at least, I'll believe her.

25

In the past ten days, I've spent more time on social media than I have during the rest of my life combined. First, I was obsessively tracking only Eviana's accounts, seeing what Simon was posting, trying to keep tabs on him. But now, I look at the accounts of almost everyone who comments on her posts, likes them, or shares them. And now I'm trying to track the fallout of my sister's alleged addiction. What addiction? That much isn't clear. Fiona wasn't specific. If she were talking about an addiction to attention—that at least, I would agree with.

I've been spending hours clicking through the posts, scrolling feeds—Fiona's in particular. It probably shouldn't consume my life like this, but what else can I do? It at least makes me feel like I'm doing something. What else is Fiona getting out of this? Does she just like causing drama or is there more to this?

My scrolling shows me a new post by Simon, an old photo of my sister drinking a latte in front of an oak tree that's heavy with Spanish moss. It's clear from looking at it that it's older. Eviana had shorter hair back when this picture was taken. I'm not sure if he didn't notice, or if he didn't think to edit it to match the other new photos. The caption reads:

Feeling blessed. Feeling caffeinated, LOL.

Then it goes on to list several of the coffee shops that Eviana has partnerships with. The post has far less interaction than she usually gets, and as I scroll through the posts since her disappearance, I realize that's a trend. Since Simon took over the accounts, engagement has dropped substantially.

I click through several of the accounts that commented on the most recent post, and I find something interesting.

Has anyone else noticed what's going on with Eviana's account? Like, I'm not going to tag it because it's clear that she's not running it anymore. These new posts are so weird. They're obviously old pictures of her being posted. Like, nothing new is happening at all. But like, what's really going on? Is she just taking a break from social media or did she hand her whole account over to a management firm?

There are several other posts just like hers, questioning if Eviana is actually in control of her account. Some repost the pictures with continuity issues. Another post pops up as I scroll. There's an image of Eviana's sonogram, a screenshot of her original post.

Are we all just going to pretend that this didn't happen? Why is no one talking about how she announced her pregnancy and now it's gone? I mean, sure, maybe she miscarried or whatever, but shouldn't she address that? You can't just say you're pregnant and then erase it from the internet. Then pretend it never happened while you post weird old content. And now these accusations of drug abuse? Did they ship her off to rehab and take over her accounts?

I flinch at the words. The images of Eviana going through nine months of a fake pregnancy are still burned into my mind. It's all just so much, almost too much to process. Trying to figure out the lies, the truth, and what Simon forced her to do—I'm not sure how to make sense of it all. Was she really abusing drugs? I didn't see any evidence of it while I was here. But maybe that could explain the lies?

My phone rings, and I look down to see Camila Rivera's number appear on my screen. I answer the call immediately, excited that she's finally returned my call.

"Hi, Blair?" Camila says as soon as the call connects.

"Yep," I say, unsure why she sounds so confused. This isn't the first time that we've spoken, and she called me.

She clears her throat. "It took me a minute to connect the pieces when I heard your voicemail. It was so rare that Eviana mentioned you that I almost forgot that she had a sister." She lets out a little laugh, as if it'll break some of the tension on the call, but it doesn't.

A thread of anger wraps around my heart. My sister rarely mentioned me? I mean, sure I know that we had a strained relationship, that she and I barely spoke—but for her to mention me so little that one of her best friends forgot about my existence, well, that stings a bit. I know that it's for the best that we don't remind anyone that we're related, connected in any way, but still, it doesn't feel great.

"I was hoping to talk to you about Eviana a little bit," I say, trying to completely gloss over her comment.

"Why? Why don't you just talk to her?" she snaps at me.

I flinch from her words. I didn't expect her to outright shut me down.

"Eviana and I aren't on the best of terms, as you know, and

I'm a little bit worried about her," I say, trying to continue my dance around the fact that she's missing. "Especially with all of the stuff about her addiction coming out..." With her being hostile toward me, I doubt I'll get far anyway, so it's for the best that I don't tell her that Eviana is missing. She'll go straight to the cops. "I've tried talking to her. I'm worried about her. And I think this is a bad position and she may not be honest with me."

"If you and Eviana aren't on good terms, then why the hell would I give you any information about her? It doesn't matter how worried you might be about her. I'm *her* friend, not yours, and I don't owe you anything. And if you knew your sister at all, you'd understand that the addiction bullshit that Fiona is peddling is completely untrue."

I reel from her words as I imagine her crossing her arms to drive her point home.

"Look, I'm just worried about her. I was hoping that you could help—if you're not comfortable with that, it's fine. But I promise you that there's nothing sinister here. I'm not trying to get you to betray her, I'm just concerned that Simon is trying to ruin her life," I say, trying to be convincing. "I'm not sure that she'll tell me this stuff on her own. I have a feeling she may think that I'd mention something to Simon and anger him. And if you know her well, then I'd suspect you also don't trust Simon."

She sighs. "I'm sorry." She grumbles audibly. "I just had one of those days, you know? And Eviana and I, we haven't been talking much lately, and I was thinking that she's pissed at me—maybe this was some kind of test to see if she could trust me or not." The more she talks, the more it's clear that the dam of her resolve is breaking. Soon, I know, the truth will come spilling out.

"It's okay, don't worry about it at all, I totally understand." I do my best to try and put her at ease, because I know that's the only way to push this forward.

"Eviana and I, well, since about six weeks ago we stopped talking so much." I can hear her take a long sip of something, the ice clinking.

"Six weeks? What happened six weeks ago?" I ask. That's well before her disappearance. And long before the fight that Danica mentioned. Is that when Eviana found out about the cheating? Was this woman somehow connected to that?

"Eight weeks ago, I found out that I was pregnant. Six weeks ago, I told Eviana about it—I was so excited. The two of us had a regular dinner scheduled, but instead of going out, I invited her over, thinking it'd be great to tell her at my place over some takeout. I really didn't want to announce my pregnancy to a friend in a busy restaurant. I just imagine everything being noisy and I start to say I'm pregnant but as the words leave my mouth the restaurant quiets, so I basically end up screaming that I'm pregnant at all the patrons, like some horrible romcom." She lets out a nervous little laugh. "So, anyway, yeah, I invited her over to my house. She showed up with eight bottles of wine."

"Eight bottles? For one evening?" I ask, trying not to sound judgmental, but polishing off eight entire bottles of wine in one night sounds like a lot.

"Oh yeah, that was actually a light evening for Eviana. She really likes to drink." She lets out a laugh like it's nothing—but I didn't realize that my sister had been drinking at all. She didn't drink while I was visiting. Was she really abusing drugs or alcohol? "But anyway, when she showed up with the wine and started pouring herself glasses, I didn't say anything at first—but when she started trying to force the wine on me, I knew I had to tell her. So, I announced the pregnancy. And... she just..." Camila goes quiet for a minute. "She went ghost white, like I just told her that someone died."

"She did?" I ask when she pauses. Why would that have bothered Eviana at all?

"Yeah, it was the weirdest thing. I'd never seen Eviana react to anything like that before. It was just... so unlike her. She's usually so even tempered, unless Simon is involved. We sat down at the table, and I made sure she ate something. She started sobbing, which was also completely out of character—I'd never seen her cry before. She told me about how she and Simon had a stillborn. And it was all too much."

My mouth goes bone dry. A stillbirth? She told this woman that she had a stillbirth? I'm wondering if Eviana was really sick or if what Simon was forcing her to do was starting to go to her head. I can't believe that she told this woman that her baby died. I doubt my sister has ever even been pregnant.

"How long ago did this happen?" I ask.

She pauses. "You know, I didn't think to ask. She was just so upset. It felt like it must have been recent, but I've known Evie for three years and she's never been pregnant during that time— not that I knew of. If she was, she didn't show and she didn't tell anyone. And she hasn't acted any different."

"Well, shit, that's terrible," I say, because I can't exactly tell this woman that I think my sister was lying to her, trying to manipulate her. It's just another thing that I add to the mental file that I have on her.

"I know. It's awful. And the fact that Simon treated her like that after the stillbirth... I think that's the worst part."

I straighten. "What do you mean?"

"Simon got so mad that the baby didn't make it he tried to blame it on her. He said it was all her fault and that they'd likely never be able to have a child, because it was clear that she was broken. She'd apparently had a few miscarriages before the still-birth, so he was convinced that she had something deeply wrong with her."

"That's bullshit," I say automatically, the anger rising inside me. It could very well be something that was wrong with him. Then I remind myself that it likely never happened, that she was probably lying to this poor woman. Why though? Why was my sister spending so much time crafting these elaborate lies? What else will I find out she lied about?

"She said that after the stillbirth, the doctor told her that she wouldn't be able to conceive again. Something about that pregnancy had damaged her ability to carry another child. So she was still grieving the fact that she would never be a mother. Me announcing the pregnancy, well, that made her relive the entire thing. I felt so awful. I wish I had known and I would have kept it from her for as long as possible," she says, clearly still beating herself up over it. "I totally understand that she doesn't want to talk to me, that it's just too hard right now. So I've been giving her the space that I know she needs."

I grind my teeth together, but I can't give her any hints of the truth. So instead, I just move along.

"Did she mention anything else about Simon that had you concerned?"

She clears her throat. "Oh, there was plenty. He was so verbally abusive toward her, he always had snide comments about her weight. He was trying to drive her toward an eating disorder so she'd always look great for the advertisers and followers. He kept pushing her to try all the fad diet products that they sell online, so if they *could actually* make her lose weight then they could sell them on her pages."

Not that anyone needs to lose weight for the approval of the internet, but my sister was already very much on the thin side to begin with. The idea that Simon was trying to make her lose weight, to control her by making her spiral into an eating disorder—well, that enrages me. As someone who has struggled with my self-image and my weight my entire life, the thought that he tried to force those issues on my sister lights a fire inside me that I'm not sure I'll be able to extinguish. But then I take a step back—was any of that even true? Was it all just another lie crafted by my sister?

"God, that's awful," I finally manage when I realize that I've been silent for too long.

"I know, Jesus Christ, she barely ate as it was. But he was always looking for some reason to pick at her. He'd suggested plastic surgery, weight loss, you name it—it seemed like he really wanted to make sure that she was insecure." I wonder if it was to keep her in line or something.

"That's a common tactic of abusers," I say. "They want to make sure that you feel terrible enough about yourself all the time that you'll never think that anyone else would want you." I don't delve into it anymore, but I've seen my friends fall into patterns like this with shitty guys who try to convince them that they're *lucky* to have their current boyfriend because anyone else would find them *gross*. It's so disgusting—and despite all of Eviana's flaws, she definitely didn't deserve something like that.

My stomach churns with unease, guilt. I spent so much time judging my sister in secret, questioning her choices constantly, thinking horrible things about her. The idea that none of this was her fault, that her husband was forcing her to be a show pony in front of the camera, and was manipulating her behind the scenes, it's enough to make me sick. I shouldn't have been so quick to judge her.

"I know. It's not all of it either. He would scream at her over the smallest things. He'd blow up. In public, he's one of those nice, charming guys who you'd never suspect anything of. He's just so charismatic. One of the good guys. But behind the scenes..." She huffs out a sound of disapproval or disgust. "It's clear he's a completely different person. There were a few times when Eviana was over at my place, Simon called her in an absolute rage because she wasn't home and he didn't have any idea where she was. She put the call on speaker, and I listened as he berated her for over an hour because of it. He called her every name in the book, accused her of lying, said that she must be cheating on him. At one point he started crying and asked why she would ever do something like this to him." A door shuts in the background, and I hear someone talking in a low voice to Camila, though I can't make out what they're saying. "Oh, hey, I've got to run, but I'll try to call you back and tell you if I think of anything else."

She rushes off the phone before I can even thank her for her time. When she hangs up, I'm left reeling as I try to digest all of her words, what she's said. Was Simon more than verbally abusive to my sister? Was he the architect of all the lies that she told, of her entire social media personality? I really wonder how much my sister was in control of.

I'm still digging through my sister's laptop. Though it's after five in the afternoon, I've got an enormous latte on the nightstand next to my bed in the guest bedroom. Despite the fact that I've been getting out of my room to walk a few laps around the neighborhood daily, I feel like I've been in this cave for far too long, as if I've been shuttered away for months, maybe years. But I can't stop now. I feel like I'm so close to the truth.

Hidden away in one of the folders buried in my sister's laptop, I find an Excel spreadsheet with a blank name. It's strange, my sister didn't have many spreadsheets on her computer. Curiosity squirms inside me, and I double click, opening it up. The rows and columns appear on the screen, covered in so much text. On the far left side, my sister has a strange list.

- *Abuse*
- *Money problems*
- *Stillbirth*
- *Drug problems*
- *Cancer*
- *Unhappy in marriage*

- *Cheating*

Next to each of the items on the list, my sister has written sentences next to the names of some of her friends as well as names of people I don't recognize.

- *Tia: Didn't respond the way I expected, didn't seem to matter.*
- *Fiona: Fell for it exactly like I expected, but seemed more like she'd use the info herself, wasn't concerned.*
- *Blair: Took the bait exactly like I expected, suspected nothing. Cancer would be too hard to fake on a large scale though. Maybe pick something that's not a death sentence?*

My mind spins as I try to process what I'm reading. Deep down, I knew my sister was lying about some things—but this is not something I ever expected. Was my sister really cataloging lies and then keeping the reactions of her friends? Was she going to use this to determine how to get more social media traction? What the fuck was wrong with my sister?

My phone vibrates with a text message from work, breaking my concentration on the computer. I respond, answering their question as quickly as I can. As I scroll through my messages, I realize that Calvin might be able to help me get into the cellphone that I've had charging for a couple days now. Several attempts to break into the phone have garnered nothing, except for hour-long lockouts before I can try again. But, if Calvin could help me get into the laptop, maybe there's a way to get into the phone as well. I shoot off a text asking for help, and within thirty seconds, my phone is ringing.

"Oh, hey, Calvin," I say, trying to calculate the time difference in my mind for my friends back in the Seattle office—then I realize it's two, so he's definitely still working.

"So, you broke into a laptop and now you need to break into a phone? Are you using your time off to become a spy or something? Did you join the CIA?" He lets out a little laugh, as if it's the most ridiculous thought in the world. I try to laugh with him, but it comes out forced.

"You caught me. Damn, you're good," I joke, hoping that he'll help me.

"Okay, so seriously, what kind of phone are you trying to get into?" he asks.

I pick it up and flip it over, hoping to get a sense of the brand. "It's not an iPhone or anything. I'm not seeing anything written on the outside," I say as I turn it over in my hands.

"Can you take a picture and send it to me?" he asks, and I oblige.

My phone whooshes as the picture is sent off, and I wait impatiently for him to examine the photo.

"Hmm, that looks like a generic prepaid cellphone. It's a few years old, not a new one, that's for sure. But the good news is the security on those types of phones isn't great. So we should be able to get you into it." He's quiet for a moment. "Whose phone is it?"

"My sister's. She can't remember her password for it, so we've been trying to get her in," I lie. It seems like the easiest lie that's close enough to the truth.

"Oh, okay. Look, I don't think I can get you into that phone. I'm better with computers. But I have a cousin who lives in Orlando. I could send you over to his shop, and he'll get you into the phone," he offers.

"That would be great, thank you," I say, appreciation lifting my words. I've never been the kind of person who's comfortable asking for favors, but I'm really glad that I went outside of my comfort zone to ask for help.

"Okay, so his shop is on OBT." He rattles off the directions, and the description of the shop and I write it all down. Then I pop the address into my navigation. It looks like a thirty-minute drive with traffic, but it'll take longer because of the wait for an Uber. "I'll let him know you're coming by. Are you going today?" he asks.

"Yeah, I'll head over there in a few minutes," I say. I've got to spend a few minutes getting ready. If I look like hell, I bet word will get back to Calvin—and I don't want my friends at work to get worried about me. If they start asking too many questions, that will cause more issues for me. As it is, I'm nervous that people are going to start to wonder why I'm taking such an extended leave. I've never taken more than three days off before.

"Okay, I'll give him a heads-up. Hope everything is okay with your sister," he says before ending the call.

Dark clouds clot on the horizon the moment I head out of the house and wait for the Uber, the brooding weather echoing the darkness swimming in my head. Heat is heavy in the air and wraps around me like a suffocating blanket as I wait. I wish I knew what I was looking for on this phone, what might await me. I've never been the type of person who likes surprises. The anticipation of what may or may not be waiting for me on this device is killing me. After finding that spreadsheet, I wonder what else my sister was hiding, what other lies she was planning on telling.

Finally, the car rolls up in front of me and I climb in. I make small talk as we start to move. The drive to the shop takes longer than I expect as the driver dodges traffic. As the car pulls into the parking lot, the clouds open and rain pelts the car. I curse under my breath as I throw open the door and run toward the building.

A bright green awning stretching out from the concrete-block building saves me from the onslaught. The few windows in the front of the shop are covered in thick wrought-iron bars. The heavy tint on the windows makes it impossible to see through even between the bars. There are faded signs all along the inside of the door that are too far gone for me to read. Even the hours of the shop have been bleached out by sun.

The door jingles as I open it. The inside of the shop smells vaguely of gasoline and engine grease. It looks like the store used to be a pawn shop but has been converted into a place that seems to repair anything and everything mechanical. There are rows of guitar amps, small appliances, TVs, vacuum cleaners—you name it, this guy has apparently fixed it and put it up for sale. In the glass cases that line the back of the shop, there are more valuable items like cellphones, computers, and gaming consoles. A short man with a thick black beard smiles at me from behind the counter. He's propped on top of a barstool, where he was hunched over an Xbox. It looks like the console is undergoing an autopsy. It's split open, the insides spilling out. He's got a soldering iron in one hand, which he sets down when I approach.

"Hi, I'm Blair—Calvin," I start, but he holds up a hand to stop me.

"Yeah, he told me that you were coming. I'm Dom." He holds his hand out for me to shake, which I do, just to be polite.

"Nice to meet you," I say.

"Yep. So, you've got a phone that you need help with?" he asks.

I take the phone out of my bag and slide it onto the counter between us, trying to be careful of the glass. Though Calvin told me the phone is old, it's in pristine condition. The screen isn't even scratched. It makes me wonder how often my sister really used this phone and how long she had it.

He scoops it up and turns it over in his hands a few times.

"This thing is old. Not sure why someone would bother with a prepaid phone that's this old. The new ones are only like a hundred bucks," he says as he scoffs at the old tech. He looks up at me, his eyes filled with questions. "This is your sister's phone?"

I nod.

"And where is she?" he presses.

"She had to run some errands, so she asked me to take care of it," I say, the lie coming out smoother than I expect it too. Maybe all the lying I've been doing lately is serving me well. Or maybe it's just in my DNA.

He raises a brow at that, clearly not believing me. But as long as he unlocks the phone, I honestly don't care if he believes me or not.

"So, here's the thing. Legally speaking, I'm not supposed to unlock the phone of a person who isn't present—unless they're a minor."

I open my mouth to protest, but he holds up a hand, preemptively silencing me.

"But I do have an 'I'm not going to ask you any questions' rate. If you can tell me that this is your phone... then I can just go ahead and unlock *your* phone for you." He looks back up at me, as if trying to verify that I've understood his meaning.

"How much is it for you to unlock *my* phone?" I ask. I'm already running on empty here. I don't know that I'll be able to raise the limit on any more of my cards.

"Seventy bucks," he says. And I'm honestly relieved the price is so low. It'd cost me at least two hundred for something like this back in Seattle, if not more. My credit card isn't going to thank me anytime soon, but this at least won't put me over my limit.

"How long does it take? I ask before committing. I don't want to have to leave this phone here. I don't want him to have an opportunity to see what's on it.

"About twenty minutes, usually." He shrugs, clearly not making a promise, but it's an estimate that I can live with. "Could take up to an hour."

I swipe my card for the payment and lean against the counter as I wait.

"You're not from Orlando, are you?" he asks as he plugs my sister's phone in and starts to work on it.

"I'm from Gainesville originally. But I don't live in the state anymore. I moved to the West Coast," I say. I don't want to give him too many details, but I also can't be too stingy with them, that'll lead to more questions.

"Huh, you don't seem like a Floridian at all," he says, and I'm not sure if that's a compliment or an insult.

"Sorry, I left my gator and my orange juice back at home in my suitcase," I say, and that gets a laugh out of him.

"Well, at least you're not wearing mouse ears." He smiles as he adds the jab.

"You know, we actually never went to Disney when I was a kid—and I don't feel like I missed out on anything."

"What? If you haven't waited in line while it's over a hundred degrees for over four hours, you can't call yourself a Floridian." He adds another laugh.

"Oh, I've done that at the other parks."

We chitchat for another ten minutes or so as I watch him work, then he slides the phone across the counter toward me.

"This thing is tapped out," he says as he raises an eyebrow.

"What do you mean?" I ask, anxious that he wasn't able to get in.

"The internal memory is full, someone also added an SD card to this thing, and that's almost full too. There's over 500GB worth of crap on this phone, which is saying something. I don't typically see phones with that much stuff on them," he says. "The performance on this thing is probably not going to be great unless you do some cleanup."

I take the phone and swipe up. Sure enough, the password is gone and I'm able to access the home screen, which is a picture of a flower. I'm not about to go through the phone here —not where someone else can see it. Especially since I've taken note of the security cameras in the corners of the shop.

"Good luck digging through all that," he says.

"Thank you, appreciate your help." I motion toward the cameras. "Could you delete me off of those?" I ask.

"They're not on during the day. I only turn them on when I leave for the night—helps with the break-ins."

I nod, though I'm not sure that I believe him. "Thanks again." I open the door and slip back outside.

Humidity slams against me, the heat like walking straight into an invisible wall. I wade through the soupy air toward the parking lot, then wait for my Uber to arrive. I unlock the phone and navigate toward the system settings. Sure enough, the memory is nearly full. What did my sister have on this phone? I go to the files and find thousands of sound clips. I click on the first one, and it takes a few moments for it to open.

"You're going to do this." Simon's voice crackles to life on the phone.

"Please, I'm so tired," Eviana says. She's practically on the verge of begging. "I can't keep doing this forever."

Something slams hard in the background, a fist against a wall maybe? A palm against a counter? I'm not sure. But the sound is so loud it even makes me jump. "Yes, you will. No one is giving you a choice. You are going to keep doing this. You cannot hold me hostage and manipulate me by threatening to quit your job. Are you really that selfish? I've been the one sitting here and supporting you for all these years and now you just get to decide how our life is going to go?" He throws the words at her, each one so sharp they may as well be darts thrown at her heart, obviously meant to strike home.

I can hear the manipulation in his words, the venom, the

way that he was clearly trying to coerce my sister. After seeing her spreadsheet, I'm not sure what to think. She had abuse on her list, but this sounds like it was real—like Simon really was terrorizing her.

"Selfish? Me needing to take a break because all the pressure that you're putting on me is making me sick—that's selfish? You're hounding me twenty-four hours a day. You don't let me sleep anymore. I don't get any time to myself."

"You're the one who made yourself into a product, and now you're going to try to flip it around on me? You're going to make this my fault? You always do this. You always try to turn things around on me and demonize me. Am I really that bad? You know there are men out there who don't give a shit about their wives. They cheat, and do drugs, and start entire other families. And I'm a bad guy because I've been here by your side supporting you?"

I clench my teeth as I listen to him try to manipulate my sister. It's so obvious what he's doing—but I wish I knew how she was feeling, how she was reacting. The audio doesn't give me any of that. My stomach twists as I realize my sister must have been dealing with this on a daily basis. Why didn't she just leave? Why didn't she tell me that she needed help? I help people for a living. This is what I do.

"Fine. You win, again," she says, then the audio clip ends.

I'm left reeling after I listen to it. Then I open the next file. It was recorded a few days later—most of these are from months ago.

"We can't do this," Eviana says, her voice cracking. There's so much emotion thick in just a few words, that I wonder if she's crying, what happened before she started recording.

"Yes, we can. And we will," Simon says. He doesn't sound close to her—or the phone, I guess. Her voice is much louder when she speaks, while it sounds like he's farther away in the house.

"Simon, if this gets out, it will tank both of us. There's no way that we can do this. This will ruin everything," she says again. And I wonder what she's talking about. "We can't fake an entire pregnancy and say that our baby died. That's just—wrong. It's cruel even. Manipulation on that scale, I mean, that's got to be bad karma. We can't just do this for a few new partnerships. That could cost us everything."

He lets out a low laugh that gets louder as it goes on. I hear his footfalls on the floor, as if he's stalking closer to my sister.

"Well, if your broken fucking uterus could give us a real baby, then we wouldn't need to pretend. But here we are. Would you rather I go knock up some other bitch to get a baby? Then you can pretend it's yours when she pops it out?" His words are so harsh that I flinch. I can't believe that he's talking to her like this—that she put up with it. Why isn't she yelling back at him? Why didn't she leave? "Do we need to adopt someone else's kid? You tell me how you want this to go since you're the one who can't give us a baby."

"Grow up. You know that I'd fix it if I could," she says, her words so low I can barely make them out.

"And you can. I'm telling you exactly how to fix it," he scoffs.

"Simon, please. You know that it's killing me inside to do this. To pretend I'm pregnant, to strap on this goddamn belly when I'll never be able to carry a child of ours—it's like stabbing me in the heart. You're making me live out something I'll never be able to have." Her words are thick with tears, and her words make my eyes burn. I never knew that she was going through this. And I thought what she told her friend were lies.

"Well, now you'll be able to have all of your followers grieve with you once you announce that the baby didn't make it. That's all you've ever wanted anyway, isn't it?"

The recording ends, and I seethe as I climb into the Uber back to Valentina's house. My heart pounds as anger takes hold and grows inside me. Why didn't my sister reach out for help? Why did she let Simon torment her like this? The idea that, though my sister was followed by millions, she was being quietly abused and isolated—it's heartbreaking. If she's gone for good, I will make Simon pay for what he did to her.

26

SIXTEEN YEARS AGO

Something has shifted in my sister. For three years, we've gone to the same college. And it's been so different than high school ever was for either of us. While I was a miserable failure in high school, somehow college has helped me blossom, find myself, and my grades have improved. But Eviana, I'm not sure that she's changed for the better. The past year, she's become reserved, a shadow of herself. And I think that something's wrong.

In our apartment, Eviana is in her room, like she always is these days. Early on, she'd spend some time in our living room, she'd cook in the kitchen—but lately, all she does is sleep. I thought that college was supposed to change everything for the better, but instead, it's eaten away at my sister, like the storm surge slowly gobbling the beach. The last year has been the worst, the pieces of her drifting away on the tides.

I've tried to get answers from her, prodding gently, my intensity growing over the past few months. I want to know what's happened to my sister, who this phantom is that I don't quite recognize. I rap my knuckles against the door. I've got one cup of coffee clutched in my right hand, another tucked between my body and my forearm—the ceramic scalds my skin, warning me of the red swelling mark that will surely mar my skin when I pull the cup away.

The sound of rustling on the bed tells me that she's alive at least. Not that I'd expect Eviana to be the type who would kill herself or something. But there are times I wonder just how far she would go for attention—or more, how far she wouldn't go. After four attempts, she finally clears her throat, though she doesn't say anything to me. I finally reach for the doorknob, losing my patience, and my arm losing the ability to keep containing the steaming mug—the stabbing pain in my forearm is warning that I've got only seconds left before I end up with a blister.

When the door swings in, I'm surprised that she didn't lock it. Usually, Eviana likes to shut out the world—and unfortunately, I am very much a part of that world that she likes to block out. There's a sour smell contained in the room, the stench of the laundry vomiting onto the floor from her laundry basket, I'd expect. The room is a shambles. Her comforter slides off the bed onto the floor like it's melting, the plastic blinds disheveled in the window sending scattered shards of light into the floor. Taco Bell wrappers cascade from her nightstand onto the floor around the bed, evidence that she's destroyed no less than fifteen tacos in the past twenty-four hours. On her desk there are stacks and stacks of papers.

"Want some coffee?" I ask, brandishing the cup, hoping that my presence won't incite the rage that I know always lingers beneath the surface of my sister. It's always waiting, like a hungry shark that could go after blood without warning.

"I'm trying to sleep," she grumbles.

"You've been trying to sleep for a week," I say, then walk over and slide the coffee onto her nightstand. To my surprise, she reaches over and grabs onto the cup, sipping quickly at the steaming liquid.

She props herself up on the bed, crossing her legs. Eviana likes sleeping in a ribbed white tank tops and shorts, showing off her long lanky limbs. When she repositions herself on the bed, I notice that her usually pale flesh is pockmarked with bruises. They trail along her forearms and feather her thighs.

"What happened?" I ask, motioning toward them.

She rolls her eyes and sips her coffee again. "Nothing that you need to worry about."

But it clearly is something that I need to worry about. Eviana has never come home with this many bruises. I've hardly seen her flesh discolored at all. When we were younger, she was never the type to fall and skin her knees. She didn't ride a bike. She didn't climb trees like I did. She was careful and cautious, and it showed on her unblemished skin.

"Come on, why won't you talk to me?" I urge.

"Why the hell should I even talk to you?" Though I know that Eviana is trying to lash out at me, her words lack the sharp edge that they need. There's a weakness threaded through her words, something that I've rarely heard from her.

"I don't know, because I'm your fucking sister?" I won't let this go, instead I challenge her again. There's always been a wall between us no matter how hard I've tried to knock it down. At times, I could see the bricks crumbling. I could see her on the other side. But times like this, I know that she's trying to widen the gap, to force me away. Why though? Why has she never wanted me to be on her side?

"So what? Blood doesn't mean shit. Just because someone is a part of your family doesn't mean that they're on your side."

I take a sip of my coffee as I consider her words. Anger rises inside me but hurt stabs through it. How, with all that we've been through, has she not felt like I was on her side?

"What did I ever do to you?" Pain lances my words as I force them out. In school, I saw siblings who were close, who were best friends, who were as thick as thieves. But here I am, always on the outskirts, trying to prove to my sister that we're on the same team.

"You never understood how hard it was for me," she says, looking at her cup.

Confusion roars in the back of my mind. "How hard what was for you?"

"Everything. Nothing." She sets her coffee down and throws her hands in the air. Frustration ripples around her, forming an aura that I can feel ten feet away. I hang near the door, like I'll need to pull the ripcord and escape at a moment's notice. It's like she's an angry dragon whose lair I need to escape. There are only moments until she roars and shoots flames in my direction.

"I want to drop out," she says, and the words catch me off guard. Eviana is on the track to medical school. She's always had straight A's. She walked the path of a perfect child who always did everything right. If she can't make it to med school, then there's no chance anyone else on the planet could—I swear it's what she was built for.

"Why?" I finally ask. I'm the child who's supposed to drop out. I'm the fuckup, the one who can never finish anything. My mom said it was a miracle that I managed to graduate at all.

"It's just not working out. I don't think that I'm cut out for this," she says, then scoops up her coffee again. She's still not looking at me. I've never seen her look this defeated. Maybe she really doesn't think that she can cut it.

"Why don't you just change majors? I thought that your grades were all good?"

She shakes her head. "My grades are fine. I just don't have it in me to do this. I'm not cut out for pre-med."

"Then what are you cut out for?" I ask.

She offers me a one-shouldered shrug. "Sometimes, I don't think I'm cut out for anything. I don't belong here, and every day that I stay here, I'm losing a piece of myself."

These are my words, coming from my sister's mouth. What is happening to her?

27

This phone is a treasure trove. There are so many recordings on here this has to be years of Eviana secretly recording their fights, their encounters, some of their regular conversations. I can't believe that she was able to squirrel all of this way in secret. But then again, Eviana was always so secretive I guess I shouldn't be at all surprised. It's once I get to the folders of images that I'm really shocked. Reading through the messages, it makes a sour taste bloom in my stomach and climb all the way up my throat. How did Eviana deal with this every single day? She's even got logs of Fiona admitting that she gets lipo and doesn't take any of the supplements that she hawks online—yikes, that would make for some great blackmail material.

Part of me wants to delete them. I don't know why she would have created a device that she filled so entirely with hate. But as I dig further, I realize that's exactly what this phone is for. She's got screenshots of anyone online who spoke ill of her, those who speculated about her, called her ugly, obvious troll comments that no one would take seriously at all. But she cataloged it all, and knowing her, I feel like in her darkest moments she went through it all again and again, obsessively.

Why would she keep all of this here? It looks like she was gathering evidence for something—but for what, exactly? Did she know that everything with Simon would eventually boil over? Did she think that one of these stalkers or trolls would come calling for her at some point? Did some premonition tell her that eventually something would happen to her?

I glance toward the window and realize that in my focus of going through the device that night has fallen. I slip from the bed, shove my phone into my pocket, and slide my shoes on. Today, I haven't gone for my usual walks around the neighborhood, and my energy level is still so high I know that I won't be able to sleep unless I burn some off it off. I've also been trying to keep tabs on what Simon's been up to. Though I have a feeling he's been cheating, I need solid evidence of what he's been up to.

Most of the time when I've walked past the house, Simon has been home or at least his car has been. The times that I walk by at night, he's nowhere to be found. And the one time I saw his car—or at least I think it was his car—it was at Fiona's. Some part of me has been tempted to follow him, to figure out where he's slipping off to in the middle of the night—but I haven't been able to catch him leaving yet. And it's not like I can call an Uber to follow him around town. I'm still not sure how to handle my burned-up rental car.

Though I expect for heat to greet me when I open the front door, there's a cool breeze in the air that surprises me. I click the door closed, lock it, then walk down the front path toward the street. The night is already thick around me, the shrill drills of the cicadas rising and falling in the trees, a chorus that is the usual background noise of Florida. A few low croaks tell me that the Cuban tree frogs are also out, hiding in the shadows somewhere that I can't quite see.

I walk past the expansive houses, and find most have their

lights off, no cars in the driveway. So many of the residents here are gone frequently, which makes me think that these must be their second or third houses. A large Mediterranean house stands at the end of the street in front of me. It's one of the few with the curtains thrown open, the inside lit up. I can see a man and woman sitting at a table together, eating dinner I'd guess.

The view, watching the couple eat together, it makes a pang of longing snake up my spine. I've spent so much of my life alone, without a person, without someone to spend dinners with —I wonder what that would be like. I know it's not in the cards for me. I'm too messed up for that, so I won't hold my breath. But sometimes, when I see a happy couple like this, I wonder *why not me*, and I know deep down why not me. I don't deserve that happiness; I don't deserve to find the other half of my soul.

A cool breeze makes the few stray leaves on the ground skitter around me, as if the weather is telling me to move on, to pick up my pace. My feet drag a little too much against the concrete, scraping as I walk. But that's fine, I don't mind being seen or heard out here. One can never have too many alibis.

As I turn down Eviana's street, it's darker than the others, less lights on in the houses. When I approach the middle of the street, and her house comes into view over the small hill, I notice that there's a car sitting across the street, the lights off, the engine quiet. A flicker of movement catches my eye, and my pace kicks up. Sweat tickles down my spine, and I stick to the shadows as I creep closer to the car. The shape of a person is sharpened, silhouetted by headlights that pass behind the vehicle as another resident turns onto a side street.

There's someone in that car, watching Eviana's house. I wonder if this is one of the stalkers. I know her neighborhood is gated, but that doesn't mean it's impenetrable. Anyone can time it and follow another car inside. My pulse pounds in my ears as I grow closer and closer to the car. I want to know who's inside, who's watching my sister. But as my eyes finally start to make sense of the dark blur of shapes inside the car—a man's square jaw, short hair, broad shoulders—the engine roars to life. I dart out of the way, behind a nearby fence, hoping that the movement didn't catch the attention of whomever is inside.

I press my shoulder into the fence, as if I might sink into the cold vinyl, as if it'll absorb me so I can hide. The car rolls forward and I yank my phone from my pocket to snap a picture of the license plate. That, at least, will help me try to track down who it is that was sitting outside my sister's house.

The lights of Eviana's and Danica's houses spill onto the front lawns, casting long shadows. I look into the windows, searching for signs of movement. In Danica's house, I see her moving in the top right window on the second floor, in what I would guess is her bedroom. Next, I scour the windows of my sister's house, and though I search, I can't find Simon in any of the windows. Is he even home? His Escalade is parked outside, but he's so skilled at deception, I wouldn't at all be surprised if he had another car squirreled away so he could move about unseen. My attention turns to the street again, which is eerily quiet. A bad feeling snakes down my spine, and the burn of eyes against my flesh warns me that someone is watching. In the upstairs window of Eviana's house, I see him, a broad figure staring out at the street. I sink farther into the shadows as I watch, my mind screaming.

Did he see me? Does he know that I'm out here?

I swear that Simon is always watching, always keeping tabs on me. He admitted that he put a GPS tracker on my rental car, but I squirm in my skin as I wonder if he's tracking me in other ways. Did he hack my phone? Is there some other way he could be keeping tabs on me?

I hide until my legs grow tired, until my eyes burn with exhaustion. Simon finally steps away from the window, and I know this is my moment, my only chance to get out unseen. I slip from the shadow and skirt through the darkness. The night presses in on me as I stalk back through the shadows toward Valentina's house. Panic swarms inside me, like an unsettled hive of bees. The rushed palpitations of my heart are a warning. *What if he saw me? What if he's tracking me right now?* My eyes sweep the neighborhood, the large houses, their empty windows, the cars still parked in the driveways—though I feel completely alone, the tingling along the back of my neck tells me that someone is watching me. I pick up my pace, the scuffs of my feet growing louder as I walk.

My heart leaps as I turn onto Valentina's street. I'm so close. I know that I only have to make it another five hundred feet or so to make it back to her house. The roar of an engine makes me turn, and I sweep around to find a large SUV at the end of the street. It's right behind me, stopped as the driver revs the engine. My stomach climbs into my throat, as a fist of terror clamps my windpipe. *Is that Simon? Oh shit, he did see me.* Dread coils inside me, warning me of what's to come. I knew that he'd come after me again, that attacking me in the woods wouldn't be the last thing he did.

You're overreacting, it's just a car. Half of the people here own cars like that. Just keep walking.

I tell myself that I'm being ridiculous over and over again. The headlights click on, bathing me in LED light that's blindingly bright. Spots explode behind my lids every time I blink my eyes. If they didn't see me before, there's no way they could miss me now. I must be lit up like a Christmas tree. I turn back around and move from the street to the sidewalk. But with every step I take, I hear the roll of the tires, the way they crackle against the pavement. The sound picks up as the car gains speed, and I walk faster in response. But no matter how fast I walk, I can't outrun an SUV. Warnings scream in the back of my mind. They're following me. They're going to run me over.

Only a few hundred feet left, I tell myself, as if that'll make me feel better. It doesn't.

My heart threatens to burst out of my chest as the car revs the engine again. Now, I know for certain that they're messing with me. No one else who lives here would act like this—it has to be Simon. I whip my head around, trying to discern if the shape of the SUV is similar to the Escalade. But I can't tell. The lights are too bright, muddling the blocky shape of the vehicle.

I break into a sprint as the car gains on me. Then it swerves, jumping over the curb with a *ca-thunking* sound. The engine roars as the tires fight against the thick grass and then squeal on the sidewalk. A scream threatens to burst from my lips, but I'm too out of breath. Panic claws at my lungs and my throat. I feel like I'm drowning on land. Valentina's house is in sight, the lights of the large windows calling out to me like a lighthouse bringing a ship in to shore. My legs ache, not used to being pushed this hard. I curse myself for not going to the gym more. The engine grinds again, something that sounds like a ferocious beast that's gnashing at my heels.

You can do this. You have to get away, I tell myself over and over, as a stitch opens in my side. I promise whatever deity that might listen that if I live through this, if I don't get run over, I'll exercise, I'll do more cardio, I'll make difference choices, I'll do better. *Please don't let me die like this. Oh, God, I can't. This can't be how it ends.* The car revs again and I swear I can feel the heat of the engine behind me. Sweat blooms down my spine in response. Pain awakens in the soles of my feet, and I'm not sure how much longer I can do this—I have to get away. I dive to the right, near the bushes that separate Valentina's yard from her neighbor's just as the telltale hiss of the engine warns me that I only have seconds to escape. My palms sting with the impact and my teeth clack together. Two large *ca-thunk* sounds tell me that the SUV has swerved back onto the road after hitting the curb. I scramble to my feet, and squeeze between the podocarpus bushes into Valentina's yard.

My chest heaves as I try desperately to catch my breath. The SUV is already halfway down the road. They've given up on me, fled. I stare at the deep ruts in the grass, the evidence of where they chased me, where they gave up. I guess I wasn't worth killing.

Not today, anyway.

28

SIXTEEN YEARS AGO

Stress does strange things to people. For my sister, she becomes a bitch. For me though, I snoop. I can't help myself. There's a deep need inside me to keep my hands busy, to discover something. I know that there's always something lingering, waiting just beneath the surface for me to find. I just have to dig deep enough. Every time I tell myself that if I find the right thing, if I find the evidence that I'm looking for, then the anxiety will die away.

It never does though.

Instead, I feel like an addict, searching for a fix.

Our apartment is quiet, the only sound is the pounding of my own pulse in my ears. The *thump, thump, thump* of my heart urges me forward. I've walked about a mile this morning, just doing laps of the apartment. I walk from my room, through the living room, around the kitchen, then past my sister's door. Each time I glance at the door, a temptation, a dare, worms its way through the back of my mind.

I check my watch and realize that I've got only a couple of hours before my sister is back from class. If I'm going to do this,

I need to do it now, otherwise I'm going to run out of time. My fingers brush against the metal handle, the cold seeping into my skin. A jolt of excitement goes through me as I turn the handle and find that the door isn't locked. Most of the time, Eviana keeps her door secured against my snooping. But I guess today she was careless.

The room smells like wood and oranges as I open the door. The source of the smell is a diffuser next to my sister's bed. It's tidier in here than usual. The bed is actually made, the usual pile of clothes on the floor isn't where I expect to find it. Against the wall across from the bed, a desk sits next to her TV stand. The desk is piled high with books, papers, and notebooks. The only clean space on the desk is where her laptop sits. I don't bother messing with her computer. I don't know the password and I know I'll end up locked out after a few tries.

I scan the shelves, her nightstand, and the top of her dresser and find nothing of interest. But Eviana has been acting so weird lately I know that something is going on. If I just look hard enough, I'll find it.

My attention turns back to her desk, and I start to scan the stacks she's got piled on the corners. Several of the papers on top are graded, all A's—that doesn't surprise me at all. Eviana has always been the best student, while I've consistently been the worst. I take the first few papers off the stack, then look at a folder she's got a bit lower. The cover is made of thick glossy blue stock. When I open it, inside I find several leaflets that are stapled together. I pull the pages out and begin to sift through them. It takes me several attempts to understand what I'm looking at. They're printouts from what were clearly cellphone pictures, snapshots of a computer screen, and pictures of pages that Eviana was holding in her hands. They're all mixed-together printouts here.

It hits me what I'm looking at, what Eviana got her hands on

—they're the answers to the big tests coming up in all her classes.

Now all her comments about not being able to cut it make sense. This is why she wanted to drop out. There's no way she could get away with this forever. Eviana isn't a good student. She's cheating.

29

The lights are too bright this morning, so bright I almost feel like I've woken up with a hangover. But as I peel my eyelids open, I realize that I was just an idiot and forgot to close the blackout curtains before I fell into bed last night. It's funny how nearly getting killed throws off your bedtime routine. I groan as I roll over, feeling the scar of my pillow still cutting across my face. It's right on a bruise—ouch. My whole body aches, muscles groaning from the echoes of last night. I try not to think about how close I came, how I almost died. My hand fumbles on the nightstand, looking for my phone. When I finally grab it, I plop it down on the pillow and squint at the screen.

I've got a few notifications, emails, the usual text messages— but nothing out of the ordinary. Valentina left for work, she texted, saying that she didn't want to wake me, but there's still half a pot of coffee left for me if I want it. I still can't believe she's being so hospitable. I've totally overstayed my welcome, but Valentina insists every time that I say I want a hotel room that she enjoys the company and wishes that she didn't live alone.

My finger finds my news app and I glance over the local

stories, wondering if anyone caught a video of the SUV that nearly ran me over. But a headline catches my eye.

Woman Found Dead in Lakeview Shores Neighborhood

A pebble of terror lodges in my throat, and no matter how hard I try to swallow it down, it doesn't budge even an inch. I click on the article and hold my breath until it loads.

This morning in the affluent neighborhood of Lakeview Shores in Orlando, police were called in the early morning hours. We have reports coming in from Orlando PD that a woman was found dead in her home. She has been identified as Danica Fullerton, wife of Albert Fullerton, an executive for a local theme park. For now, her cause of death has not been reported, but police have mentioned that foul play is suspected.

Just days ago, Danica was attacked in the backyard of her home, an incident that police think may be related to her death. We are waiting for further comment from Orlando PD, but for now they ask that if anyone has any details about her death that they please come forward.

I read the story at least twelve times before it finally starts to sink in. Danica's dead? It just can't be true, it can't be real. Is this some kind of horrible nightmare? Why can't I just wake up? I saw her last night in her windows. A wave of nausea slams into me. What if I was one of the last people to see her alive? If I'd stayed longer, could I have prevented her death? This is so terrible. I can't believe that someone would kill her.

The events of last night roll through my mind again and again like I'm watching a movie. Did I have it all wrong? Was that person watching Danica's and not Eviana's house? The two are so close together, it's possible. I can't believe that I could have read this situation all wrong. Is the person who tried to run me over the same person who killed Danica? Could it have been Simon?

My mind spins as I go over and over the options again and again. Something about it is so strange. The person in the car had to have been related to Danica's death. A memory from last night awakens in the back of my mind. The license plate. I snapped a picture. That might help put all of these pieces together. I swipe away my news app and open up my photos. There at the end of my roll, I find the picture of the license plate. Though I expect for it to be difficult to read or blurred, instead it's pretty legible.

As I read over the letters on the license plate, trying to commit them to memory, I wonder if I should try and research this on my own or if I should send the plate in as an anonymous tip. I want the police to find whoever did this to Danica, so I don't want to keep the information from them. But at the same time, I need to know who did this too.

I know it's a huge ask, but maybe—just maybe Lucia could get the information for me. I text her the plate number, along with info that someone hit my rental car in a hit-and-run. My phone vibrates with a response faster than I expect.

> I cannot give you the information of a person
> based on a license plate. If your car was
> damaged, come in and file a report.

I grind my teeth together, before replying that I'll go into a local PD to report it. There's no reason for me to drive all the way down there to do it. Is there some other way I can figure out the owner of a car? At the very least, I can drive by and compare the plate to Simon's—that could check him off the list. I need to figure out who tried to run me over last night.

It takes me half an hour to get ready. The morning sun seems too bright as I crack open the front door and slip outside. Humidity is already thick in the air as I walk down the street. I glance at the marks on the road where the SUV jumped the curb last night, and continue down the street, before finally weaving my way onto Eviana's block. There's a squad car still parked in front of Danica's house along with a crime scene investigation van. My heart is heavy as I look at the house. Danica had been so nice, so helpful.

I creep slowly past her house, then glance at the plate on Simon's Escalade. It's not even close to the one that I took the picture of last night. And I'm not sure if that's a good or a bad thing. Part of me wanted so badly for it to be Simon, maybe because I know what he's capable of and it'd be easier in my mind if he'd done it. But the idea that a stranger tried to run me over, somehow that's more disturbing. Because what could I have done to a stranger to deserve that?

As I stroll past, I look up toward the house, and I see Simon framed by the window looking down, watching me. He glances toward Danica's house, then back at me, before a sick smile creeps across his face. Panic awakens inside me. I know what he did, what he's trying to tell me. He must have killed her— because Danica knew too much. She heard the arguing, she saw him slip out the night that Eviana disappeared. Is Simon now trying to destroy all the evidence, all the things that point to him being the person who killed my sister?

I walk to the coffee shop and grab a cup of coffee. Though I should go back to the house to keep investigating, I can't bring myself to stay secluded today. Something tells me that I'm safer here in public than I am back at the house—despite the walls, the surface-level safety, I'm still so shaken by last night that I'm not sure I buy any of it. Danica died in that neighborhood. Hell, maybe my sister did too. High walls and a gate won't do anyone any good if a killer lives within those walls.

30

SIXTEEN YEARS AGO

It's been three months, and she still hasn't dropped out. She hasn't made any changes at all. Eviana keeps going to classes and going through the motions—but I see the hollowness behind her eyes. I can't figure it out. I can't put the pieces together. This was what she wanted. She wanted pre-med so bad, she wanted this to be her path—so what's changed? Why is she pretending this isn't what she wants? If Eviana really wanted to drop out and to escape this life, she would have already done it. But at least she's going to class. That's better than hiding in her room and letting the world pass her by.

I walk across campus, the heat of the afternoon beating against my neck. Though I've got on a tank top and a skirt, it's still so hot I'd swear that Satan was breathing down my neck. Sweat clings to every part of my body, and I have to force myself to keep going. The iced coffees in my hands are half-melted. The five-minute walk from my last class to Eviana's has taken its toll on the drinks—and my hair. I can feel the sweat clinging to my hairline, dripping down my spine.

On the horizon, dark clouds hang, coalescing, warning of the storms that I know are coming. Every afternoon in Florida during the spring and summer are exactly the same. Fast and furious storms roll in, dumping rain and lightning across the entire city. I'm thankful that the storms are still at least a half hour away. Hopefully I'll make it back to our apartment before the sky opens up. I dart into the med building, heading toward Eviana's class. The burst of air conditioning is refreshing and makes me long for the cooler season that I know is still months away.

I turn down the hall, passing classroom after classroom until I finally reach Eviana's. The door is open, showing the staggered seats that take up half of the room. In the front there's a podium, a projector, and a whiteboard that covers most of the wall. An open door at the back stands open, my sister's silhouette framed by the door. Though I'm far, the acoustics in the room let me hear slivers of the conversation.

"Come on, don't be like this." A male voice echoes through the room.

"I can't keep doing this."

Though I can't see anyone in the room with her, I assume that she's talking to her professor. I don't remember her schedule exactly, but I think that this is a class that's required for her to finish off with pre-med.

"You have to," the man's voice says, the emotion behind his words not quite matching the statement. It's off somehow, like he's not fully convinced of what he's saying.

"I don't have to do anything. You could get in trouble for this," she says.

"If you want to pass, you do. This class is a roadblock on your path to med school. If that's what you really want, then you know what you have to do. There aren't really any other options—are there?"

I clear my throat, and my sister whips around. I can see something in her hand, but she shoves it away into her pocket.

Probably her phone, I guess. Her eyes are wide as she stalks toward me, her backpack slung over her shoulder.

"What are you doing here?" she seethes as she approaches. I look over her shoulder, waiting to see if anyone emerges from behind her in the office—but no one does.

"I brought you a coffee," I say as she approaches, thrusting it toward her.

"Why are you always following me around? It's ridiculous. Don't you have a class to be at?"

Why is she so angry with me? I was just trying to do something nice. I swear, she's always got an attitude recently. I can't do anything right when it comes to her.

"My class got out early because my professor wasn't feeling well. I figured I'd swing by since I knew you were getting out. Sorry I pissed you off," I say, a bit more defensive than I mean to be.

"Stop causing drama," she says as she swipes the coffee out of my hand. She takes a long swig of it, then pushes past me, her shoulder slamming into mine as she walks by.

"You're welcome," I hiss after her as she stomps toward the exit of the building.

I glance back into the room, waiting to see who my sister was talking to. But there's still no one there. The room is still empty. All that echoes there now are the angry footsteps of my sister disappearing into the empty building.

Eviana, what are you up to?

31

Though I don't have much to go on yet, I think that there might be something else hidden away among the blackmail on Eviana's phone that will tell me with more certainty what happened to her. I haven't spent much time going through the phone yet—not like I did the laptop. As I open up the phone, the hiss of the espresso machine rises and falls, filling the coffee shop with a dull roar. I get a text from Tia checking in on me, and I respond quickly. She wants to meet up, so I recommend the coffee shop.

I stroll back to table, my phone in hand. As I click on Eviana's social media accounts, I notice something that I hadn't seen on my own phone—there's a small icon next to her photo at the top right. As I click on it, I realize that she has several other accounts set up in her phone. I switch to the first account, Dudeudeudeo2. This account doesn't have any posts of its own, but that's not to say the account wasn't used for anything. When I go to the messages, I find hundreds of outgoing messages to other accounts, acting as what I can only describe as a stalker.

This account that Eviana used seems to have been only for

harassment. She harassed hundreds of other influencers, doing everything from body shaming to telling people to kill themselves. I swallow hard, trying to digest what I'm seeing. Did she seriously send this stuff? I can't imagine my sister doing this. But then I also realize she was using this account to harass her own accounts. There are so many threatening messages she left on her own pictures.

As I click through the notifications, I can see angry responses to comments that this account made. I scroll through the comments finding lots of public harassment and statements that border on stalking. I feel sick as I keep scrolling. Once I've had enough, I move to the next account. I find more and more of the same. Each account is filled with toxic comments, stalking, harassment. How much of her time did she spend trying to attack other influencers who it appears she thought were her competition? I can't believe that she wasted her time doing this.

There are over twenty accounts, all of them identical to the first. I guess this is how she filled her time when she wasn't making content. As I get to the last few accounts, I recognize the names. I've definitely seen them before—they were accounts that threatened my sister. In the DMs I find strange conversations that Eviana seemed to be having with other people who posted threatening comments on her posts—as herself. In a few of these conversations, she sent some of her real harassers the address to her house while pretending to be someone else. Was she trying to lure these people to her? Did Eviana want someone to show up at her house? Was this all some kind of ploy to make content out of stalkers showing up on her doorstep?

I think about what I know of my sister, how badly she craved attention sometimes. Was she trying to orchestrate something for attention? Or was she trying to scare Simon? I wish that she would have given me a hint of what she was up to while I was visiting. It kills me that some of these messages were sent while I was here, with her, in that house. Eviana was often on her phone, but I never imagined that *this* is what she was doing.

On Eviana's main account, as I scroll back to the beginning of her conversations, a name that I recognize catches my eye, Tia Wang. This stands out to me because Eviana had conversations on here with only one other friend—Fiona, as they were coordinating posts together. I click on the thread and begin to skim over the messages.

The first few messages are nothing out of the usual, sharing posts and recipes back and forth—which is interesting, since my sister didn't cook unless she had to for some of her partnerships. After the first messages, I notice some screenshots from what's clearly a chat between Fiona and someone else.

At the top of the message chain, I see Simon's name listed as the contact—the screenshot is clearly from an Apple device.

> Oh, come on, you know you want to come over to get some of this tonight.

> You know I can't. We're going for a shoot at the beach.

> Blow it off. Make her go alone.

> I can't but I'll see you in a few days.

> What will it take for you to actually leave her and stop stringing me alone?

> Along*

> You already know the answer to that.

There's a hard lump in my throat. This is what I have been looking for. This is my proof. Simon was cheating on my sister. But with whom? And the question resonates in the back of my mind—who wanted my sister dead more, Simon or his mistress? Is this why he got rid of my sister?

The front door of the coffee shop jingles, and I glance up to see Tia as she strolls through the door. She offers me a tight smile as she walks over. She's got on a pencil skirt and a gray silk button-up. A breathy sigh escapes her as she sits down.

"Ugh, my afternoon has been wild," she says, her words heavy with either frustration or exhaustion. Tia is a lawyer, working mostly in contract law from what I heard from Eviana. I imagine a job like that is incredibly difficult and stressful.

"I'm sorry. Days like that are the worst. Need to vent or want a coffee?" I offer.

She waves her hand, dismissing both ideas. "Coffee this late in the day will just up my anxiety, thanks though. I was actually hoping to talk to you about something." Her tone is serious as she crosses her legs and adjusts her position at the table.

"Oh?" I ask when she doesn't offer up what she wants to talk about. Instead, she glances toward the door.

"So, I had someone send me something that I think Eviana should know about, but I don't think that I'm the right person to tell her," she says as she finally looks back at me. She stops talking long enough to dig her phone out of a teal purse. I wait impatiently while she taps on the screen before sliding it onto the table between us.

On the phone, it's opened to her photos. There are a lot of saved screenshots of text message conversations. I skim over them, trying to decipher what I'm seeing.

"They're between Simon and Fiona," she finally says as I read through the pages and pages of sexting.

"Does Eviana know?" I ask.

She sucks in a sharp breath, her posture stiff. "Honestly, I don't think so. But I don't want to be the person to ask... so... could you..."

I nod. "Yeah, I'll break the news to her," I promise. "Where did these text messages come from? I know that she's going to ask."

Her jaw tightens. "I can't say."

I press a few more times. Each time Tia is more insistent that she can't tell me the source of her screenshots. And though I ask her about the previous screenshots that she sent to my sister, it's been so long that she can't remember who sent her those—or who Simon was exchanging messages with. There's one thing that's clear to me though: this has been going on for at least a year—and Eviana has been sitting on this knowledge the whole time. We wrap up our chat when Tia gets an urgent call from work and has to run. As I leave the coffee shop with the proof about Simon that I've suspected for so long, I don't feel vindicated. Instead, I feel hollowed out. I'm no closer to finding Eviana. Instead, I'm here stacking up more reasons that someone might have killed her.

32

SIXTEEN YEARS AGO

Time is elastic, moving so fast when it's inconvenient, and so slow when you have something to say. I've been waiting for Eviana for hours. I've looked over the test answers so many times I'm sure that I could ace her tests at this point. She's late. Much later than she should be for a Tuesday afternoon. My palms are slick with sweat as I look at the time on my phone, then glance to the door again.

When Eviana finally walks through the door, there's an iced coffee sloshing in her hand. Her lanyard with her keys on it is hanging off her pinky. Her hair is balled up on top of her head in a bun, her makeup a bit too nice for class. It's clear that she doesn't know that I'm here, sitting on the couch, waiting for her.

"Can we talk?" I ask as she walks toward her room.

She gasps, then stops and glances at me, her eyes wide.

"Jesus Christ, you're just sitting here in a silent room? Ugh, you're so weird."

"Vi, seriously. Can you sit down?" I motion toward the couch. For a moment, I half expect for her to tell me to shut up, and for her to disappear into her room. But instead, she takes a seat across from me.

She crosses her legs, takes a sip of her coffee, then stares at me expectantly. "Okay, so what do you want?"

"Do you want to tell me about what's going on?" I ask. I want to keep my question vague because I know there's more going on here than meets the eye. I'm sure she has other secrets, so maybe if I'm not clear enough about the information I'm trying to get out of her, I'll end up with more.

She props her elbow on her knee, then begins to chew on her thumbnail. "What do you mean?"

"You know what I mean," I say, keeping my voice even.

She raises a brow and appraises me, as if trying to see straight through me to the truth I'm trying to glean from her. "No idea what you're talking about," she finally says before taking a sip of her coffee.

"Look, I know that you've been cheating," I finally manage.

She lets out a low laugh but doesn't deny it. "And? What? Are you going to tell on me?"

I scoff. Honestly, I'm somewhat relieved to find out that my sister isn't perfect—that all this time she wasn't really that much better than me. The golden child wasn't golden at all. She just gilded herself. I try not to smile at that knowledge, at the realization, but I'm not so sure that I manage it.

"So you are? You're really going to be a bitch about this and tell someone? Did you already go to Mom about this?" Her voice hitches, rising in octaves, and I can tell that Eviana is about at her breaking point. I've never seen my sister like this, usually things go her way, she doesn't have a reason to throw a fit.

"Of course I'm not going to tell on you. Why would I do that? And besides, no one would believe me. If it was my word against yours, there's absolutely no way anyone would think that I was telling the truth."

Her shoulders relax and she leans back into the couch. A

look of satisfaction quirks her features because she knows that I'm right, that it's true.

"So, then, why are you even talking to me about it if you're not going to do anything?"

"Because I just want to know the truth. There have always been walls between us, and I want to feel like at least with one thing you've let me in, that I'm not an outsider." Baring my soul like this, it's a risk. I know that Eviana is more likely to throw harsh words into my face than she is to even consider what I'm asking. Her moods are so hot and so cold that I never know which version of my sister I'm going to get. Beneath that stony exterior, there's compassion, I've seen it before—but it's so rare, and it's not usually squandered on me.

She bristles, but her usual resolve is shattering.

"I just want to feel like you trust me with *something*," I add, trying to break the dam that I know is holding back all of her secrets.

"Fine." She throws her hands up in the air. "What do you want to know?"

"I want to know everything," I say, desperate for my sister to confide in me about anything and everything in her life. I want to know her secrets, what she's been hiding, how she gets away with it all. "When did it start? How did it start?"

She sighs, places her coffee down on the table between us, then crosses her arms. "Freshman year, right after I started high school, that's when it all started. Things between middle and high school shifted too much, and it was difficult for me to keep up. For a little while, I paid someone at school to print me out fake report cards so that Mom wouldn't have any idea that I wasn't doing well, but I realize that wasn't sustainable."

I take it all in, relishing the fact that my sister is finally trusting me with something. I don't dare open my mouth, because if I remind her that she shouldn't be telling me these things, I'm terrified that she'll stop—that she'll come to her senses and I'll get nothing.

"One day, I was in my algebra class talking to the teacher about problems I was having with an assignment. She had to leave the room to take a call, and while she was gone I noticed that there was a stack of papers with test answers sitting on her desk. A good person would have just ignored them, but we both know that I am not a good person. While she was out there on her call, I copied down all of the answers that I could."

She picks up her coffee and takes a sip before continuing, and I am absolutely rapt by her story. I would have never dared something like this, I would have been too afraid of being caught.

"I aced that test with the answers. The whole time I was absolutely petrified that I would get caught. But I didn't. And it became like an addiction. That's how I made it through high school. I almost got caught a few times, but in general, as long as you get a few answers wrong on purpose, it's difficult for them to figure out. Teachers are overworked. As long as it looks like you're paying attention, that you ask questions, they assume you're doing well because they're a good teacher."

Nerves prickle inside me as I imagine trying to pull off what my sister did. "How did you almost get caught?"

"There were a few times that I was trying to get the answers, and a teacher walked in on me. But as long as you're pleasant, it's pretty easy to play it off like you were just waiting for them." She laughs a little, as if it is a pleasant memory, while my guts twist like oiled eels at the thought. I'd probably puke on the floor if I got caught trying to steal test answers.

I swallow hard, knowing that my next question might piss her off. "So, you weren't sleeping with your teacher then?" I had been so certain that's what I was seeing when I'd walked into that classroom.

She lets out a humorless laugh. "That would have been

easier, honestly. If I could have pulled that off, I probably would have gone that route. But that would have been too difficult to juggle."

"If Mom finds out, she's going to kill you," I say.

She offers me a one-shouldered shrug. "I'd like to see her try."

33

Sometimes, when news breaks, it's hard to believe. Then other times, it hits you so hard, it takes your breath away. A woman sits on the screen of the local news, her bright green dress practically glowing under the stage lights. The grim look on her face hasn't changed since she started speaking, as if she froze all of her facial features into place before the camera started rolling.

"Police have confirmed that they've arrested a suspect in the murder of Danica Fullerton, a resident of Orlando. For now, they haven't released any information regarding motive, or how exactly Danica died. But we are keeping in close touch with Orlando PD."

I hold my breath, waiting for them to say Simon's name—for them to say what I know he's capable of. In the back of my mind, I hear them saying Eviana's name too, that her body was found dumped in the woods somewhere. Next to the anchor, the face of a man appears. But it's not Simon. In fact, it's a man I've never seen before in my life. I swallow hard, feeling like I'm pushing razor blades down my esophagus. How is this possible? Why would a random person kill Danica?

The news is short on answers. They don't know how the

man got past the guard. They don't know why Danica was targeted. I'm short on patience as I listen to it all, the evening sky purple and gold through the window, warning me about the impending night. I want to walk over to Simon's to catch him in the act. Because I know he must be up to something. He's still over there, pretending that my sister isn't missing—that she's home posting, and that everything is just as normal as can be. I need to catch him in this. I need proof of what he did so I can take him down. Maybe I can't bring my sister back, maybe it's too late to save her—but I can make him pay for what he did to her. The idea that I may never see my sister again wrenches my heart. She didn't deserve this end—despite all of her faults.

An image is burned into my mind, Simon smirking from the upstairs window as if he's trying to keep me in the dark, as if he's messing with me on purpose. I refuse to let that asshole win. I grab my phone, shove my feet into sandals, then storm out of the house. Though the sun is edging down on the horizon, somehow it's still so hot outside that it may as well be noon.

Anxiety and frustration war inside me and I grind my teeth together. Do something, my mind demands over and over. I look down the street, considering my options. The last time I walked in this neighborhood, I nearly got run over. But the guy who did that has been arrested—so I should be safe now, right? My mind replays the scene, and the panic that swarmed inside me last night. But I can't let fear keep me from figuring out what happened to my sister. I've retraced all her other steps; I've tried to see where she went—but Simon told me she disappeared in this neighborhood. So, shouldn't I spend more time here? Shouldn't I comb these streets to find out what happened to her? I need to walk by Fiona's to see if Simon is there again. Eviana's house will be my last stop.

Anxiety is so thick inside me, it's a palpable force. But I swallow it down. It doesn't matter how I feel about it. I banish the fear to the back of my mind. My sister is counting on me.

No one else is fighting for her, no one else even knows that she's missing. So it's up to me to save her. The neighborhood is sprawling, filled with over ten streets and hundreds of houses. But toward the back of the community there's a pool, clubhouse, and a walking trail.

The last remnants of the evening sun burn against my skin as I walk, and though the sunlight should help with the anxiety twisting inside me—it does little to assuage my worries. My heart pounds as I work my way through the meandering streets toward the back of the neighborhood. Sweat seeps into my shirt, making it stick to me like a second skin, the heat and my outfit threatening to suffocate me as I walk. As I approach Fiona's house, I realize that there's an Escalade in the driveway—but it isn't Simon's. It's a dark gray but not black like his. I kick myself and wonder if it was actually his car in the driveway at all. She is married. How likely is it that she'd be inviting Simon to her house anyway? If they were having an affair, surely they'd be smart enough to go to a hotel.

I keep walking toward the trail my sister pointed out to me while I was here. As I pass Fiona's, I see the front door is open. I jog out of the way, behind the cars in the driveway, and toward the trail next to her house. I don't want to be seen.

My mind is clogged with thoughts, dark images of my sister disappearing off of these streets at night. I need proof of what Simon did so that I can go to the police. I should have just gotten rid of this asshole for my sister. Why didn't she tell me that she needed help? Why didn't she let me help her like I did before?

Above me, the tree branches weave together into a thick canopy that blots out the heat of the sun. Though I'm thankful for the reprieve, the looming darkness makes fear prickle down my spine. I swallow hard as the neighborhood gives way to a forest. The row of trees is broken by a trail that's barely visible before being gobbled up by the darkness. My shoe sinks in the grass as I walk, each step a bit more tense than the last. But as I finally make the break in the trees and step foot on the dusty path, I wonder what Eviana thought the last time she was walking through these woods.

The sounds of the forest rise around me, the cicadas singing, the crackling buzz of their wings rising higher and higher before slowly dying again. I can see why Eviana came out here for walks. I imagine if you're not worried about getting murdered, this would be a nice place to clear your head. The branches groan as a stray breeze slips through the trees and I look up into the swaying canopy. My chest tightens as my boot catches on the edge of a protruding root. I throw my hands out in an attempt to right myself and regain my balance to barely avoid toppling onto the dirt. I stop for a second to catch my breath, glancing behind me—but there's no one following me, there are no signs that anyone else has been back here for a while.

Ahead of me, the dirt is smooth, as if no other shoes have marred the surface for a long time. I wonder if the rain the other day smoothed everything out, if it washed away the evidence of my sister being back here over a week ago. The farther and farther I walk, the more clotted with Spanish moss the trees above me become. How long is this trail? Did I set myself up for a mile-long walk and I didn't know it?

The path curves left and right through the trees, passing a few overturned trees; their roots are exposed, twisted, still caked with dirt. They look as if a giant pushed them over and crushed them into the ground. As I finally get toward what looks to be the end of the trail, I find something I don't expect, a small gazebo. Spanish moss hangs low above the roof, tickling it. The structure has been out here for so long that green has started to stain the white paint. An intricate railing works its way around the pillars that create the frame. I approach carefully, wondering why I've never seen this place before. This gazebo seems like the perfect fixture to appear in my sister's shots from time to time. Actually, now that I think about it, I may have seen it on her account a few weeks ago.

My feet sound hollow when I step on the wooden floor. Though it's weather-beaten, it still looks sturdy, solid. Thankfully it doesn't feel like the wood will collapse and my ankle will end up stuck in the boards. As I investigate the benches that are built into the gazebo, I notice a dark brown substance that's been splattered all over the white boards. I swallow hard as I examine it. And it has to be blood—there's no other way it's anything else. I've seen dried blood before.

Next to the blood, a few inches away beneath the small bench that's built into the structure, there's a note that's written on a sticky note. I pick it up and turn the paper over in my hands. There's a time written at the top of the note in handwriting that's similar to my sister's, then beneath that, it says a name. Fiona.

34

SIXTEEN YEARS AGO

"Fuck, fuck, fuck, *fuck!*" my sister screams, her voice cutting through the apartment as she throws open the front door, then slams it behind her. The whole house vibrates with her rage, her anger traveling through the wood, filling me with a sense of dread.

Eviana rarely has outbursts. If she's freaking out like this, something is seriously wrong. I walk toward my closed door, trying to see if she's talking to someone. When I don't hear any hints that she's on the phone, I slowly open the door and peek my head out.

She turns around, I guess sensing my presence, and glowers at me. Anger is clear on her face, in her rageful eyes, the way she's pulled her lips tight.

"What do you want?" She hurls the words at me like daggers, but they don't land the way they usually would. She's like a caged animal lashing out because she's frightened.

"I heard the door slam." I shrug.

"And?"

"What's your problem?" I fire back. Usually, I'd just let

Eviana burn herself out with her attitude, but something seems off. She's way more angry than usual. This isn't just PMS.

"I fucked up." She throws her hands up in the air before walking over to the couch and plopping down onto it.

"Fucked up how?" I ask, leaning against the doorframe to my room.

"I was trying to get the test answers for my calc final, and my professor walked in. They knew exactly what I was doing, they already had suspicions. I'm fucked." Tears pool in her eyes, shimmering in the low light in the room.

I'm taken aback, watching her, seeing her dissolve like this in front of me before she buries her head in her hands and starts to sob—hard. She mumbles something that I can't make out. And I'm so unsure of what to say. So instead of saying anything, I press my lips together and look at the floor.

"They already told Mom. They took my bag. They saw how many other answers I had. They think that Mom was involved because I'd managed to hack into the email accounts of a few of the teachers and take answers from there too."

I chew my bottom lip as I listen to Eviana confess all of her sins to me. Somehow, it doesn't feel as good as I thought it would. My guts churn with unease. I should be happy that the golden child has fallen, that it'll now finally be obvious that she's really not any better than me—but instead, I don't feel any of that.

"So, what are you going to do?" I ask once she goes quiet.

"Drop out."

I let those words roll over me for a bit. I never thought I'd hear my sister say those words. She always wanted to go to med school or, at worst, to follow in our mother's footsteps and become a professor too. Hearing her say that she wants to drop out, it's like the world has been turned on its side. Eviana has never been the type to just give up.

"You can't just give up like that." Though I say the words,

they ring hollow. If I were in her position, I'd probably drop out too.

"I've got to go back to Mom's to talk to her about everything that's happened. Will you come with me?" she asks, finally looking up at me. Her cheeks are stained with mascara. It streaks down her face and drips from her jaw.

I chew my lip, biting so hard that I almost draw blood. I avoid my mother's house like the plague. But if she really needs me to go with her, I know I can't deny her that. I've always wanted a way to bond with my sister more—maybe this will be the moment that we finally do.

"Fine, I'll go," I say, but the moment the words leave my mouth a bad feeling blooms inside me.

35

There are a lot of steps to stalking that I've learned, to peeling back the onion to figure out who someone really was, where they went, what their routine was. But what I'm looking for isn't routine. I need to figure out where my sister went, why she went there, and what happened before she died or disappeared. The phrase *no body, no crime* echoes in my mind every time I consider her whereabouts. Dead or disappeared? Which one is it? The more I find out about my sister, the less clear the answer becomes. One minute, I'm convinced she must be dead, while the next minute I'll know deep down she's not—that someone must have her.

On my sister's burner phone, I open up her map app, then navigate to her history. I've googled how to find someone's past location on their phone. Thankfully, on this phone, she didn't bother to turn the tracking off—I guess because she never thought that anyone would get into this phone or even learn of its existence. Trying to figure out where she met Fiona before she disappeared, sure, I know the time, but there's no place.

She's used this phone to navigate to a lot of places—the history goes back at least a year. It looks like she mostly went out during the day, early in the morning, probably after her run to the coffee shop. She stopped at the parks I already investigated, the one where I found the bracelet. But there's another location she frequented almost as much as the coffee shop—the gym. Now that I know Eviana frequented the gym because Simon made her feel like crap about her body, seeing all the visits, sometimes multiple visits per day, forces frustration to ripple through me. The gym looks like her last location before she disappeared. Maybe that's where she met Fiona.

Luckily I'm already dressed in leggings and a baggy tank top, so I won't look out of place if I slip into the gym. The makeup on my face is thick enough to cover my lingering injuries. That at least will help me blend in as well. When I walk in the front door of the gym, the air is thick with the sharp scent of cleaner and the musk of sweat. It's more humid inside the gym than it is outside, which is saying something for Florida. The place is huge, two stories that I can see, filled with rows of equipment from wall to wall. A woman behind a large circular desk offers me a smile, and a look that shows she clearly doesn't recognize me.

"Here for a guest pass?" she asks.

I nod, knowing that'll be the easiest way for me to do a quick sweep to see if anything of my sister's remains here. Or if there are any clues she met Fiona here. It makes me uneasy, sneaking into places like this, looking for evidence. I try to shift my frame of mind—I'd do this for one of my kids, for one of my cases. I'd investigate anything I needed to if it meant I could get them out of danger, to help them find a better life. I swallow down my discomfort as I try to tell myself that's all I'm doing now. I'm helping Eviana. I'm looking for evidence to help with her case. That's all this is.

"Okay so, as you can see all the equipment is here. If you head to the back, there's a sauna, a pool, tanning beds, lockers, showers, all the stuff that you might need after a workout. Do you want a formal tour or are you comfortable checking it out yourself?" she offers.

"I think I'm okay showing myself around." I pass her my ID and she finishes checking me in for the guest pass. It takes a few minutes of her typing on the computer and me anxiously tapping my foot before I'm free to wander the gym.

The woman offers me one last smile before giving me a sticker to indicate I've got a guest pass for the day. I curve around the desk, past a row of treadmills, then begin to scan the place. Where the hell in this gym could my sister have left something?

As I weave through the gym, I open Fiona's social media accounts and scroll back to the day that Eviana went missing. Sure enough, she posted several videos and pictures at the gym that day. I make a mental list of what I'm looking for and continue past people working out on machines. The sound of grinding metal, grunting, and the clink of weights creates a dull roar.

My first stop is the spin studio, which is essentially an aquarium filled with bikes. Anyone in the gym can see inside here—so I seriously doubt this is where she met my sister. I work my way through the pool, the locker room, then finally the sauna. Back in this section of the gym, there are at least ten different sauna rooms all only big enough to hold about six people. If they were looking for somewhere quiet to talk, this is obviously where they would have retreated to.

The air in the sauna rooms is so hot, my chest tightens in response. I hate suffocating heat. It's one of the reasons I left this state in the first place—that and it's so hard when you have curly hair. I look like a poorly groomed poodle from April until October. I throw open the doors of the first few rooms, finding them empty. As I approach the last two rooms, I realize there's a door at the end of the hall in front of me—a way out. Eviana and

Fiona could have left from here—that is, if they ever met here in the first place.

I open the last door, having found nothing so far—and I'm startled to find someone sitting naked in the last room. I'm too temporarily blinded by the unexpected nudity that it takes me far too long to realize that Fiona is sitting on the wooden bench.

She hasn't even laid a towel down to sit on. Yuck.

"Blair! Hey!" she says before pushing herself up and striding over to give me a hug and a peck on each cheek. She furrows her brows. "What happened to your face?"

I did not expect to find her here. And I guess my makeup isn't doing the job I'd hoped. Though I want to confront her about Eviana, the last thing I want is to have an argument with a naked woman.

"Nothing, just an accident." I try to shrug it off, to move on.

"How are you doing?" she asks, her voice saccharine sweet.

"Oh, you know. How are things with you?" I ask. The heat is already getting to me, despite having the door propped open behind me. My chest is tight as sweat blooms down my spine. Though I've only been in here a minute, my tank top is already sticking to my flesh like a second skin.

She offers what looks like a forced smile. "Great. Perfect actually. How's Eviana?" she asks, with a sharpness in her eyes that's unsettling. "How's she doing after all that ugliness on social media?"

I ignore her comment. I'm not going to give her any feedback on her attempts to mess with my life or my sister's. But it's interesting that she can act so cheery, so *normal* after threatening to destroy our lives. She tried to get me fired, for God's sake. People like Fiona feed on attention. Simon didn't post anything about the drug allegations, and in forty-eight hours, there was another social media scandal that lit a new fire on the internet. The world has moved on from Fiona's posts, though I'm sure she hasn't.

"You know, I was actually going to ask you about something. My sister mentioned that the two of you got into a fight."

I throw the statement her way casually, just to see how she reacts, the same way she spoke to me about the mess she tried to cause for Eviana.

Her botoxed brows rise slightly, but her widened eyes show the shock the rest of her frozen features can't.

"A fight? With Eviana?" she laughs, like it's the most ridiculous thing she's ever heard, but there's a tightness in her posture. Her features don't match the levity of her words. "There was no reason for us to fight *before* she didn't hold up her end of the bargain. Now though, there are reasons. Plenty of them."

"Yeah, Eviana's neighbor mentioned she heard the two of you fighting," I add, trying to see if I can get even a sliver of the truth out of her. I know now that it wasn't Claire who Danica overheard Eviana fighting with. It must have been Fiona. That's the only thing I can piece together.

She's silent for a second, then glances to the floor. "Oh, that. I don't think I'd call that an argument. It was more of a misunderstanding. She misheard something."

"What level of misunderstanding?" I'm not going to let her get out of this without giving me *something*.

She crosses her legs and leans back on the bench. "She thought that I had been speaking to Simon, and I hadn't been."

"By speaking, you mean that she thought that you two were sleeping together, right?" I hammer the point home a little harder than I normally would, but I want to wrap this up. The longer I'm stuck here with this woman, the more uneasy it makes me.

"She thought that, but Simon?" she sputters. "Oh God. No. Have you seen my husband?" she asks as she seems baffled by the thought. She grabs her phone from the bench next to her, taps on the screen a few times, then shows me a picture of a muscular shirtless man. Not at all my type, but I can tell she's quite happy with the guy. I'm still not so sure I believe her though.

"You know, I saw screenshots..." I start as she sets her phone back down.

"Those were just innocent flirting. It was nothing. Everyone flirts in this business. That's just how you say hello." She presses her lips together and I swear I can smell the lie in the air. Why would she bother flirting with Simon if she wasn't interested and she was so happy with her husband? I don't care what industry you're in, that's not how anyone says *hello*. "Is Eviana done with her stupid digital detox yet? There are some things that the two of us need to hash out. It's been sitting for too long, and honestly, it's kind of pissing me off. No one puts me on the backburner like this."

"Look, I've got to get going, before you decide to twist some of our conversation and send it to my boss," I say, the heat really starting to get to my head. I know that Fiona isn't going to give me anything anyway. I'm just wasting my time. And I'm not going to discuss with her again how she thinks my sister owes her posts or something.

The air in the hall feels icy when I slip out of the sauna. I gulp down the air as if I've just emerged from the bottom of a swimming pool. Sweat is slick on my face, rolling down my cheeks then my throat before soaking into my tank top. My head feels fuzzy, like it's thick with static as I walk down the hall. I don't understand how anyone can enjoy that.

"Hey! You can't just walk out on me," Fiona's shrill voice calls as she bursts into the hall. Her bare feet smack against the tile floor, but when I turn, I'm relieved to see that she at least wrapped her towel around her body.

"Actually, I can. I don't work for you." My words are filled with more venom than I expect for them to be. I don't ever talk to people like this—it'd be too much of a risk to my career. I can be firm, I can present evidence, but being this snappy... that's new, and it feels kinda good. Rage kindles inside me. I hate people like this—wealthy people who seem to think that everyone else is at their command. I don't owe this woman anything.

"Oh shut up, Blair. You sound like more of a brat than your sister did," she says. And I take note of her talking about Eviana in the past tense. It's an interesting choice.

"We're the brats? While you're out here trying to ruin people's lives. I did nothing to you, and yet you're trying to get me fired? Then you tried to spread lies about Eviana being an addict on the internet. You need a reality check. There's something seriously wrong with you."

"You and your sister have cost me a lot of money. I gave you the opportunity to go to Eviana to fix this. But you chose not to. All you got is what was coming to you—just like Eviana did. And it sounds like you haven't learned your lesson. It sounds like you need to be punished more." She crosses her arms over her chest and cocks her head. "And Eviana wasn't some angel; she blackmailed me and told me that she'd expose me as a fraud on social media. That's the only reason I offered up that partnership in the first place."

I wonder if she's talking about what she blasted all over social media or if she's talking about something far more sinister.

"*I* didn't cost you anything. I barely know you. You can feel free to blame the rest of the world for your problems, but I am not one of them. And whatever beef that you have with my sister, that's not my problem either." Anger rises inside me, and though I try to get a grip on it before I start screaming at this woman, I'm not sure I can handle it much longer. I clench my fists at my sides, trying to contain it.

She stomps toward me, her feet smacking against the floor with each step. Her hand slashes the air as she points an acrylic finger at me threateningly. "You sure did cost me. You aren't innocent in this because you're working with *her*. You're both exactly the same, all high and mighty. I'm sure it's only a matter of time before you try to blackmail me too."

"Grow up. You don't even know me." I turn around and start heading for the door.

"Yeah that's right, walk away. And just you wait, Blair. I'm only getting started."

I burst through the doors to the outside, my heart pounding as I'm blinded by the midday sun. When Fiona says she's only getting started, I hate that I believe her. But at the end of the day, whatever it is that Fiona thinks she's capable of—I'm capable of worse.

36

SIXTEEN YEARS AGO

The weather matches my mood, a storm is brewing on the horizon, the air charged with an energy that feels like it could be dangerous. Eviana is driving, and I'm in the passenger side of her ancient Civic. The way she's driving has me on edge, whipping around corners so quickly that my whole body slides across the seat. I've got my bare feet resting on the dash, though she's warned me that if we crash, I'll break both of my legs—a warning I seriously doubt the validity of. Rain starts to pelt the windshield as we grow closer to our mother's neighborhood. Just seeing the familiar stores, the roads I walked down just years ago, it's enough to knot my insides. Anxiety skitters beneath my skin, tightening my chest. I don't want to be here again. I want to be far from this place and to never have to think about it again.

We turn into the neighborhood as thunder crackles overhead, a sound so loud that I'd swear it split the sky in two. I count down the houses until I know we're at our mother's house. It feels smaller than it did when I was younger, though I know nothing has really changed. As I slip out of the car, I swear I can smell her cigarette smoke already—though I know it's likely all in my head. Eviana gives me a long look as she stands frozen by the driver's side of the car. I don't say anything because I want her to change her mind. I want both of us to get back into the car and not to go in there.

"Ugh, we should go," she finally says, motioning toward the curtain that's shifted in the front window. Our mother knows that we're here, there's no turning back now.

"If you say so," I say. I hesitate as Eviana walks toward the door, debating if I should just slip back into the car. Once Eviana is inside, it's not like she's going to come back out here to grab me.

When she reaches the stoop, she pauses and glances back at me, glowering until I start walking. It's as if her stare has an invisible tether forcing me forward. I drag my feet. They scuff against the concrete walkway as I approach the door. The dread already pooling inside me rises, becoming a tsunami that threatens to bowl me over. My heart pounds as Eviana opens the door and ushers me inside.

What if she's bringing me here so she can blame all of this on me? I've always been the one that Eviana has thrown under the bus. That could be her real intention here.

I curse myself for not realizing sooner that Eviana could be planning to do this. I never assume the worst when I should. The stench of cigarette smoke pours from the house like a toxic fog. Eviana clears her throat, reminding me to follow her inside. My feet move automatically, and I trail after her.

We find Mom at her usual spot at the dining room table. She's got a cigarette clamped between her fingers so hard that it looks pinched. I wonder if she'll break it in half. Her cheeks are redder than usual, and her eyes look bloodshot. There's something wrong, I can see it already in her face. The bad feeling already swirling inside me turns into a warning siren, urging me to get the hell out of this house.

"Is it my birthday already?" she asks, her sharp tone something I'm quite used to—but for her to aim it at Eviana is new.

"We just wanted to stop by to see how you're doing," Eviana says, nudging me hard in the ribs until I nod in agreement.

"Bullshit. I know why you're actually here." She snuffs out her cigarette, shoving it so hard into the ashtray that it breaks in half. "Did you come to gloat or to plead?" Our mother stalks toward Eviana, and I step back reflexively.

I watch them, thankful that for once I'm invisible to the both of them. Something tells me that there's more to this fight than I realize.

"Because of your antics, I got fired today. Do you know how long it took me to get tenure? I worked my ass off for this. And for what? For you to throw it all away for me because you wanted to cheat?"

I digest what mom is saying. For as long as I can remember, being a professor has been her entire identity. She got a book deal last year, one where she was going to divulge her path to success.

"You ruined my career. My book is going to be canceled. What else did you come to take from me? Are you after your inheritance now?" A cruel laugh slips from our mother. And I can't help that I feel sorry for her. She may have always treated me like shit, but I know this is all she has. I would have never wished that this be taken from her—despite everything.

"You ruined your own career. You're the one who had unrealistic expectations and forced me into this. I told you when I was struggling in school, but you didn't care. You couldn't have a daughter who struggled in school, no, that was too embarrassing." She flashes a look at me, and I glare at her.

"What the hell do you mean? I already had to deal with that!" Mom says, an edge to her words as she throws her hand in the air toward me. "Blair couldn't even ace P.E.. I was hard on her because I knew she could do better if she applied herself. You were meant for success. You were so quick to learn, you basically taught yourself to read."

I chew the inside of my cheek. I do not want to be in the middle of their fight—especially when it's now becoming about me. I swear I can feel myself shrinking as my breaths come faster. Smoke from an abandoned cigarette spirals from the center of the table, the column rises high toward the ceiling before disappearing—and oh how I wish I could do the same.

"I might have taught myself to read, as you put it. But I needed help as I got older. And every time I asked for it, you shooed me away and forced me to find my own way. So I did. I figured it out just like you told me to. Hell, I almost made it to med school from cheating. I'd say that's a hell of a run." Eviana is clearly very proud of herself. She's got a grin from ear to ear.

Mother's face is a mask of rage, the air is thick with it. The pounding of my pulse in my ears kicks up a notch, and I take another step back, away from them. Eviana stumbles back away from our mother, but a fist flies toward Eviana's face.

"What the fuck!" Eviana says as she throws her hands up to shield herself.

"You ruined my life. I should have never had you, either of you. You've done nothing but take and take and take. And now you've taken the only thing I had left." My mother's voice cracks as she rages.

Eviana backs up, her back hitting the cabinets behind her. She's trapped between our mother's rage and a wall. There's no way she can escape. I'm frozen, completely unsure of what to do. Time slows as mom's hands reach for Eviana's throat. Eviana pounds against our mother's chest with her fists. When that does no good, she tries to wedge her forearms in front of her to push our mother away. But it does no good.

"Help," Eviana manages to squeak, and that kicks my ass into gear.

She's really going to kill my sister if I don't intervene. I have to do something. Eviana's face is bright red as she struggles.

"Leave her alone!" I shout as I rush toward Mom. My body moves automatically, my arm circling her throat. With a swift movement, I yank her back enough that Eviana can get free.

An elbow slams hard into my stomach, knocking the wind out of me. I stumble backward. In the space between us, Mom turns, her wild eyes focused on me. She lashes out, and the movement is all a blur—a fist hitting my cheek, black spots invading my vision, the lines of the kitchen slipping and sliding away as I lose my focus. My heart and panic roar inside me, a ferocious storm that paralyzes me.

As I stare at the enraged face of our mother, her teeth bared, nose flaring, I barely register what Eviana is doing. Fight or flight has me firmly in its grip. I want to flee. I want to get far, far away from here. The sound of crinkling fills the kitchen and suddenly there's a plastic bag over my mother's face. It's wrapped so tightly around Eviana's fingers, they turn white in between the gray pieces of plastic. Mom's back slams into Eviana, forcing them both backward. She scrambles, her hands clawing at her face as she struggles to breathe.

My mind swarms with thoughts, the reality of what's really happening. If I don't stop this, Eviana will kill our mother. But if I do stop her, I know Eviana will end up dead, hell, Mom might kill both of us. Eviana motions for me to help, and I move automatically. Tears fill my eyes as I wrap my fingers around mom's wrists stop her from struggling. The plastic crinkles as our mother struggles for breath. The sound of it grates on me, worming its way into my ears. It moves faster—then slows. Then, her body sags against me. I let her fall, thudding to the floor with a sound that's too hollow.

I take a step back. Eviana's hands are angry, swollen from the grip she had on the bag. Adrenaline still courses through me, forcing breath in and out of my lungs so quickly that I'm a bit lightheaded.

I can't believe that we did this.

I wonder if my sister planned this. If she knew that our mother would have to die. She's too calm, staring down at the body as if she expected this all along. I feel sick, like I may vomit all over the kitchen floor. This isn't what I wanted, what I thought would happen. My head swims, and I take a seat at the dining room table so that I don't faint.

"We have to get her body into her car. We'll put her in there, start the engine, and make it look like a suicide. It'll make sense, she just got fired," Eviana rambles off as if she had this all planned out already.

"She's dead."

"Yeah, I know. But we've got to get this plan in motion now or it'll be clear that we killed her." Her words don't match the severity of the situation. She's explaining it like we've got to take hamburger meat out of the freezer to thaw.

"She's fucking dead, Eviana."

She takes a step toward me, her face tight with anger. "Don't you think I know that? Do you want to go to prison? Because if you don't, you'll get off your ass and help me drag this body to the garage so we both can just move on with our lives."

When I don't move, Eviana loops her arms under mine and hoists me up from the chair.

"Grab her feet, I'll grab her chest," Eviana says, and I follow her directions automatically.

I try not to think about what I'm doing as we drag the body through the house to the garage. We open the car, prop her up inside, and I have to force myself not to vomit on the floor as Eviana shoves the keys into the ignition and starts the car. I

walk lead-limbed back into the kitchen and look down at the
plastic bag still lying on the floor.

"Come on, we have to go," Eviana says as she walks back
into the kitchen, as if nothing has happened.

She looks down at the plastic bag on the floor and scoops it
up, shoving it into her pocket. I follow her out of the house. She
talks our whole ride back about how we can't talk anymore, that
she's going to drop out, that once our mother's body is found
and we attend the funeral—after that, we can never talk again.

Eviana talks about getting away with murder like it's something she's been planning for a long time.

37

YOUTUBE

A woman sits wide-eyed in front of the camera. Her makeup and hair aren't done like they normally are. The room is darker around her than usual, letting her viewers know that this particular video was shot hastily, in the middle of the night. Tiffany's hair is pulled back, and her desk is free from her usual tea.

"This is going to be a quick video because I guess you could call this breaking news. For those of you who didn't see, a video was posted on Eviana's social media accounts tonight. It has since been deleted, but I saved the video."

She grimaces as the camera zooms out, allowing for a black box to take up half of the screen next to Tiffany's face.

"Sorry, there isn't going to be much to the video. It's the audio here that matters. But I'm posting the full thing here so you can see it all."

Tiffany's audio cuts out, as a loud rustling and static fill the feed. The rustling gets louder, then softer, followed by what sounds like far-off thuds. Though the video feed is still unclear, the feed shifts a bit, as if there's light trying to break through the picture. Tiffany pauses the video and leans in toward the camera.

"So here," she says, pointing to the black box. "I think that we're hearing someone running with a phone in their pocket or something."

The video resumes as Tiffany presses her lips together, as if she's forcing herself to remain silent.

The thudding grows louder in the video feed as it resumes. Rustling crackles, then dies out. "Help!" A woman's shrill voice is audible over the rest of the background noise. The video pauses again as Tiffany takes back control.

"So, obviously I'm not an audio expert or anything, but that voice sounds super similar to Eviana's. Obviously we've never heard her scream for help in any other video that she's posted, so it's kinda hard to be certain, but to me, it definitely sounds like her."

She waves her hand to the video as it starts again. This time, the darkness shifts, as if the person has retrieved the phone from their pocket. A midnight sky forked with jagged tree branches cut into the screen. The owner of the phone isn't visible, but the blur of the trees and the streaks of the stars above make it clear that whoever it is—they're running from something or someone.

"Please, someone help," a voice says before being snuffed out by sobs. The words are thick, clumsy. "Please, anyone." The woman calls one last time before the video dies.

38

Like all people, I try to tell myself that I'm a good person. But I'm not. Especially after seeing the new video that's been posted on my sister's social media account. I can't sit idly by anymore. I have to act. So, when I text Simon that I'm going to turn him in to the police, it's not a kindness, it's not me giving him a heads-up—it's a threat. I want him to overreact, to tip his hand. I'm still not sure who was the mastermind, Simon or Fiona, but I know that telling Simon will light a fire under both of their asses.

I've been debating texting Simon while I've walked to the coffee shop. Halfway through my walk back, I finally pulled the trigger. I glance at my phone over and over. Somehow, the silence from Simon's side is worse than the anger I was anticipating. With silence comes planning, stewing, action. I knew how to handle his anger, how to play it against him, but I don't know what to do with his silence.

Darkness looms over the neighborhood as I slog back to Valentina's. The sun has slipped below the horizon, casting the clouds in deep red and purple. As I approach the street I need to turn down, the flash of blue and red lights captures my attention and raises my heart rate. My pace picks up. In front of Valentina's house, three cop cars are stationed with their lights flashing. I push myself from a jog to a full-on sprint toward the house.

Did something happen to Valentina? I swear to God, if Simon hurt her, I'll kill him myself. I won't let this man hurt any more women in this town.

When I get to the police cars, a woman in uniform gets in my way and stops me from approaching the house.

"Do you live here?" she asks.

"I'm staying here with Valentina. Is she okay?" I ask, nearly out of breath.

"What's your name?" the officer asks.

"Blair Casteel," I say, scouring the windows for a hint of what's going on inside the house, but with the tint on the windows, I can't see inside. "Is she okay?" I ask a bit more forcefully this time. What if the same thing that happened to Danica happened to her? Simon must have done this.

"Would you mind stepping over here with me?" she asks, and motions toward a squad car with the door open.

I hesitate, then follow when she looks over expectantly. When I approach the car, she motions for me to get in the back.

"Let's go to the station so we can chat for a little bit," she says.

My stomach bottoms out. Something has to have happened to Valentina. Why else would they want me to go to the station? I glance back to the house one more time before I slide into the squad car. The seat is much harder than I expect, it feels like a hard plastic chair. The cold seeps into my legs as I sit on it.

The woman climbs into the front of the squad car and throws the car into drive. She accelerates and radios to dispatch that she's driving to the station.

"What's your name?" I ask.

"Officer Ramirez," she says simply.

"Could you tell me why we're going to the station?"

She doesn't respond, so I look out the window and watch the trees fly by. By the time we pull into the station, my armpits are damp and I feel like vomiting all over the back seat. She opens the door for me, and I slide out, happy that, though I feel guilty getting out of the back of a cop car, at least I'm not in cuffs. Officer Ramirez stays close and leads me through the station, past a bullpen filled with cops. The station is half-full, some of the cubicles filled with plainclothes officers typing away on computers. It feels closed in, labyrinth-like. There are no windows in here. Finally, she shows me into what looks like an interrogation room.

I take a seat when she signals for me to. And I feel very much like I've gotten sucked into an episode of *Law & Order*. How the hell did I end up here? I hope Valentina is okay. There's been too much death already.

"Do you need a drink or a snack?" she offers.

"I'll take some water." At this point, my heart is already beating like a hummingbird and if I add any more caffeine onto the anxiety raging inside me, I'll probably have a panic attack.

"The detective will bring some in for you," she says before disappearing. The door clicks closed behind her with finality.

I examine the white walls, the camera planted in the top right corner of the room—watching my every move, I'm sure. Sweat prickles on my palms, my neck, and I feel as though I'm seconds away from liquefying on the floor. A few minutes after Officer Ramirez disappears, a pale middle-aged woman in an ill-fitting pantsuit opens the door, followed by a man with dark hair, thick-rimmed glasses, and piercing blue eyes. His suit doesn't fit any better than hers; his pants are wrinkled and look too loose.

"Hey. Blair," she says with more familiarity than I'm comfortable with. She takes a seat on the other side of the table in front of me, and who I assume is her partner follows suit. "I'm Detective Hanson and this is Detective Alders."

"Is Valentina okay? Did something happen to her?" I ask, completely shedding niceties. I'm not going to play nice before I know what happened to Valentina. I don't understand why they're keeping me in the dark—unless she died and they think that I killed her.

She raises a brow. "Valentina, the woman you were staying with?"

I nod.

She waves her hand through the air as she pulls a notepad from her blazer pocket, a little laugh erupting from her thin lips. "Oh, she's fine."

"Then why were there three squad cars in front of her house? Why was I brought here?" I ask.

Detective Alders glances to his partner, and a hint of a smile plays on his lips. "No one told you why you were brought here?"

I shake my head. "No. I was taken from Valentina's house and Officer Ramirez didn't tell me anything."

Detective Hanson laces her fingers together and places them atop the table, while Detective Alders pulls out a notepad.

"What can you tell us about your relationship with your sister?" she asks.

I tense up automatically, not able to put the pieces together. "Why do you ask that?"

"Why don't you just answer the question?" Alders interjects as he sits, poised to take notes.

I consider my answer, trying to figure out what would be the best thing to say. "I'd say our relationship was a little bit complicated," I finally land on.

"Complicated, how?" she presses.

"We just grew apart after college. We went our separate ways. She focused on growing her online presence while I went out and got a career," I say, trying to summarize it as best as I can.

"Your sister had a career in marketing. She worked for a very successful AI company from what I understand," Alders adds, his words a bit of a dig.

I grind my teeth together. "Yeah, she did before she became an influencer. She started working for an AI company while she was in college, then stayed there for a few years after she dropped out."

"It sounds like you might have a little bit of animosity about what your sister did for work," Hanson says, her eyebrows inching up her forehead. Her words border on accusatory.

"I wouldn't say that," I say a little more defensive than I mean to be. Maybe a few weeks ago it was true that I had issues with my sister's career, but now that's changed. I see things were different than I realized. Eviana was being forced to continue influencing even though she wanted to step away.

"Then what would you say?" she presses.

I grind my teeth together again and pick at my fingernails under the table. I don't know what to say to them or how to say it. Sure, I threatened to go to the police about Simon, but I didn't think about what it'd really feel like to tell the police.

"Did you know that your sister has been missing for over a week?" she asks.

Surprise hits me so hard and so fast, I feel like I've been punched in the side of the head. Did she really just ask what I think she asked? They know that Eviana is missing?

"Yes, I did," I finally manage to say.

"And why didn't you come to the police? Why didn't you make a report?" Alder asks, his tone harsh. The look on his face tells me that he's already made up his mind about me.

I swallow hard and I calculate what to say—how to say it. "Because my brother-in-law threatened me and said if I came to the police, that he'd make it sound like I was responsible for Eviana's disappearance."

They exchange a look that tells me in no uncertain terms that they don't believe me even a little bit. I can't exactly tell them I didn't want to involve the police because Eviana and I murdered our mother and made it look like a suicide.

"And why would he do that?" Hanson asks as she cocks her head to the side.

"Because he doesn't want anyone to think that he's responsible for his wife's disappearance or death," I say, as if they're both idiots for not piecing it together. "He also wanted to keep making money from her brand."

"Her death? Why would you insinuate that your sister is dead?" Alders asks.

"If she hasn't shown back up by now, where else would she be? She's dead or someone kidnapped her, right?" I ask pointedly. I don't want to bring up the bracelet or the note. Those things could still make me look too guilty. But I think it's clear to everyone in this room that if Eviana had left on her own, there would have been some sign of her by now.

Hanson nods, then shoves up from the table. She disappears out of the room for a minute, then returns with a large white box in her hands. The table jumps when she drops the box on top of it, then she takes out an evidence bag and plops it in front of me. Through the clear plastic I can make out the phone that I found in Eviana's car before it burned up, a phone that clearly wasn't destroyed like I expected it to be.

"Whose phone is this?" she asks.

"I think it's my sister's burner phone," I say, deciding that honesty is probably the best policy for this—since my fingerprints are all over this phone.

"And how did *you* get this phone?"

"I found it in my sister's car."

"The car that you set on fire in the woods to hide that piece of evidence?" Alders accuses, his voice rising before Hanson serves him a cutting glance. "Along with your rental?"

Anger surges inside me. I can't believe that they're trying to throw that on me. Why would I have done any of this? I've watched enough *Law & Order* to know this is all circumstantial. "I did not set that car on fire. Simon did that," I say, sounding a bit more like a pedantic child than I'd like to.

"Uh-huh," Alders adds as he nods.

"Why the hell would I set my sister's car on fire? What would I gain from that?" Frustration sharpens my words, and I hate how shrill it makes me sound. But no matter how much I try to tamp down the emotion, there's nothing I can do to stop it. But their silence says the words that they don't. I obviously destroyed the car to cover up my sister's murder.

She reaches into the box again and pulls out my sister's laptop. "Is this your computer?" she asks pointedly.

"No, that's my sister's." I feel like I'm digging myself into a hole that I won't be able to climb out of. I curse myself for having it in my backpack. If it were back at Valentina's, they wouldn't be able to hold that piece of evidence against me at least.

"And where did you get this laptop from?"

"My sister's house..." Though I say the words, I don't feel like they're needed. They clearly went through my room at Valentina's house. Why would they go in there to go through my things? There's only one reason that they'd do that: Simon told them to come after me. But how? Why would they believe him in all of this?

"So, you *stole it*. And this?" she asks as she drops another clear bag onto the table before I can argue that I didn't *steal* anything. This one brings a tear to my eye. The bloody bracelet. The piece of evidence I didn't think I'd ever be able to explain away.

"I found that on a hiking trail that my sister liked to walk on." My words fall flat. I can't believe that Simon got the jump on me. But I won't let him win this. I grab my sister's other burner phone from my pocket. "I know what you're both thinking. I know how this looks. But before you really convince yourselves that I did this, I want you to listen to this." I play them the recording of Eviana being screamed at by Simon, one of their uglier fights. Glass shatters in the background, punctuating angry words. Occasionally, Simon slams his hands or fists against something. I wish I could see the fear on my sister's face, the fear that I hear in her words as she begs him to stop, for him to calm down.

The detectives exchange a look. My heart pounds as I wait to see if they're going to take me seriously.

"How long has this been going on?" Hanson asks as she motions toward the phone, then pauses the playback.

"I don't know. I didn't know that this was going on at all until I found this phone in my sister's car before Simon torched it." I sigh and shake my head. "I saw my sister the day before she disappeared. She asked me to come visit her in Florida because she had cancer. That's the only reason I came. After I left, I got a voicemail from Simon stating that Eviana disappeared. But after staying at his house, the voicemail got deleted. But I can show you the call on my phone logs. I know it happened."

"So, Eviana didn't tell you about any of this fighting?" Alders asks.

I shake my head. "She was the kind of person who I think would be too proud to admit that something like this was happening to her." I motion toward the bruise that's still barely on the edge of my cheekbone. "But Simon gave me this before I left that house. I know exactly what he's capable of. I wonder if he asked me back here so he could take me out of the picture too."

"What did he tell you about keeping Eviana's social media accounts live while she was missing?" Hanson presses, questions playing behind her eyes. I can tell that she's hungry for answers.

"He told me that he and Tom, her manager, decided that was the best option because they thought that she didn't disappear at all—that she just took off because she needed a break." I roll my eyes at this idea, making it clear that I don't agree with it at all. "But she didn't mention to any of her friends that she was planning to leave. Eviana isn't the kind of person to plan something in a vacuum. She would have told someone about her plans," I explain.

"Simon mentioned to us that he thought that someone had abducted Eviana, and that it was likely they'd ask for ransom. He thought that by keeping her accounts active and by not making her disappearance public knowledge, that it would keep the kidnapper from being able to ask for more money," she explains. "He then explained that he called you back here, because he thought that you were the top suspect in your sister's disappearance."

I shake my head. "Did you ask him why he's so concerned about money? My sister was rich. Why wouldn't he just pay the ransom then? And again, what do I have to gain from my sister disappearing or dying? It's not like *I* was in her will. I didn't get anything if she died."

And you just went along with his plan? I want to ask. But I don't. It seems like Simon wrapped these two around his finger and convinced them of the best path forward, and not the other way around.

"But it's been over a week and no one has come forward asking for ransom. So why hasn't this gone public?" I press when neither of them speaks.

They share a knowing glance again, and I really wish I knew what they were thinking. But some part of me thinks that they didn't want the media attention on the department.

"It's not uncommon for public figures to take time away, to

take a break," Hanson explains. "We wanted to be sure that we gave Eviana the time that she needs... just in case it was just a misunderstanding."

"This isn't a misunderstanding. I'm telling you that Simon did something to my sister," I say, an edge to my voice. I don't want to lose my composure, to come off as one of those women who overacts, because then I know they won't take my concerns seriously. "I don't say it lightly when I tell you this. Before I heard that audio, I'm not sure I would have been convinced that Simon was capable of something like this."

"There were some red flags during our interviews with him," Alders explains. The cutting glare that Hanson shoots him tells me that he was definitely not supposed to give me that information.

"What can you tell me about their relationship?" Hanson asks.

"They got together about a year before Eviana started her social media accounts. It was a very fast engagement and marriage—which didn't seem like my sister at all. She was always a planner, the type of person who needed control over everything. I honestly didn't expect her to ever get married. She didn't invite me to the wedding. I saw it on social media. Shortly after that, she started her social media account, apparently at his urging, and began her foray into influencing. Some of her friends have shown me evidence of Simon's infidelity. I'm not sure if that's directly related to the abuse or not though."

She nods. "And there weren't any posts that seemed to indicate that there may be abuse going on?"

I shrug. "I didn't keep up with her posts like that, so I'm not certain." It's not entirely a lie, but I really wasn't scouring my sister's posts looking for evidence in the past. My view into her life had been through a very different lens.

She nods, then pulls a phone from her pocket. I watch as she clicks on the screen several times, then slides it across the table toward me. She's got my sister's social media account opened up to a post. She's scrolled down to a comment that says,

You're such a dumb bitch. You should be dead, not posting this bullshit on your social media account. You don't deserve this fame or a single goddamn like. You deserve to be dead.

I swallow hard as I read the words, then look back up at her.

"Why did you write this to your sister?" she asks.

I raise a brow. "I didn't write that. I'd never write something like that to her."

A thin smile creases her lips. "Yes, you did. We were able to reach out to the company who runs this social media outlet. They confirmed some of the details on the account that link back to you."

I swallow hard, feeling like shards of glass are coating the inside of my esophagus. My account was clearly hacked or this is some poor attempt to connect me to my sister's disappearance. Scenes from *Law & Order* flash through my mind, but they're not very helpful. Do I ask for a lawyer? Do I demand for them to let me go?

"Are you going to charge me with something?" I finally manage to ask. If I'm not being arrested, at the very least, I know they can't hold me long term.

"No, we're not charging you with anything right now," Alders says, frustration threading through his words.

"Am I free to go then?"

"You're not going to answer the question about this threat?" Hanson presses again.

"I've never seen that before in my life," I say as I shove up from the table. "So I have nothing else to say to either of you."

I can feel them both staring at me, but instead of looking back, I look toward the door.

"Down the hall to your right, that'll get you to the parking lot," she says.

"And how do I get a ride back to Valentina's house?" I ask.

"You've got Uber on your phone, I'd expect?" Alders quips without pausing.

39

I'm going to kill Simon, I think as I sit in the back of an Uber. The car is musty, as if I'm sitting in the back of a rolling antique shop. I don't see how it's possible, the car is probably only a couple years old—and yet... something about it is so off.

As we drive, my mind skips between murderous flashes of rage in which I imagine myself snuffing the life out of Simon's smug face, and wondering if the seats I'm sitting on were yanked out of the back of an eighties Astro van, because that's the only way I could understand the stench.

We turn onto Valentina's street and I'm thankful to find that the cop cars are all gone. Though I climb out of the Uber, I have no intention of going back to her house right now. No, instead, I'm going to give Simon a piece of my mind. How could he have tried to orchestrate all of this to make me look like I wanted to kill my sister? As if I wanted her out of the way so badly. None of this makes any sense.

The car rolls to a stop out front. I climb out, slam the door, and face my sister's monstrous house. I swear, even from the sidewalk, I can feel him watching, staring me down. But he has no idea who he is messing with. I'm not someone he can just push around and pin a murder on.

The heat bears down on me as I walk up the drive to Eviana's house. Simon's too comfortable. He's slid into this life without my sister as if it's the most natural thing in the world—as if he'd been planning it for far too long. As I approach the front door, I can hear something inside. Voices. I pause and press my ear to the door. Though I should probably care that I'll be seen by a neighbor eavesdropping, at this point, I don't give a shit.

"You dumb bitch!" Simon rages on the other side of the door. Glass shatters so loudly, it sounds like he threw a chair through one of the plate-glass windows in the back. I tense up at the sound, my body readying for an impact that never comes.

"Simon, please stop!" Eviana screams. And I swear I feel all of the blood drain from my face.

I take a step back from the door, blinking in disbelief. Eviana... she's here. She's inside. She's not dead? My mind unravels, swarming with thoughts, unable to make sense of what I'm hearing. I reach for the handle, then push the door in. To my relief, it's open. I slip inside the house, and click the door closed behind me—locking it before I walk toward the kitchen. From the foyer, I can see the living room, the wide-open space at the center of the house. But wherever the fighting is coming from, they're not in here. Though I search the ground for signs of broken glass in here, I find none.

When I reach the kitchen, I turn right, and a pool of blood on the floor catches my attention. Time skids to a halt. I stop dead in my tracks as I take the scene in. Simon is on the floor, his pale face staring up at the ceiling. His eyes are fixed, unblinking. His mouth is open slightly, as if at any moment he'll take a breath—but I can tell from his pallor that it won't happen anytime soon. Blood has leaked from stab wounds in his chest and dribbled onto the floor, congealing in the grout, spreading out from the scene. The knife still stands erect in the middle of his chest at the center of a cluster of stab wounds. It takes so long for my mind to process it all because it can't be real.

I feel as if I'm wading through water as I take a step closer. My body is moving automatically. How did this happen? What is this? Why can't I make sense of any of it? The pool of blood is so large, it looks like he must have been here for a while. There are no smears, no smudges on the ground.

"Please, Simon, don't!" I hear my sister scream. My eyes snap up, searching for Eviana. But she's not here. No, all I can make out is a small device on the counter on the other side of the kitchen. That's where the noise is coming from.

I take a step forward so I can grab it, stop it. But a noise behind me makes me stop in my tracks. Lights explode behind my eyes, pain wraps around my skull, then I'm falling as the world slips out from beneath me, and the darkness swallows me whole.

40

The air is sharp, fragrant with a cleaner that is so pungent, my nose rebels against the smell. I feel my nostrils flare, and something smooth and cold stuck in them ensnares my attention. Though my eyes are closed, the light shining through my eyelids warns that the room is bright. My mind spins as I try to grasp a memory, but they feel so far off, so slippery that I can't catch a single one. When did I fall asleep? Why does my head hurt so bad? I open my eyes carefully, squinting against the blinding sun. Maybe if I can just open my eyes this will all make sense.

White walls and vague shapes come into view as my eyes try desperately to adjust. It looks as if I'm viewing the world underwater, as if I haven't used my eyes in a long time. Where the hell am I? The realization clicks into place that I must be in the hospital. A dark shape shifts beside me, a person, I think. Then warmth wraps around my hand. When the shape leans in, the perfume—orange, vanilla, and cinnamon—clicks the pieces together for me before I can even see her.

Eviana.

My mind churns as I try to remember, as I try to answer all the questions simmering in the back of my brain. Did I see her?

Did Eviana come back? Am I dead? All I can remember is the pain... and yet. There was something else. I try to grip it, to tear the memory from the back of my mind so I can see it again, but as soon as I feel I'm close it slithers away.

"You were so brave to try to save me from him," she says as she squeezes my hand.

Blood. I know there was blood. The memory fades in and out, like trying to remember something that happened when I was five years old. It's too far gone, too far away from me.

The blurred silhouettes in the room harden bit by bit. Every time I blink my eyes it seems to wash away the haze. Her face finally appears, the curtain of her hair, the sharp details of her eyes. There's something swimming behind them—but that's nothing new. Eviana is always calculating. Eviana always looks like a venomous snake held in captivity.

My phone buzzes on the nightstand beside me—I guess the nurses were nice enough to plug it in for me—and I grab it, looking at a notification from work. Are all my kids okay? Did I miss anything while I was out? How long has it been?

Eviana's words spear my mind as I slip my phone under the blankets next to me. I need to refocus on her, what she's saying. I saved her from who? From Simon? I don't remember that. I scour my mind for memories, for what happened before I ended up here, in the hospital. Simon was already dead when I walked into the house, and it looked as though he'd been dead awhile.

"The police know that Simon was abusing me. That he was forcing me to be on social media constantly, that he was pressuring me to do things that I wasn't comfortable with. They know that I had to leave for a little while, to pretend that I'd disappeared. And once I got a plan in place and I tried to come back to tell Simon we were getting divorced, he flew into a rage." She pushes her hair back and shows me a large bruise on the side of her face.

I swallow hard, my throat so dry I wonder when the last

time I had something to drink was. Her lies are hard to swallow.
The memory comes rushing back, the blood, the phone playing
a fight on it, Simon's dead body on the ground. God, I was so
wrong. So, so wrong. Simon wasn't really the villain I made him
out to be. Eviana picks up a cup with a straw hanging out of it
from the nightstand and offers me a drink—a gesture that is just
so unlike her. I sip carefully, waiting for her to yank it away
from me, to stab the straw into my lip—something. But she
doesn't. When I'm done, she places the cup back and offers me
a sharp smile. She's never taken care of me like this. It feels
wrong, unsettling.

"I told them that you came into the house as Simon was
attacking me. That he knocked you out, and I had to stab him to
save both of us. Because he would have killed us." She says the
words with such confidence and certainty I know that she has
practiced them. Probably the entire time she was gone she spent
rehearsing this act.

"I saw the recorder. You were playing a fight on it," I finally
manage. And now, I wonder if any of the fights I heard were
real.

She glares at me and cuts a glance toward the door. "The
cops are right outside. I could tell them that you were in on this
with Simon. That both of you were planning to take me out so
that you two could be together."

My lip curls involuntarily at that thought. I would never
sleep with Simon. Even with all of the shit I may have threatened my sister with over the years through my jealousy, I would
never lower myself to something like that.

"You know I wouldn't do something like that." I growl the
words at her, but I keep my voice low.

The look on her face shifts, something feral simmering
behind her eyes. "You might not, but with the software I have, I
can make it sound like you two were conspiring. I can make it

sound like you both planned to kill me, to get rid of me." Her words sound like a hiss as they escape her thin lips.

"That's not possible," I say. But the reality starts to click into place in my mind. That's what those fights were. Were they fabrications on her part? She created them? After finding the spreadsheet, I knew my sister was a liar, but this—I never imagined...

"Oh, it is. The AI software company that I worked for, we specialized in replicating the speech patterns and inflection of real people. Which isn't all that remarkable... but the remarkable part, we taught the AI emotions. We could tell the software that the speech pattern needed to match a fight. It was a conversational model. So, I could scream at the software, and it would scream back." A slight smile curves her lips. "When the company went under because they couldn't secure more funding, I realized just how special the program was, and I took a copy of it before we were all laid off."

Oh, Jesus Christ. My sister has software that can replicate anyone's voice and make them say *anything* that she wants? A stone plummets to the pit of my stomach and I feel like my abdomen is filled with greased eels. This isn't possible. How could she have something like this? It could be so dangerous.

"Why did your little show even matter? Simon said the cameras in the house weren't working."

She lets out a little laugh. "They weren't working because I turned them off before I *disappeared*. Took you long enough to find my hideout, by the way. That's kind of embarrassing for you."

So she was staying near the house where I found her car? I couldn't imagine my sister staying in a place like that.

"When I was ready to put my plan into action, when it'd been long enough that I could tell the police that I left because I was scared of Simon—and when I wanted to get my things to leave him for good—he tried to kill me. I turned the cameras back on remotely."

Exhaustion grips me to my core. "Why? Why go through with all of this? You could have just divorced him."

"Nope. If I divorced him, he won. He was cheating on me. This is the ending he deserved, so that's exactly what he got." She crosses her arms and sits a little straighter, like she's so proud of herself.

"Was any of it real? The abuse? The baby?"

A sick smile splits her lips. "Oh, damn. I am a good liar. I had you fooled." She barks out a laugh.

I'm quiet for a long moment as I try to digest it all, then I ask, "So that's it? I play your little game, or you have me locked up? I lie for you so that you can get away with murder again?" I croak the words out. It was different with our mother; Eviana actually was in danger, and so was I. Who knows what our mother really would have done. But this? This was just cold-blooded murder. Even if Simon was a cheater, did he deserve this? Could he have done anything to really deserve this end?

"You protected me once before, and now it's time to do it again," she says, her words a clear demand.

Even if I told the police what she did, they wouldn't believe me. I calculate my options, and I realize that I have no choice here. Eviana is going to get away with her lies. Again. And I know if I don't go along with it—one day, she'll kill me too. So, I nod, a silent agreement formed between us before she slips from the room. I watch her go, a part of me knowing that it'll likely be the last time I see my sister. I expect to be sad, for my subconscious to want to chase after her, to smooth things over. But whatever part of me that would do that died the moment I saw Simon dead on the floor.

For once in my life, I looked in my sister's eyes, and I saw her for what she really is. A monster.

41

The airport swarms around me, the sound of chatter and conversation easing my nerves. My hands have been trembling since I made it through security. There's a flutter in my chest, as if my heart is trying to break free. I imagine it bursting through my chest and hopping down the tarmac without me. All around me, the seats in the terminal are packed. I glance up from my seat, looking at everyone else staring down at their own laptops.

The computer feels heavy as I settle it on my thighs, but I know it's all in my head. Sweat creates a film on my fingers as I unlock the machine and navigate to my browser. While Eviana was gone, I moved all of her login details onto my personal computer—just in case Simon found a way to get her laptop back. I refresh her feeds, noting that I'm thankfully still logged in. She hasn't figured out that I still have access, that she isn't the only one in her accounts anymore.

I load the scheduling tool she usually used for her posts and cue up several videos and audio files. It takes me longer than I'd like to admit to get it all right, for the posts to automatically repost themselves every fifteen minutes over the next twenty-four hours, just in case they get deleted.

"Flight 113 from Orlando to Seattle, we're going to start boarding in five minutes." A voice erupts over the speaker, and I know that my time is nearly up. I have to pull the trigger. It's now or never.

I schedule the posts, then change Eviana's passwords and link all of the accounts to my phone and email. It takes a few minutes to switch it over, but that's all I need. I know that Eviana will get them back eventually, get it all unlocked, but I just need a window where she has no control—no ability to delete everything before it can be seen. A bad feeling kicks around inside me like I've swallowed a baby shark. I've never done anything like this, stood up for myself. But I can't keep covering for her anymore—no matter what might happen.

After it's all done, I close the laptop and get in line to board the flight. It's all a blur, until I buckle myself into my seat. As the cabin shifts around me, the grunts of people lugging their bags, the clicks of seatbelts, the low chatter of children watching cartoons on devices, I slip in my earbuds and look down at my phone. I refresh, seeing the first of my posts hit my sister's social media feed.

And there it is, the audio, her confession—Eviana, telling the world that she's a killer. I hold the side button on my phone until it shuts off. I close my eyes as the plane starts to taxi, and before I know it, we're rising up into the sky, leaving my sister behind. There's a hard pebble in my throat when I try to swallow. I want to feel better about it, I really do—but I'm the kind of person who feels like I need to fix things, to fix people. It kills me that this time, I didn't close the case, I didn't do what I thought that I would.

I couldn't save her. And now I know I never will. As hard as it is for me to move on, for me to look at this from the right point of view, I know that this time it's different. This time I realize the person who needs saving is different. This time, I need the saving.

ORLANDO SENTINEL

In the early morning hours of March 13, police arrested Orlando resident and influencer Eviana Casteel-Pendelton for the alleged murder of her husband. The body of Simon Pendelton had been found in their shared home in Orlando, within the community of Lakeview Shores, earlier this week. Police had originally indicated that they were not investigating the death as a homicide, but instead it was being considered as self-defense based on details that Eviana had disclosed to Orlando PD.

On March 11, audio and video were leaked on Eviana's social media accounts, where she confessed that she was responsible for her husband's death and used AI technologies stolen from a previous employer to stage the scene for security cameras in her home.

This story is still developing, and we are waiting for comments from Eviana's manager and Orlando PD.

ONE YEAR LATER

I've never been comfortable with attention. And finally, slowly, the attention has receded like the tides have finally gone out. Some days I wonder if this is all a hurricane and I'm in the eye. I wait constantly for the other shoe to drop, for Eviana to figure out some way to take me down. In the year since Eviana's arrest, I fled Seattle seeking quiet, some insulation from my sister's crimes. And I found it in a small community along the coast in Washington. The cases are smaller, the town quieter, but here I can help the kids as much as I'm helping myself.

In the misty mornings as I stare out at the rocky coast over the dark waters, I feel like out here there are no shadows. I've left something behind, baggage, my sister, the bad memories. I know I'll never be free of it all, but here, at least for the moment, I can breathe.

I slip out my front door and walk down the cobblestone path of my small cottage to the mailbox. As I ease it open, I pull out a stack of envelopes. A cool breeze rustles my hair as I stride back into the house, thumbing through the letters. There are three from Eviana, just like there are nearly every single day. I sigh as I look down at her loopy handwriting.

The small fireplace in the corner of the living room crackles, as if reminding me of its existence, beckoning me forward. There's a tight knot in the center of my chest as I look down at the letters, wondering what she has to say, if she's changed. There will always be some part of me that wonders, that imagines how things could have been. But I can't keep trying to build a version of my sister who doesn't exist. These demons have to stay dead.

I walk to the fire, and slip the letters in. Flames reach out expectantly, is if they were waiting—a hungry pet that I haven't fed frequently enough. Fire laps at the envelopes, and they glow orange. The loopy script darkens as the white paper slowly turns to ash.

Goodbye, Eviana. Today, and every day from here forward, it's me who I have to save, not her.

A LETTER FROM DEA

Dear reader,

I want to say a huge thank you for grabbing a copy of *Have You Seen Her?* If you enjoyed it, and want to keep up to date with all my latest releases, just sign up at the following link.

Your email address will never be shared and you can unsubscribe at any time.

www.bookouture.com/dea-poirier

I hope you loved *Have You Seen Her?* If you did, I would really appreciate if you could leave a review. I'd love to hear what you think, and it makes such a difference helping new readers to discover one of my books for the first time.

I love hearing from my readers—you can get in touch on my Facebook page or through Twitter, Goodreads, or my website.

Thanks,

Dea Poirier

KEEP IN TOUCH WITH DEA

www.dhpoirier.com

facebook.com/dhpoirier

twitter.com/DeaPoirierBooks

instagram.com/deapoirier

goodreads.com/dhpoirier

ACKNOWLEDGMENTS

I am so thankful for my incredible editor, Laura Deacon, and the amazing support team at Bookouture (thank you all so much for everything that you do). I can't believe that this is our fifth book together.

To my critique partner, and the best friend I could ever ask for, Elesha Halbert-Teskey, as always, I appreciate you. You're the best <3.

To my readers, thank you so much for joining me for my eighth book—whether this is the first of mine you've read or the eighth, I'm so happy you're here. All of your support, kind words, and reviews are wonderful. Thank you for helping spread the word about my books and helping me find new readers!

To my family—thank you for everything. *Kiss noise.*